PRAISE FOR R.J. PINEIRO

THE FALL

"It's a thrill-a-minute story, with good here-and-now technology, and a striking scientific premise at its heart."
—*Wall Street Journal*

"R.J. Pineiro breaks the sound barrier with *The Fall*, one of the most original and electrifying science-based thrillers I have read in a long time. The opening chapter—the incredible "fall" itself—is mind-bending enough, but it only gets better, with cutting-edge science, vivid characters, and a plot that accelerates to a mind-warping climax. Highly recommended."
—*Douglas Preston, New York Times bestselling author of The Kraken Project*

"Imaginative premise." —*Publishers Weekly*

"This alternate world sci-fi thriller is packed with high stakes and moves at a high speed." —*Kirkus*

"Jack's adrenaline is contagious - *The Fall* will keep readers on the edges of their seats, waiting to find out what crazy stunt Jack will perform next and to learn the fate of this charming, daredevil hero." —*Forces of Geek*

WITHOUT MERCY

"Constant action, sympathetic heroes, believable evildoers, and absolute authenticity on every page."
—*Publishers Weekly*, starred review

"The authenticity of the story makes the tale particularly terrifying, especially at a time when real-life international relations appear unstable. A fine apocalyptic thriller right up the alley of Clancy and Thor fans." —*Booklist*

"A masterful thriller written by men of deep experience. Epic in scale yet swiftly paced, *Without Mercy* is as convincing as it is chilling. First-rate and very highly recommended!"
—Ralph Peters, *New York Times* bestselling author

"The ultimate terrorist scenario, with authenticity steeped into every page. Col. David Hunt and R.J. Pineiro put their credentials on display in stellar fashion. Readers who enjoy Tom Clancy and Brad Taylor will find a new favorite." —Ward Larsen, *USA Today* bestselling author

WITHOUT FEAR

"Outstanding… This military adventure thriller deserves to become a genre classic."
—*Publisher's Weekly*, starred review

AVENUE OF REGRETS

"*Avenue of Regrets* is **a superb psychological thriller**, a gripping tale of violence, tension and intrigue. From the very first chapter it propels the reader into a dark world haunted by the demons of the past and the horrific evil of the present. **Highly recommended!**"
--Douglas Preston, #1 bestselling author of the Pendergast series of novels.

"An engrossing novel of domestic suspense...a fast-paced tale of murder and horrific crime with **twists and turns worthy of Hitchcock**. Along the way, Pineiro, who's best known for his military/computer thrillers, dishes up some wry reflections on humanity, trust, and forgiveness."
—*Publishers Weekly*

"A man becomes entangled in a conspiracy of murder and deceit with ties to a years-old murder charge for which he received an acquittal. Pineiro's novel thrives on copious plot turns . . . high stakes perils unfold throughout, and surprises persist all the way to the epilogue. **Zigzagging plot rife with suspense and character detail**."
—*Kirkus Reviews*

"Greed, violence, and the hope of redemption are the defining themes of *Avenue of Regrets*, a **nonstop action thriller** . . . perfectly paced, with clues revealed in small doses...the writing is tight and smooth and keeps to the nail-biting pace."
—*Foreword Reviews*

BOOKS BY R.J. PINEIRO

CHILLING EFFECT

A Novel

R.J. PINEIRO

Chilling Effect: A Novel
Auspicious Apparatus Press

Copyright © 2019 by Rogelio J. Pineiro
Published by arrangement with the author

ISBN: 978-0-9966628-8-8

TABLE OF CONTENTS

"The supreme reality of our time is the vulnerability of our planet."

—John F. Kennedy

For my mother, Dora Irene Pineiro,
with all my love. TQM.

ACKNOWLEDGEMENTS

Marty Greenberg from Tecknobooks thought it would be a good idea for me to write a book revolving around ecological terrorism. That was over twelve years ago. The book began to take shape over the course of the following six or seven years off and on in between other projects. The research alone took a significant portion of that time. My agent at Sanford J. Greenburger, Matthew Bialer, reviewed early versions of the manuscript and, as always, provided very useful and insightful feedback. But it took another five years before it arrived to its current form, and with the help of Todd Barselow from Auspicious Apparatus Press, it has finally reached your hands. I hope you enjoy reading it as much as I did writing and researching it.

I would also like to thank Alice Frenk as well as my wife, Lory Pineiro, for their thorough proofreading of the manuscript and for providing the final touches. Every author should be so lucky to have such amazing allies in his corner.

A special thanks to Saint Jude, the patron saint of impossible causes, for continuing to make it possible.

Finally, a special thanks to all my fans for your support through the years. Please keep writing and offering suggestions. I do my best to answer every one.

For more information on my novels, please visit www.rjpineiro.com or my FB page at: https://www.facebook.com/rjpineirobooks

CHILLING EFFECT

A Novel

R.J. PINEIRO

PROLOGUE

**EAST OF JAKOBSHAVN ISBRAE GLACIER.
GREENLAND. AUGUST 18, 2027.**

*You never know what you are capable of, until the monster
inside of you pushes you beyond your moral line in the sand.*
William Kiersted stared out of the Airbus H225 helicopter contemplating that thought while cruising over the
fjord amidst towering flotillas of silvery icebergs drifting in
the half-light of an Artic summer evening.
A full moon hung high in the star-filled sky at the top
of the world. Its gray light fused with the wan orange glow
from a sun reluctant to set on the distant horizon, casting
an amber double shadow of the large helicopter across the
surface of the inlet.
The light and variable winds this evening suited
William as he filled his lungs with the cold air inside the
spacious cockpit. He savored its chilling effect while flexing
his gloved hands in anticipation.
*You never really know . . . until you realize there's no such
thing as morality in the world.*
Not anymore.

Lying ahead were the last few miles of the large iceberg-dotted bay before reaching Jakobshavn's tongue, the glacier's three-hundred-foot-tall seaward end floating on the waters of the fjord.

Like an icy Amazon River, the four-mile-wide Jakobshavn Isbrae flowed to the sea during the summer months at a speed of up to 150 feet per day from the heart of Greenland. The glacier, a dome of frozen fresh water over a mile thick covering an area larger than the Great Lakes, dumped nearly 20 cubic miles of ice each year into the Davis Strait, which led into the North Atlantic Ocean.

His eyes gravitated to the west. Somewhere beyond the blushing horizon lining the pallid sun, dozens of merchant vessels made the now-routine journey along the North-West Passage. The sea route ran along the Arctic coastline of North America previously clogged with thick ice. But three years ago, climate change made it ice free through the summer months, shortening the route from Europe or the Eastern Seaboard to Asia by nearly 4500 miles, drawing a lot of traffic away from the venerable Panama Canal.

Sitting in the copilot seat, William shifted his gaze from the majestic sight to the slim profile of his pilot, Lian Guo, wearing a green David-Clark noise-cancellation headset. Her face was awash with the soft glow of the 12-inch Primary Flight Display directly in front of her.

A former captain in the People's Republic of China's Air Force, Lian had abandoned her military career years ago lured by a smuggling business that promised wealth far beyond her government-issued Shanghai condominium and Hyundai sedan.

Lian remained focused, her fine features tight, dark eyes scanning her instruments and the picture beyond the

Plexiglas windscreen. The fingers of her right hand worked the cyclic, or control column, and her left hand held the collective lever as she kept them steady and well below radar.

Not that I expect any trouble this far north.

Most governments failed to recognize that this desolate spot along the North-West passage held the key to not only accelerating the rise in sea levels but also triggering a mini ice age across western Europe.

The weather in the Old World was heavily influenced by the Greenland ice shelf as well as by the meltdown in the Arctic Sea, which pumped fresh water into the ocean. Over the course of a few decades, it would start diluting the salty sea enough to weaken the Gulf Stream, which carried warm water from the tropics to Europe. As the tropical water released its heat in the North Atlantic, it sunk and flowed back to the equatorial regions along the ocean floor. This sinking effect formed the engine that powered the Gulf Stream, which in turn, warmed Europe. A massive and sudden meltwater gush into the North Atlantic from a catastrophic event in Greenland would exponentially accelerate the salt water dilution process to the point that within a matter of weeks the tropics-bounded current may not be dense enough to sink.

Killing the Gulf Stream.

And freezing Europe.

William glanced toward the cargo secured in the rear compartment, which he planned to deliver to the heart of Jakobshavn's Isbrae.

He shook his head at the unfortunate turn of events that had propelled him down what international security forces considered the road to perdition.

They've labeled me a goddamned climate terrorist.

But William saw himself as a climate *liberator*.

The Earth had survived meteors, continental floods, volcanic eruptions, and countless ice ages. It would also survive an event he simply planned to accelerate.

But mankind would suffer.

Especially the assholes that screwed my father.

He continued regarding his surroundings.

If the world realized just how damn critical Jakobshavn's tongue is to global climate, they would be protecting it as if it were the fucking White House.

But lucky for him, those were the same arrogant scientists and politicians who had dismissed his father's theory on the relationship between solar activity and cloud coverage.

Henrik Kiersted, the once respected chief of the Danish National Space Center in Copenhagen, had spent a lifetime collecting solar activity and mapping it to decreasing cloud coverage, which resulted in a warmer Earth. Unfortunately, he had been ostracized for suggesting that his research could share the climate change stage with greenhouse gases.

The politically-driven scientific community had ridiculed his father to the point that he had taken his own life. And six months later, William's mother had mourned herself to death.

You never really know what you're capable of.

Until an amoral world erases your moral line in the sand...awakening the monster.

A climate researcher and former member of the *Fromandskorpset*, the Danish version of the U.S. Navy SEALs, William had sworn then to dedicate his life and his family's fortune to exacting revenge against a global political system who had so maliciously wronged his parents and—

The sudden upward acceleration pulled him out of his reverie.

As they approached the soaring headwall of Jakobshavn's tongue, Lian had twisted the throttle at the end of the collective, soaring the Airbus under the power of its twin turbines.

William blinked away the memory of his parents as the helicopter gained altitude, the wall of glistening ice rushing down in front of them, vanishing in the semidarkness. They crested this floating end of the glacier, which rose vertically three hundred feet above the fjord, before thickening to one thousand feet as it reached land.

He pressed a button on the console, illuminating a red light in the main cabin to give his team the ten-minute warning. A moment later, he noticed the scowl forming on Lian's face.

The operatives suddenly moving about in the main cabin was upsetting the careful trim of the helicopter, taxing her flight skills.

William double-checked the GPS coordinates on the 12-inch Multi-Function Display. It showed their position over Jakobshavn's tongue, a floating ice sheet that continued rising steadily as it neared ground. A magenta line led to their destination twelve miles to the east: a narrow cleft in the ice—a moulin—positioned near the glacier's grounding line along the western coast of Greenland.

William's data, which came from research conducted by a group of graduate students from the University of Colorado four months ago, indicated that this moulin reached halfway down the thousand-foot-thick tongue.

Lian kept the H225 locked on the navigation route while holding altitude even as the racket in the rear increased.

The outside air temperature reading on the MFD indicated minus two degrees Celsius, or about twenty-eight degrees Fahrenheit—a mild summer night in the region. The satellite weather overlay on the GPS showed a snow shower over their target zone. There was also a blizzard in the forecast but not for another hour, providing William and his crew with ample time to deliver their package and head out before detonation.

"All set back there?" he asked, speaking into the microphone of his own David Clark noise-cancellation headset.

"Ready when you are, Billy," came the deep and thickly-accented voice of Mathias, a Nigerian operative who, like William, had also spent time with his own country's special forces some years back.

"Good to go," added Hans-Jorgen, a former colleague in the *Fromandskorpset*.

"Five miles," Lian reported in the common language of his multinational team. "Snow flurries ahead."

William began to check his gear, including the Heckler & Koch MP7 submachine gun strapped across his chest and the Sig Sauer P220 .45-caliber pistol secured to his utility belt, which also held a half-dozen smoke grenades, spare magazines for the MP7 and the Sig, a utility knife, and an ice hammer.

"Two miles."

As the snow intensified, William checked the Velcro straps on his ice boots, which were integrated to a battery-powered body suit designed to keep him warm in sub-zero temperatures without the excessive bulk of passive thermal suits.

"I'm setting it down fifty feet from the target," she said as the Airbus entered a hover while William increased the resolution of the MFD, which depicted the start of the fissure with an accuracy of three feet.

Three rivers of meltwater fed the crevice. Lian would land between two of the rivers, on a dry area roughly one acre in size flanked to the north and south by the gushing water and to the east by the abyss, their target.

"One minute," William announced before removing his headset, briefly wincing as the loud rotor noise blasted against his eardrums. He donned a thermal mask with a built-in mic and ear piece to remain connected with the team.

The noise in the rear intensified as the team went through final preparations and shifted around the cabin, sabotaging Lian's otherwise smooth decent. It forced her to change pitch constantly and bank while slowly lowering the collective and reducing throttle, progressively decreasing lift until settling the helicopter on the ice sheet.

"Time!" William shouted, pushing open the side door and jumping onto the ice, bending his knees as the serrated soles of his boots bit into the slick surface locking him in place.

Mathias and two others joined him an instant later, as snow peppered their white thermal suits. The large African with arms as wide as William's thighs hoisted a waterproof case the size of a large footlocker from the rear of the helo and gently set it on the ice. It rested on a pair of built-in skis to make it easy to transport. The other two operatives hauled a mix of ropes, ice hammers, pitons, and other climbing gear.

"Move out!" William screamed over the noise of the rotor as Lian waited for everyone to get out except Hans-Jorgen, who settled behind the dual handles of a side mounted M2 Browning .50-caliber machine gun.

Lian took off into the white out to hold a defensive hover a quarter mile away.

The foursome moved swiftly, with purpose. Mathias led the way, pushing the case towards the moulin a few dozen feet away. William and the other two men followed single file under a rapidly darkening sky. Snow clouds thickened, blocking the burnt-orange glow from a sun looming just above the stark horizon, signaling that the blizzard was blowing in faster than forecasted.

Fingers of meltwater rushed into the wide fissure with a roar that increased in pitch as the helicopter turbines faded away.

William walked up to Mathias standing five feet from the edge of the dark chasm devouring massive amounts of grit-laden water. It reminded him of a miniature Niagara Falls as surface water gushed to the bottom of the melting glacier.

While William and Mathias kept watch, scanning the snowy surroundings, the two operators secured the heavy case to a pair of long ropes devised to lower it half way down the cleft, where the detonation would achieve maximum impact.

"Ready, Billy," Mathias said.

William set his MP7 on the ice and took a knee while removing a key from a Velcro-secured pocket. He used it to open the case, exposing the implosion-type nuclear device he had purchased from a corrupt Pakistani colonel.

You never really know what you are capable of.

He entered a ten-digit code on a keypad, and a 5-inch screen came alive with a menu of options. William selected the timer and programmed it to fifteen minutes. Five minutes to lower it into position and ten minutes to escape the blast zone. He entered a second code to arm it. Finally, he enabled the tamper mechanism for immediate detonation should anyone try to open the case again after he closed it.

He started the timer on the device and on a digital chronograph strapped to his right wrist. Finally, he closed and locked the case, an irrevocable action that made it impossible to deactivate the device.

"Ready," he ordered.

They had practiced this many times before. While Mathias pushed the case to the edge, the other two men anchored themselves to pitons fired into the ice and clutched the ropes connected to the top of the metallic housing. In unison, they began to lower it.

The light breeze turned into a steady wind, blowing snow into his eyes, stinging them, forcing William to don a pair of ski goggles as he witnessed the device disappear in the darkness.

"All good, yes?" Lian asked over the operational frequency.

"So far," he replied as Mathias stepped up to him. "We'll be done in four minutes."

"Copy that."

"We also need to—"

A gunshot cracked across the barren glacier, the round stabbing the ice next to one of his men lowering the device.

William and Mathias reacted in unison, dropping to the snow-filmed ice while scanning the horizon. "Lian! We're taking fire! Help!

"On our way!"

"Can you tell where the shot came from?" he asked Mathias.

"I think from over there!" the Nigerian replied, pointing beyond the wide river fifty feet north of them.

William passed the information to Lian, squinting while probing beyond the falling snow to get a better fix on the threat. "Need that Browning now!" he added.

"Thirty seconds!" she replied.

"Someone double-crossed us, Billy!" Mathias shouted.

William frowned as he pulled two smoke grenades from his utility belt and threw them in the general direction of the shooter. Mathias did the same.

The African was right. Canadian Command, chartered with patrolling the crowded North-West passage this time of the year, seldom ventured up this fjord, well north of the shipping lanes. In addition, few people knew about this mission as William had taken care of eliminating all loose ends, including the research group of grad students from the University of Colorado.

I killed everyone.

Except Jimmy.

William recalled his former research colleague who worked under his father. It was Dr. James Payden who had first pointed out the delicate pivot point where the glacier's tongue touched land.

Did he cross me?

Red smoke spewed from the grenades, mixing with the falling snow, forming a curtain, but not before two additional reports echoed in the distance. One of the operatives lowering the device fell back, dead.

"Goddammit, Lian! Where the hell are you?"

"Almost there!"

In the same instant, the man holding on to the second rope collapsed as a single shot nearly tore his head off, letting go.

Mathias dove toward one of the ropes, clutching it with one hand while sliding towards the crevice. Swinging an ice hammer wildly with the other, he stabbed the glacier twice before arresting the slide just short of the edge.

William snagged the second rope, gripping it with both hands while sitting on the ground and anchoring the spikes lining the bottom of his boots against the ice. Once he had a good enough hold, he reached for an additional smoke grenade with his left and tossed it in the direction of the shots. Mathias did the same.

Momentarily shielded by the swirling gas and the falling snow, they started to release the rope in unison and at a faster rate. He felt the heat building up in his thick gloves.

More shots gashed the ice just to their right.

"We need to get out of here, Billy!" Mathias shouted.

"We need more depth!"

"Two hundred feet!" Mathias shouted as a yellow rope marker rushed by in between his hands.

More gunfire erupted from beyond the protective curtain, peppering the ice a few feet from them. The snow and the smoke were buying them precious seconds as they continued to lower the case.

"Three hundred feet!" the African announced.

The Airbus's rotor noise increased, but along with it came the downwash that started to blow the smoke and the snow away.

"Four fifty!"

William could now see the opposite end of the river and spotted movement on the ice. Figures camouflaged in white crisscrossed each other clutching automatic weapons, muzzles flashing. And that also meant the threat could see them.

The Airbus rushed overhead toward the enemy while Hans-Jorgen opened the Browning on them.

William checked the chronometer. Four minutes had elapsed and—

Mathias fell back as a round tore into his face, and he released the rope.

The resulting forward tug yanked William to his feet, but he managed to hold on to the remaining rope. In the same instant, a stabbing pain jabbed his right thigh.

His grip weakening from the sudden pain arresting his leg, William reached for the ice hammer and drove the spike into the ice, hard. Looping the rope around it, he secured it, keeping the crate from dropping to the bottom of the moulin and destroying its content before detona—

A round exploded through his right arm just below the elbow, leaving exposed bone and cartilage in its wake. Blood splattered the ice by his boots, a macabre Rorschach blot.

The blizzard gathered strength, pounding his face as he watched his gloved hand and the bottom half of his forearm slide away.

Momentarily disoriented, William felt the urge to vomit when an invisible force punched him in the face, yanking off the goggles. His world turned red, and the excruciating pain broadcast from the right side of his face made him lose control of his bladder. He had been shot through the right cheek, and he suddenly could only see out of his left eye.

Feeling lightheaded, William used his surviving hand to push himself in the direction of the incoming rotor noise.

The blizzard intensified, turning everything around him blinding white. Growing weaker, staining pristine ice crimson, he dragged his body toward the—

Another round tore into his legs, tossing him across the frozen hell with animal force.

His thoughts became distant, unfocused, propelled to the periphery of his mind as the blood loss and the extreme cold took their toll. Finally, he went into shock, trembling, shaking violently, the—

Something stopped his momentum—something that also began to tug him steadily by his left arm

He tried to mumble, tried to see and hear, but the rotor noise and the howling blizzard blocked everything.

The pain reaching maddening levels, William forced his good eye open, blinking rapidly, struggling to see through the whiteout. For an instant, he recognized the slim figure of Lian back-dropped by the roaring helicopter.

A moment later the wind vanished as he landed on something hard before he felt hands undressing him. He cringed when the cold stung his exposed skin, heard the ripping of Velcro and the tearing of paper mixed with shouts from Lian and Hans-Jorgen—all muffled by the rotor noise outside and the bellowing wind. He winced at the sudden pressure of multiple field dressings on his legs and right arm, against his torso and face, and he tensed at the stabbing jabs of hypodermics. But he relished in the ensuing intoxicating warmth of sedatives searing through his veins, banishing the pain into oblivion, along with his mind.

The helicopter noise rose to an ear-piercing crescendo, and he sensed upward motion as the Airbus soared in the blinding turbulence.

He closed his good eye, the chemicals relaxing him, signaling that he just might survive this.

The Airbus pushed its way through the storm with intense vibration, its structure trembling as Lian revved up the turbine, accelerating the machine to the breaking point, apparently ignoring the turbulence and the pounding snow. The maneuvers clearly violated the helicopter's design specifications.

William suddenly understood why.

The bomb.

The timer.

As he heard Lian scream something about being followed by an American gunship, William tried to see his chronograph but he had worn it on his right wrist.

Surrendering to the enveloping chemical haze and the thickening fog clouding his thoughts, he let it all go, the pain, the maimed limbs, the loss of his team as Lian pushed the machine. She skillfully rushed them away from Ground Zero, from the kill zone of a device packing the power of a Hiroshima.

The whirling cyclone shrouding his world dropped a dark curtain around him, shunting all sound, all sight, all thought.

But not before a blinding flash pierced his substance-rich, dream-like state with the force of an apocalyptic bolt of lightning.

The shockwave that followed pushed him beyond the brink, and everything went dark.

* * *

"Don't lose them!" shouted Rachel Daly as she sat behind Air Force Captain Harvey Lee, the pilot of the A-10NG Warthog close support fighter in pursuit of the climate terrorists.

A senior officer of the CIA's Global Climate Counterterrorist Unit, Rachel had tracked William Kiersted across Europe and Iceland. But she had lost him in Reykjavik, only to reacquire him this morning, north of Nuuk, Greenland, when Canadian Command reported an unidentified aircraft at the edge of their radar range traveling north from the capital city.

She had coordinated the HALO jump of a team of Navy SEALs out of Naval Air Station Oceana in Virginia Beach while also securing a ride aboard an A-10NG from Thule Air Base, the U.S. Air Force's northern-most base.

She had monitored the attack by the SEALs, who had dropped from a C-17 Globemaster over the unsuspecting terrorists, catching them by surprise.

But it appeared that despite their best efforts, some of the terrorists, including Kiersted, albeit heavily wounded, had managed to get into a helicopter and were now trying to depart the area.

Bastards!

As the SEALs attempted to recover the cargo the terrorists had lowered into a moulin, Rachel ordered the Warthog-NG pilot to go in pursuit of the helicopter and obliterate it from existence.

"Range four miles," reported Lee, whose voice came through clearly in the headset built into the helmet Rachel wore as she squinted to see beyond the blizzard peppering the windshield. "Armed sidewinder. Seeking lock."

Although the A-10NG's dual turbines were classified as stealth, they had remained several miles back to provide silence for the SEAL team as they dropped on the terrorists.

Turbulence now pushed her into her restraining harness as the storm intensified.

"It's gonna get rough," Lee announced.

"Don't let them get away!"

"Yes, ma'am."

She returned her attention to the screens dominating her navigation console, depicting a real-time image of the SEALs reaching the Moulin and beginning to—

Alarms and warning lights filling the cockpit, Rachel brought both hands to her visor, shielding her eyes as the night turned into day from the brightest flash she'd seen in her life.

Jesus! What in the world—

Then the thought slapped her, and the realization made her shiver with fear: the blinding flash had resulted from a nuclear explosion.

"My screens are toast!" screamed Lee. "I'm losing control! Need to head inland!"

The flash ended before Rachel could reply.

As the entire world spun out of control while the pilot struggled to keep the Warthog-NG flying, Rachel managed to get a glimpse of the rapidly developing column of fire rising up to the sky just a couple of miles to the west.

"Mother of God," she whispered.

* * *

The fireball's initial thermal energy of 100,000 degrees Celsius sublimated twenty-five cubic miles of ice—nearly half as much as all of Greenland had lost in the past year—along the glacier's grounding line.

A column of incandescent air rose to the heavens, reaching ten thousand feet and expanding radially at an initial velocity greater than the speed of sound. Pressure exceeding a thousand tons per square inch broke off the four-mile-wide Jakobshavn's tongue while also obliterating the flotilla of icebergs crowding the fjord, sublimating an additional fifteen cubic miles of ice and melting twice as much.

A massive wave of ice and water propagated outward from the fjord at two hundred miles per hour. Nearly one hundred feet tall, the tsunami rushed towards Baffin Bay, across the crowded North-West passage, rapidly approaching the northern coast of Baffin Island, lying between Greenland and the Canadian mainland.

As the tidal wave swept in a southwesterly direction, cool air rushed back towards Ground Zero to fill the partial vacuum created by the explosion. A surge of heated ocean collided against the thousand-foot-high headwall, jetting several cubic miles of water deep beneath the dying glacier, prying it off its bed.

Uncorking Jakobshavn Isbrae.

Lacking the buttress effect of its tongue, the glacier accelerated into the ocean at almost fifteen hundred feet per day, ten times its previous rate.

* * *

The A-10NG fell from the sky as a heat wave scorched all exposed surfaces. The screens blank from the EMP effect of the nuclear blast, Rachel shifted her stare to the back-up analog altimeter as it dropped below seven thousand feet.

"We need to eject, Captain!" she barked.

Silence.

"Captain!"

Six thousand feet.

"CAPTAIN!"

The heat flash gave way to a powerful shockwave that shoved the A-10NG to the right, almost as if Lee were executing a maximum-G turn.

Rachel felt lightheaded from the pressure as the windblast engulfed her, stressing the armored skin of the Warthog-NG, threatening to rip the wings off. But the rugged jet held together as they dropped below three thousand feet.

"We need to eject!" she shouted again, recalling the minimum ejection altitude.

Silence.

Two thousand feet.

Damn!

One thousand feet.

The mushroom cloud visible in the distance, Rachel saw the shiny surface of the glacier come up to meet them. At an altitude of five hundred feet, she pulled on the ejection handle, an action that synchronized the activity of both ejection seats. Rachel, in the copilot seat, would go first and Lee a second later, otherwise the booster from his seat would burn her on his way out.

The world still seemed to catch fire around her as the clear canopy blew upward, and she followed under the power of the Martin-Baker ejection seat's solid rocket booster. It shot her up five hundred feet, and she lost track of Lee, but caught a glimpse of the Warthog-NG crashing below them a moment later.

Rachel felt the intense heat as the ejection seat pushed her through the twilight like a cannon ball

Nearly crushing her chest, the windblast turned her upside down and to the side as she darted across the sky in a parabolic trajectory.

Visions of flames, mushroom clouds, icescapes, and stars flashed in her eyes, but the images barely registered as a deep sense of isolation drowned her, a feeling of complete helplessness.

A hard tug and the canopy blossomed overhead, separating her from the ejection seat, which fell away in the night.

The windblast turned into a soft breeze that seemed to caress away the shock of what she had just experienced, and the terrible vision of fire and destruction on the western skies, unlike anything she'd seen before.

The ultimate nightmare had unfolded in front of Rachel. Yellow fires billowed in the distance. Explosions, like sheet lightning, illuminated the shaft of the towering cloud menacing over what had been the tongue of Greenland's largest glacier.

Through the inferno, Rachel could make out white vapor boiling skyward as enormous amounts of ice were sublimated in the aftermath of a nuclear blast.

And the worst is yet to come.

At that moment, she was being bombarded by an invisible force: gamma rays. Although she could not see it, smell it, or feel it, the radioactivity that filled the air ravaged her body. Her flight suit offered no protection from the isotopes attacking her living cells.

And as she landed softly on a large and flat surface of ice, Rachel shortened this realization into a single thought.

I'm fucked.

Removing the safety harness, she checked her body for damage but found nothing aside from a general soreness from the ejection. But she knew adrenaline lessened the effects of the windblast and the spinal compression from being shot out of the Warthog-NG like a damn bullet.

Meaning you're gonna be hurting soon.

She removed her helmet and brushed back her soaked, very short dark hair with a gloved hand. Her reflection in the visor of the helmet made her think of her parents. Rachel was the product of an Irish immigrant who married a local girl from Harlem, New York. She had her father's light-green eyes and straight nose, and her mother's full lips, rounded cheeks, and dark honey skin. She stared at her somewhat tomboyish face right next to the reflection of the rising mushroom cloud, alive with sheet lightning.

Rachel tried to work through the shock and reached for the survival butt pack she had automatically attached herself to when strapping in at the start of the mission. It had remained with her through ejection and parachute landing.

She extracted the URT-44 radio, which contained an Emergency Locator Transmitter already broadcasting an emergency signal in the older 121.5 and 243 MHz beacon frequencies. The radio also transmitted her position in the 406 MHz digital data beacon aimed at the search and rescue satellite (SARSAT) system. Given her location, it was the latter that presented her with the best chance of detection by rescue crews.

From another pouch, Rachel pulled out a portable GPS and quickly determined she was indeed in the middle of nowhere, with the nearest town over a hundred miles away.

Great.

She looked about her, trying very hard to ignore the distant column of smoke, wondering where Lee had landed, and spotting his parachute swirling nearby in the rapidly advancing twilight of the region's night.

She tried to walk but realized that her Air Force-issued flight boots lacked the required traction to traverse on ice. So, she opted for sliding in his direction, taking her well over five minutes to cover a few hundred feet, and falling several times in the process.

Kneeling by the helmeted pilot still secured to his parachute harness, Rachel checked for a pulse and felt none.

Her eyes drifted to the helmet. As she stared into her own reflection on Lee's lowered green visor, she reached over to pull it up, and felt that it was warm to the touch, even with her gloves on.

What the—?

Then she pieced it together, and the realization made her breathe in deeply, eyes closed.

It was the angle, Rach...the fucking angle.

She realized how lucky she had been, and how *unlucky* Captain Harvey Lee had been.

The heat flash had occurred as the Warthog-NG spun out of control toward Earth, scorching all exposed surfaces, including those inside the cockpit. Unfortunately for Lee, because of the angle of the plane with respect to the heat flash during that crucial fraction of a second, he had been exposed directly to the incinerating blast. Rachel, on the other hand, had been sitting behind him, protected by his shadow and also by the rear of the cockpit and fuselage looming over her.

That had been the reason why he had not responded.

Poor bastard was already dead.

Taking a deep breath, cursing William Kiersted for what he had done, Rachel rubbed her aching temples as she took in the distant billowing cloud again.

And another realization reached her mind.

The blast, if placed just deep enough, would have not only dislodged the glacier, which meant an acceleration in the melting of Greenland, the rise in sea levels, and the deceleration of the Gulf Stream. But more immediate, its proximity to shore also meant a tidal wave.

* * *

Captain Alberto Massi stood on the bridge of Carnival Cruise's *Polar Voyager*, one of three pleasure mega ships recently built by the large cruise line for the new and increasingly popular North-West Passage route, treating tens of thousands of passengers each year to the unique beauty of the Arctic in summer time.

Tonight, Massi was relaxed. The forecast for the southwest channel of Baffin Bay was calm, and that meant the 2657 passengers under his watch would enjoy a smooth evening beneath the soft orange glow of another Arctic evening. There were blizzards over Greenland to the east, but they were not expected to venture his way.

Above, the moon hung high in the polar sky surrounded by a sea of stars.

They had left the port of New York two days ago, and he expected to reach the Alaska coastline in another two. There, passengers would enjoy glacier tours, whale watching, and many other polar activities, including excursions into Glacier Bay. *Polar Voyager* would continue south from Alaska, following the Canadian coast, and finally taking in at Seattle to drop off one-way passengers and pick up another replacement load for their return trip to New York. The New York-Seattle cruise had become one of the premier summer vacation spots since the passage opened.

Massi scanned the array of color displays casting a dim glow on his crew. He found the effect almost—

A flash on starboard made everyone on the bridge whip their heads to the panoramic windows along the right side of the bridge.

"What the *fuck* was that?" Massi hissed a moment later to his executive officer, Lieutenant Bruno Salvador, as the low rumble of an explosion rattled the bridge.

A tall and thin Spaniard with twenty years of experience on various cruise lines, Salvador rushed over to a set of multifunction displays linked to an assortment of satellites.

After a few seconds looking over the shoulders of two operators, Salvador glanced up and reported, "Captain, the infrared satellites indicate a large detonation over the southwest coast of Greenland. Possibly nuclear."

"Nuclear? How far away?"

"Looks like sixteen miles, sir."

"Did it happen over land?" Massi asked, also looking at the screen while standing next to Salvador.

"It was along the coastline…in the fjord."

"Get me Canadian Command immediately," Massi replied much calmer than he felt. "And turn to starboard. Right full rudder."

"Aye, sir," Salvador repeated while staring into his superior's eyes, realizing the danger they were in. "Turn starboard! Right full rudder!"

The 145-ton megaship, the largest of its class, began a long and slow turn to the east.

Massi grabbed a pair of binoculars and scanned the ocean in the direction of Greenland.

Thirty seconds later, he saw the monster.

"We're not going to make it," he mumbled at the tidal wave roaring towards them at incredible speed, before lowering the binoculars and closing his eyes.

The tsunami, as tall as the ship, struck broadside at almost four hundred miles per hour in an explosion of foam, glass, and twisted metal. At that speed, the wave of icy water felt like a wall of reinforced concrete as it collided with *Polar Voyager*'s superstructure.

Millions of rivets popped like synchronized machine guns as the hull bent, twisted, and cracked in multiple places. The colossal momentum transferred to the superstructure, causing it to roll three times in its powerful wake.

A third of the souls on board perished during the seconds following initial impact, including everyone on the bridge. The starboard decks above the waterline gave to the tidal wave, buckling in nearly fifty feet, crushing cabins, dining halls, casino floors, corridors, and stairs. Freezing water burst through the hull into the core of the crumbling vessel, cascading to the lower decks. It flooded movie theaters, dance halls, and restaurants, drowning all surviving passengers and crew, before leaving the *Polar Voyager* broken in four sections. Three of them sank right away. The stern, which bobbed in the water with its shiny bronze screws pointed at the stars, disappeared from view five minutes later.

The fast-moving surge continued its deadly sweep, sinking every vessel, including two other cruise ships, several merchant vessels, fishing rigs, and even a large container ship and a pair of oil tankers. It sent thousands of souls—plus over a trillion dollars in cargo and equipment—to an icy grave at the bottom of Baffin Bay.

The tsunami finally reached the cliffs, coastal plains, and glacier outlets of Baffin Island, leveling dozens of thriving ports built in the past five years to cater to the increased summer commerce in the region. It continued inland for miles, flattening every structure, and finally colliding against the sharply rising terrain at the foot of the Artic Cordillera. An explosion of foam, mud, and debris marked the final moments of the tidal wave, before the waters receded.

The once-fabled and now thriving North-West passage, the silver lining of a planet deep in climate change, became witness to the worst disaster of the twenty-first century. Hundreds of cubic miles of sublimated ice, released as water vapor into the atmosphere by the detonation, returned in the form of Biblical rains across the region over the following week, hampering relief operations.

This unparalleled meltdown of freshwater, combined with the dozens of cubic miles of thawed icebergs in the fjord and the accelerated flow of Jakobshavn into Baffin Bay, exponentially diluted the salt water content of the North Atlantic.

As the world mourned the consequences of a despicable act of climate terrorism, the Gulf Stream slowed down, causing temperatures across Europe to drop by a seasonal average of eight degrees Fahrenheit, throwing the continent into an early winter.

By the end of October, as Europe endured the coldest blizzard on record, global sea levels rose by almost two feet, wreaking havoc in coastal areas around the world, including the Gulf Coast and the Eastern Seaboard, plus Bangladesh, Singapore, the Netherlands, Shanghai, and a host of other sea-level territories. It resulted in the deaths of thousands, the displacement of millions, the loss of tens of thousands of square miles of continental lands, and trillions of dollars.

And the worst was yet to come.

CHAPTER ONE
SURPRISES

"Greenhouse warming and other human alterations of the earth system may increase the possibility of large, abrupt, and unwelcome regional or global climatic events. Future abrupt changes cannot be predicted with confidence, and climate surprises are to be expected."
— U.S. National Academy of Science

NORTH SLOPE BOROUGH. ALASKA. JULY 6, 2029.

They flew in from the south, high above craggy mountain ridges that abruptly turned into a sea of thawing ice and tundra. A massive expanse of meltwater lakes and rivers disappeared into a horizon dotted by glacier-carved cirques surrounding monumental walls capped with snow.

Glaciers, ice on slanted terrain set into motion by the earth's gravity, streamed out of high mountains, pushing aside all which stood in their way. They spread vast blankets of white that slowly turned into meandering fingers of thawed ice as it reached the distant coastal plains.

Sitting directly behind the pilot of the two-seater amphibious Piper Cub, and wearing a noise-cancellation headset and dark sunglasses, Dr. Natasha Shakhiva followed the shadow cast by the single-engine plane over dozens of glassy lagoons of icy water stained with vivid hues by the day's first shades of sunrise. It created dazzling mirrors of infinite shapes and sizes surrounded by distant sleepy volcanoes dotted with snowy forests—all stained in hues of orange and yellow-gold.

From a distance the land looked peaceful, tranquil, seemingly immune to the global effects of the attack in Greenland.

From a bloody distance.

But even before the Greenland event drowned the world and froze Europe, climate change had steadily eroded the quality of life in Alaska.

And the rest of the world for that matter.

African countries had suffered the most. Multiple cycles of droughts and floods had spread disease, primarily malaria, dengue fever, and cholera. And that resulted in large population migrations north, to Europe, taxing the continent's already besieged infrastructure.

Closer to home, the United States struggled to contain the largest wave of refugees from Latin America in history as food sources declined south of the border from incessant droughts. But America was also coping with its own natural disasters. Monster tornadoes, wildfires, heat waves, mudslides, flash floods, and hurricanes continued to plague all fifty states. And there were those recent baseball-size hail storms right here in Alaska, which were becoming commonplace in the summer months for reasons no one could explain.

And yet, it seemed as if the world's super powers kept turning a blind eye to the reality staring them in the face.

But that's why you're here, to raise awareness of the danger we're in.

The fifty-year-old global climate specialist leading this year's International Arctic Research Center team—sponsored by the University of Alaska, Fairbanks—looked beyond the cosmetics of the magical sight, ignoring the dawn-streaked ice. Her veteran eyes surveyed the lake levels and compared them to the graphical information displayed on the FlexScreen she unrolled on her lap like a scroll.

The IARC logo momentarily filled the screen as the built-in camera scanned her face, unlocking the system. The logo vanished and the screen filled with the real-time satellite data linking her paper-thin system to hundreds of GPS sensors deployed across this melting land.

The images confirmed her observations—and those reported by the IARC team stationed near the shores of Shirukak Lake twenty miles away: record-low lake levels correlated with the increased loss of ice mass from the glaciers that fed them during the summer months.

And that also correlates to the three-degree-Centigrade average higher temperature than just ten years ago.

The Ukrainian-born scientist bit her lower lip, considering that while watching a flock of northern fulmars hunting in patches of bluish water bruising the thawing ice sheet. The native birds picked prey just beneath the surface while making their way to their roosting nests high in the cliffs of the Brooks Mountain Range, where Natasha had spent the past three days hiking to clear her head from IARC work.

Her legs sore from the long climbs, she momentarily enjoyed the sight, watching the slick fulmars drop to the water like fighter jets, stabbing the surface. Briefly disappearing from sight, they surged back up, winging skyward with their writhing prize clamped in their black beaks.

The light aircraft banked to the right and began a shallow decent towards the west shore of Shirukak Lake.

Natasha stared into the northern horizon, her mind going just a little farther, to the Arctic Sea ice that had shrunk steadily 7% per decade for the past three decades, to an ice sheet that had lost 50% of its thickness since the 1990s.

Dropping her gaze to the FlexScreen, she tapped the upper left corner and accessed the British Arctic Survey site through the dropdown menu. It brought up the latest images of the Arctic Sea ice cover and compared them to still shots of this time of the year in prior decades back to 1979. Running her forefinger on the left side of the FlexScreen's surface, Natasha switched over to the decreased ice volume in Antarctica. During the 1990s, the continent lost around 49 billion tons of ice annually. That number was now approaching 300 billion tons per year.

And there it is, she thought, staring at the significant ice cover retreat in the past half century.

In all of its bloody ugliness.

That, of course, had some effect on sea levels, but most of the recent rise, which had triggered evacuations all around the world and had also mortally wounded the Gulf Stream, was caused by the rapid loss of the ice blanketing Greenland in the past two years.

"We'll reach the base in five minutes, Tash," the pilot announced over the intercom.

"Thanks, Mario," she replied in English tainted with a Slavic accent. She pulled up a graph on the sea level rise potential from the British Antarctic Survey site, which ranked global ice masses according to their potential contribution to sea-level rise. A complete meltdown of the ice on the Earth's surface would result in a sea level rise of around 220 feet. Antarctica alone contributed nearly 87% or 191 feet. The Greenland ice sheet soaked up 24 feet, or around 11%, leaving just 2% or around 5 feet for all of the world's glaciers, polar caps, and sea ice.

And since the Greenland event, sea levels have risen almost two feet.

The thought evoked images of evacuations along the Gulf Coast as Florida, Louisiana, and Mississippi lost over 10% of their land. New York City and Boston were experiencing chronic floods. New Orleans was in trouble, as well as Biloxi, Pensacola, Miami, Tallahassee, and other cities down the Florida peninsula. And all of the above were now more vulnerable to seasonal hurricanes.

The Caribbean had lost nearly 10% of its land. Even the Texas coastline suffered marked losses, mandating the emergency buildup of higher levees to contain the rising ocean from eating up Houston real estate. Shanghai was also fighting off the ocean, as well as the Netherlands in the evolving geography of Europe, which was now in a permanent winter.

Natasha heard the engine's reduced RPM as Mario Escobar started his descent. The young Bolivian-born bush pilot and glacier researcher had joined her IARC team a year ago, soon after she first arrived in Fairbanks as a transfer professor from the University of Kiev.

Escobar used to study the tropical Andes glaciers of his home country until a relentless series of El Niños devastated them over the course of twenty years, forcing him to head north in pursuit of ice. Taller than her own five-foot-nine and sporting the fair skin and blue eyes of European descent, Mario Escobar had seen his beloved glaciers shrink as El Niños diverted the moisture away from the tropical Andes, starving the glaciers of their sun-blocking snow and triggering rapid meltdowns. But Natasha had not recruited Escobar because of his thorough knowledge of glaciers or aviation—both very handy skills in these regions. Natasha had selected the Bolivian climatologist because of his passion, because of the fire burning in his belly, and because of the anger etched in his lined face after spending two decades watching his country's ice melt away in the wake of undeniable climate change.

Passion.

You have to have passion for this, my dear Tash.

As they continued their descent, Natasha remembered her late husband, Doctor Sergei Shakhiva, a world-renowned glacier scientist who had lost a battle to an aggressive strain of malaria in New Zealand on his way back from an Antarctic expedition three years ago.

Without passion, you won't endure the hard battle ahead, the politics and criticism for the work we do by the large corporations—and the governments they control.

Twenty years her senior, Sergei Shakhiva had died while living life by his own rules, which was precisely how Natasha had sworn to live hers: at the outer reaches of a changing world doing the work few could endure, many criticized, some misunderstood, and most had ignored.

Until two years ago, when that bastard unleashed Jakobshavn, awakening an indifferent world.

But Natasha had not come to Alaska to study retreating glaciers or to measure the thickness of the ice shelf or to investigate sea-levels. That work was carried out by hordes of traditional global climatologists through multi-million-dollar grants from conglomerates seeking endorsements for renewable energy sources.

Doctor Natasha Shakhiva had been lured to this part of the world by renegade scientist and long-time colleague and close friend Dr. Konrad Malone. The controversial dean of the department of geology of the University of Alaska, Fairbanks, had recruited Natasha to spearhead a non-traditional study of the Alaska permafrost. The frozen soil formed 11,000 years ago, at the end of the last ice age, covered over 85% of Alaska and most of northern Canada—in addition to the Northern Eurasia permafrost domain spanning an area equivalent to the United States.

Malone was known as the "Ice Man" for having spent most of his adult life studying ice somewhere around the world while running research projects for UAF that eventually earned him the appointment as dean of geology. Malone had taken part in her husband's final Antarctica expedition three years ago and he too had contracted malaria in New Zealand. But Malone, forty years old at the time and in good physical shape, had managed to survive the malaria strain which had consumed her older husband.

Malone had eventually caught up with Natasha last year at a joint U.S.-Russian East Siberian Sea (ESS) cruise, where he convinced her to come to Alaska for a change of scenery.

The change will do you good, Tash. Sergei would have wanted you to move on.

Natasha sighed.

Although their relationship had started up as merely professional, there was something about Konrad Malone that made Natasha feel different, alive—even young. Perhaps it was because Malone was nearly seven years younger than her, or maybe it was his energy, his determination. Maybe it was the passion he had for his work, a passion that equaled—if not surpassed—that of her late husband, and her own.

Natasha wasn't sure, but she did know that somehow Malone had managed to pull her out of a two-year-long state of depression on that ESS cruise a year ago. So, when he had asked her to join him at UAF, it had only taken her a few days to finally agree.

And there was that bottle of Stolichnaya we shared in his cabin.

Natasha remembered that final night aboard the ESS cruise with fondness, as they toasted to a new beginning. They drank vodka the Russian way, eating pickles in between shots, before…

She smiled, then frowned while staring at her reflection in the Piper Cub's side window. Natasha had been beautiful in her youth, with striking hazel eyes crowning high cheekbones on a triangular face. But the damage from years of exposure to extreme elements had started to take a toll on her once silky skin. And those fine lines of age, a reminder of the cruel passage of time, had only deepened during her mourning years, when she had stopped taking care of herself.

Until Koni came along.

A part of her still felt guilty for the joy Malone had brought back into her life. She had loved her husband dearly, but he was gone, and she still had some life in her.

A life Malone had reignited in that cabin a year ago.

Natasha grinned again, then looked beyond her image on the Plexiglas, her stare gravitating toward the distant Brooks Mountain Range. Malone had brought her up to the mountains during her first week here. Alaska's cool breeze, clean air, and clear skies had kicked off the healing process.

Hiking in the mountains became her escape from the world. It was those brief but frequent hikes, when Escobar would drop them off by the shores of lagoons at the foot of the range, which allowed her to add perspective to her life. There was something about being alone for a few days every few weeks—just Koni and her, their backpacks, and Alaska's beautiful yet rugged scenery—that gave her an appreciation for the gift of life, for the time she was being granted on this Earth, and for the opportunity to live again.

And although Malone had gone to Africa for a few months to study a dying glacier atop Mount Kilimanjaro, Natasha had continued this hiking tradition at least once a month, before heading back to the realities of a world very much in trouble.

Back to work, she thought, watching the distant shores of Shirukak Lake materializing in the distance.

Her mission in this remote section of Alaska, however, was not to assess the thawing permafrost's risk to buildings' foundations, roads, or infrastructure on this unstable soil. It also wasn't to study the increasing number of the so-called drunken trees in forests rooted in softening soil. Those unfortunate but largely cosmetic results of the thawing of the surface-level permafrost were inconsequential compared to the global implications of the thawing of the deeper permafrost. Malone was concerned about this frozen shield protecting the world from almost two thousand gigatons—or billions of metric tons—of trapped methane gas.

A year ago, Malone had convinced a reluctant UAF Board to allow him to conduct a deeper permafrost study in spite of the pressure the university received from corporate sponsors to focus grant money on the infrastructure effects of surface-level frozen soil. The world of profits and balance sheets was more interested in preventing the destruction of roads, railroads, buildings, and airports than in the research Malone believed to be more important to the survival of our species.

Malone had also been successful a year ago convincing the Pentagon to direct the Army Corps of Engineers to dig a new permafrost tunnel near the shores of Shirukak Lake.

Just as he convinced me to lead the tunnel project while he disappeared in Africa to document the final months of its last tropical glacier.

The Piper Cub dropped to three hundred feet over the lake's smooth surface and Escobar pointed the plane's nose into the wind while lowering the flaps and further retarding the throttle.

The IARC base camp loomed into view, reminding her of the ten long months she had spent here working on Malone's controversial project in the shadows of better funded and staffed IARC initiatives. But Natasha's mind drifted to another time and place, to the overarching reason her long-time colleague and recent lover was so obsessed with probing deep beneath the surface.

To understand just how close we are to another Permian-Triassic extinction event.

To the unthinka—

"Tash, looks like Koni's military *amigos* have arrived," Escobar said in his thick accent, pointing to a pair of V-22 Osprey tiltrotor military aircraft tied down at the west end of the base.

"Well, he talked them into digging the bloody thing," she replied in the English she learned while getting her undergraduate degree at Cambridge a lifetime ago. "About time they showed up to see what they got for their taxpayer's dollars."

The thought of the months invested by the Army Corps of Engineers to build a new permafrost tunnel for the IARC team—a deeper and longer version of the one they dug in the 1960s in nearby Barstow—inexorably led her mind to the Permian-Triassic extinction event. Two-thirds of the world's species were wiped out 250 million years ago—long before the much more publicized Cretaceous mass-extinction event that killed the dinosaurs 66 million years ago.

The Permian-Triassic event, whose cause had been rigorously argued by the best scientific minds of the world for the past century, had just recently caught the attention of the Department of Defense due to its potential global implications. This was an event that made the terrorist strike in Greenland two years ago—and its devastating effects on the world—seem like child's play.

And if Koni's right, history is about to repeat itself.

CHAPTER TWO
THREAT MULTIPLIER

"Climate change will provide the conditions that will extend the War on Terror."
—Admiral T. Joseph Lopez, USN (Ret.)
Former Commander-in-Chief Naval Forces Europe and of Allied Forces, Southern Europe

PARIS, FRANCE. JULY 7, 2029.

I hate this fucking town.

Rachel Daly frowned while watching the scene beyond the window of the weathered Tesla SUV as they caught a red light.

No one could be trusted; neither the Muslim taxi driver zigzagging through thinning Parisian traffic this bitterly cold evening nor the cyberjunkies wearing SmartShades crowding the street. She saw them shooting up nanohallucinogen cocktails while huddling by the neon-washed wireless portal of a sidewalk Internet bordello on the Boulevard de Clichy, in the heart of Montmartre.

It amused and saddened Rachel.

Beyond the snow-pelted glass they injected themselves with concoctions designed to maximize the virtual-reality sexual high downloaded directly to their SmartShades from the cyberpimp tending the glimmering lavender access port.

Summer in Paris.

With snow on the ground.

Rachel shook her head at the way in which the world had turned to shit, especially since Greenland.

Plus, she was turning forty today.

At some point in her life, she wouldn't have minded spending this milestone in a place like this, drinking heavily to help her forget the fact that she was definitely into middle age and that the past two decades had rushed by before she could get her personal life in order.

Not only had the City of Lights lost its luster as a desirable place to celebrate such life events, she was also on assignment tracking down a critical informant.

And there was the frigid weather, of course, which continued to plague the continent after William Kiersted kicked the Gulf Stream in the balls two year ago.

And to put a cherry on her birthday shit cake, this past year she had also powered through the effects of radiation sickness. From reduced salivary gland activity and thinner hair to damaged cells lining her digestive system, placing her on a special diet. Plus, she had to undergo a double mastectomy and full hysterectomy as the gamma rays from that glacier ravaged her breasts and her ability to reproduce. But at least the good surgeons at the VA were able to save her nipples to crown her brand-new c-cups, which she saw as her cancer present to herself.

And the best is yet to come, she thought, remembering what doctors had told her just last week, as they released her back to CIA duty and she boarded a plane to come here. Her next decade was bright with possibilities, from lung and kidney cancer to lymphoma, melanoma, and leukemia.

So, happy fucking birthday to me.

Rachel leaned back and forced the poker face already painted on Case Patterson, the veteran CIA officer sitting in the rear of the Tesla next to her.

Albeit from very different backgrounds, Rachel considered Case and her professionals, a reality not shared by the Muslim driver. His hungry eyes kept undressing her through the rearview mirror on the other side of the thick glass pane protecting him from the rough clientele in this part of town.

Or is it repulsion he feels because my face isn't veiled?

Rachel looked away, ignoring the pervert's stare, though not out of fear of unwanted access of the wireless interface coating her recently-installed SmartLenses. Her ocular firewall was always enabled, preventing anyone with the latest optical malware from hacking into her computerized lenses and displaying unwanted advertising or even worse, triple-X videos. The porn industry was always reinventing itself, taking advantage of cutting edge technology to spread the gospel of dirty, kinky love far and wide.

The Tesla accelerated under the power of hydrogen batteries, its electric motors humming as it revved up, leaving behind the sidewalk cybersex party.

She shot another glance at the government escort she had met just this morning at the embassy.

The man assigned to accompany her was an old hand at the Agency, and he had the lined face to prove it, and also the quiet demeanor of someone who had been around the block. Case calmly stared out of his window, which sported a picture-perfect view of the lower section of the Eiffel Tower in the distance beyond the light snow flurries dancing in the stale air. The tower's top third had been missing since Islamic extremists blew it off back in 2026, the year that Europe finally slipped away from the Europeans.

Rachel frowned at the unfortunate sequence of events triggered by a significant decrease in cloud coverage, which led to a rapid decrease in precipitation starting in 2021 that continued to today. That further led to reduced flows of the Jordan and Yarmuk rivers, resulting in severe water shortages in Israel and Jordan. Combined with similar droughts in Iraq, Oman, Iran, and Egypt, widespread famine and disease were no longer biblical tales but reality.

Enter the largest wave of Muslim immigrants in history.

Unfortunately, the number of extremists amidst the hordes of Middle Eastern and African refugees was such that within a few years, Europe—France in particular—became the new Mecca for Islamic insurgents, the new promised land of suicidal fanatics.

The Beirut of the twenty-first century.

"Almost there," Case said, stretching the index finger of his gloved right hand towards one of a dozen bars lining his side of what had once been a vibrant, light-filled boulevard. Now, cyberbordellos mixed with traditional ones, for those still willing to risk contracting an STD to get a taste of the real thing.

A cluster of U.N. soldiers, mostly Pakistani, Ukrainian, and Malaysian—dressed in their now year-round winter uniforms—patrolled this sector of red-light district. Here, most buildings depicted varying degrees of damage from the wave of car bombings that razed the city six months ago.

Rachel glared at the soldiers through the glass. They were armed with enough weapons to start a small revolution, but in classic U.N. tradition, their presence was largely cosmetic. They couldn't use any of their advanced hardware unless directly approved by the Secretary General—even when under attack.

Useless bastards.

She considered these security forces as powerless as the World Health Organization, which was still struggling with the rapid spread of malaria across Africa and Latin America. And more recently Europe, North America, and Asia as climate change allowed the anopheles mosquito to populate new regions of the planet. And the little winged bastard always seemed to fly alongside its compadre-in-misery: the Aedes aegypti mosquito, primary delivery system of the cruel Zika virus.

Following the on-board navigator Case had programmed via remote when boarding thirty minutes ago by the Place de la Concorde, near the American Embassy, the Muslim stopped in front of La Scène, a strip club on Boulevard de Clichy less than a block from the Moulin Rouge. The former world-famous nightclub was now a run-of-the-mill whorehouse packed with Asian, African, and Middle Eastern women catering to a diverse crowd, including lonely U.N. enlisted men.

Peeling back the thumb of his skin-tight glove to tap the fingerprint scanner on the side of his credit card, Case wired the fare to the cab's meter. The 12-inch screen on the dashboard flashed a green *MERCI* a moment later, signaling the posting of the payment.

The magnetic locks disengaged, releasing the curb-side door. A hydraulic arm swung it open over a clump of brownish snow surrounded by stained concrete.

Case slipped on a pair of Agency-issued SmartShades, the black FlexFrame conforming to his face, creating a perfect fit. Its mirror-tint film was nanorized, providing a first line of defense against all known strains of ocular malware.

And anything that might get through would be stopped by his surgically-implanted CIA-issued SmartLenses.

He stepped out first, boots sinking in snow as he surveyed the bustling crowd—mostly off-duty U.N. personnel looking to trade their hard-earned Euros for sex, even if the majority of the surrounding hookers used SmartLenses and chemical blockers to keep their minds from remembering the experience.

That was another unexpected but interesting twist of high technology: selectively jamming unwanted experiences through black-market software, hardware, and injections, making it too easy for women to sell their bodies in the evenings without any day-after mental scarring.

Rachel mused. With the right blocking software, proper vaccinations, and a good pimp, they could, in theory, go on with their daily lives while making quite the income at shit holes like this a couple of nights per week.

In theory.

The reality was that the blocking software and chemicals had their quirks, resulting in the occasional unpleasant—and oftentimes shocking—*awakenings* of part-time hookers halfway through a trick.

And the realization of the limitations of today's software and hardware was precisely why Rachel, although in possession of SmartLenses like Case's, reached for a similar pair of SmartShades in a side pocket, holding them in her left hand as they exited the taxi.

Stepping over the snow accumulated by the curb, she settled next to Case in time to catch a glimpse of the Muslim checking her through the large side mirror before the door shut and the Tesla sped off.

"I think you made a friend there," Case said. He was slightly taller than Rachel and husky, strong, with light-olive skin, and very short brown hair. A powerful chin and chiseled features beneath the mirror tint of his SmartShades glared back at her as the right end of his lips lifted almost imperceptibly. Case had been with the Agency over a decade, and before that he had spent time with the SEALs—at least according to the dossier she had read on the flight over from Washington last night, before meeting him at the embassy.

"Fuck him," she said, using the SmartShades as a pointing device.

Breathing in the cold air, she stared at the departing pervert before surveying the freezing, gray, and basically utterly depressing surroundings under an equally miserable sky the color of gunmetal—the lovely place Uncle Sam was forcing her to spend her fortieth birthday.

For an instant, she caught her reflection in his SmartShades. What was left of her short hair hugged the sides of her very dark and now also very bony face, a mere shadow of her former self.

Rachel did what she could to counter the radiation-induced borderline-emaciated look through make-up. Although her new gaunt image had done wonders to accentuate her green eyes, cheekbones, and lips, like those skinny models in a *Vogue* magazine, she sometimes felt like she was just one step away from resembling a starving Ethiopian refugee.

As she stared at her reflection a final moment, she wondered if any of that expensive makeup really made a difference.

Like lipstick on a goddamned pig.

In her mind, no amount of mascara could hide the death mask of radiation sickness staring back at her every time she looked in the mirror.

But, hey, at least I'm back on my feet and feeling pretty darn strong.

Rachel had passed all of the necessary Agency physical requirements to be back on duty.

That's gotta count for something, right?

"So," Case asked. "Where's Payden?"

"Inside," she replied, slipping on the SmartShades, double-bagging her eyes from malware attacks.

Case's features tightened as he frowned while regarding the surrounding decadence. "Your boyfriend sure loves shitholes."

"Jimmy's not my fucking boyfriend."

"Then you won't mind when I nail his balls to his forehead if he refuses our offer?"

"I'll do the talking. I know this guy," she said, remembering the months she had dated James Payden back at the University of Colorado towards the end of her senior year. But then, Rachel, who funded her college through the GI bill, had to pay back Uncle Sam upon graduation by using her degree in glaciology to assist the U.S. Navy in a variety of expeditions to Antarctica. Upon her release from the Navy, she joined the CIA's emerging Global Climate Counterterrorism Unit.

"You may know this particular asshole, but I know this *kind* of asshole. Trust me, he only understands *one* language."

Rachel ran a hand through her thinning hair. "We do agree on one thing."

"What's that?"

"That he's an asshole."

"Amen to that."

"But, he's also *my* asshole, Case, so I get first crack at him."

"Fine."

"And if the information we obtain is useful, he gets a full pardon, some cash, and WitPro," she said, referring to the witness protection program.

Case kept looking about them, surveying the surroundings. "Pretty fucking ironic, isn't it?"

"What is?"

"That a petty crook gets ten to twenty for holding up a liquor store but this asshole, responsible for enabling the bastard who fucked up the world, gets a pardon and a condo on Nantucket Island?"

The dossier had warned Rachel that Case, like so many CIA officers with strong military backgrounds, tended to see the world in fewer shades of gray than your average CIA officer. But the dossier also suggested that what the man lacked in moral flexibility he more than made up in operative skills.

"Don't know about a condo on Nantucket, Case. Probably more likely a double-wide in some unknown town in the Midwest. But either way, not our call. The powers that be in Langley say he gets a deal if he cooperates."

Lifting his shoulders an inch, Case held one of the smoked-glass double doors open. A pair of Pakistani soldiers in the company of petite Mongolian whores wearing fake minks rushed out of the dark establishment. He waited for them to pass by, then extended a gloved palm towards the murky entryway.

"A gentleman?" Rachel said. "Didn't read that in your file."

"I have my moments."

The dossier had also revealed Case married very young, had two kids, and got divorced seven years ago, very likely due to his profession. Spies and families never mixed well, which at the end of the day was probably the best explanation for her still being single. In a way, she felt a bit jealous. Albeit divorced, at least Case *had* children. She, on the other hand, was completely alone—deceased parents, no husband or boyfriend, certainly no biological kids in the future, and with her bleak health outlook, adoption agencies would likely turn her down.

She stepped inside. An air saturated with the smell of booze, cheap perfume, cigarette smoke, and body odor washed over her.

"We do agree on another thing, Case."

"What's that?"

"This is a shithole."

Under the violet and emerald glow of neon lights, a long bar stretched down the left side of a warehouse-like room. Patrons sat on stools surrounded by scantily-dressed women of varying ethnicities while bartenders in dark uniforms busily moved about serving drinks.

Behind them, holograms composed of Trixels—3D pixels—of whores and ridiculously-endowed men performed sexual acts on a raised stage. The Trixel show was backed by high-definition natural scenes, from rain forests and tropical beaches to icy mountain peaks.

Rachel eyed the glaciers for a moment, bringing back memories of her years with the Navy. She had been happy then, working outdoors at the far reaches of the planet. The air had been fresh and invigorating; the scenery clean, pure, and unspoiled by humans.

Definitely in sharp contrast with the filth and decadence filling this bar—and this city.

Why did I ever leave that world?

The answer was always the same: the glaciologist in Rachel Daly had fallen in love with the hypnotizing beauty of Antarctica to the point she became obsessed with protecting it from ecoterrorists.

Rachel frowned while surveying the room.

The second-generation Trixel holograms lacked atmospheric-particle-balancing software and became partially distorted when cigarette smoke coiled through them, altering their effect to something almost comical rather than sexual.

A mix of whistles and howls from the bar and tables, the clattering of glasses and bottles, plus the surround-sound moans and screams from the cybershow mixed with a Cuban tune flowing out of unseen speakers. The steady Salsa beat reverberated across the packed room.

"Classy joint, indeed," Case observed. "Maybe I'll book it for my birthday party."

Rachel briefly closed her eyes, not knowing how to reply to that.

Case took notice and asked, "You okay there?"

"Yeah. Just peachy."

He dropped his eyebrows at her before continuing to survey the place, finally stretching an index finger at the rear of the establishment. "Your boyfriend."

Rachel frowned while peering through the thick haze, not certain how Case could see anyone in the back. But then her SmartLenses worked in combination with her SmartShades to resolve the image by averaging out the smoke and amplifying the available light. The result gave her a better view of the lone figure wearing a brown wool jersey and a cowboy hat sitting at a table sipping from a longneck Kirin.

Rachel filled her lungs with re-circulated air, remembering.

James Payden had been a superstar global climate student at the University of Colorado when she met him. Upon completion of her school work, she left to serve in the U.S. Navy while Payden became inspired by the research of Doctor Henrik Kiersted from the Danish National Space Center in Copenhagen. There, Payden joined the highly controversial climatologist in his theory that the sun played a major role in global warming. The theory proposed that energy particles from interstellar media, mainly from supernova explosions, entered the magnetic field streaming nonstop from the sun to create clouds in our atmosphere. If solar activity was high, as had been the case for some time, less of these cosmic rays would get through the magnetic field, and therefore that would lead to fewer clouds, which would result in climate change.

And this, of course, was considered heresy by the world's scientific community as it implied climate change was not primarily due to greenhouse gases.

Overnight, Kiersted was ostracized by his peers and took his own life shortly thereafter.

Payden became tainted by association, and his job opportunities dried up, forcing him to become a shadowy consultant for oil and chemical conglomerates. He made a living by helping corporations loophole their way through environmental policy. And when that work also ended, he went underground, assisting the Chinese get around the agreements from the Kyoto Protocol of 2005 which extended the 1992 United Nations Framework Convention on Climate Change in support of a global agreement to reduce greenhouse gases. In addition, rumor had it he even developed—or maybe stole—global climate computer models to help anticipate droughts and floods for the benefit of insurance companies and financial institutions that the Global Climate Counterterrorism Unit believed were tied to climate terrorist groups.

They proceeded towards the back of the club, zigzagging their way through a sea of tables packed with off-duty soldiers and whores, beyond a handful of bouncers and pimps keeping a watchful eye on the merchandise, ready to evict anyone abusing it.

They approached Payden's table, past a group of Pakistani soldiers in the company of African prostitutes. One of them glanced her way and smiled as Rachel glided by.

"Hey, sister," the young hooker said in heavily-accented English, the common language in this multinational part of town. She was an African girl probably still in her teens. "Fancy shades."

Rachel ignored her and focused on Payden. Behind him, doors led to the restrooms adjacent to a large metal door, the rear emergency exit. A neon **SORTIE** sign hung above it, its crimson glow pulsating from the club's stroboscopic lights slaved to the Salsa beat.

"Hey Jimmy."

Payden looked up slowly, his dark eyes under the brim of his old Stetson squinting for a moment, before glinting recognition. He didn't wear any SmartShades, which meant he was either in the possession of the latest generation of SmartLenses or he was abysmally stupid, especially in this town.

Payden briefly sized up Case before looking back at Rachel, his eyes still narrowed, perhaps taking in her new look, though the SmartShades did a pretty good job hiding some of her sunken features.

He broke the eye lock abruptly, took a sip of beer, and stared at the distant cybersex show before saying, "Hey,

Brown Sugar. What's with the shades? Afraid someone's going to fuck those pretty green eyes?"

Rachel frowned at hearing the stupid nickname he'd given her in school after dancing to that old tune from the Rolling Stones. She had not seen him in almost 15 years and this was the first thing he could think of saying?

"And those are new," he added, stretching an index finger toward her chest. "Got yourself some implants, huh?"

She sighed at the thought she had actually dated this man; though at the time James Payden had been a clean-cut good-old boy, and also a bright student with a promising future. Unfortunately, he had gone off the deep end with Kiersted's solar theory.

Ignoring his remarks, Case and Rachel sat across from him as he took another swig, set the Kirin on the seamless alloy surface, and added, "If you don't trust me enough to look me in the eye, I suggest you go back to whatever shithole you came from."

Rachel almost chuckled at the irony of the comment considering where they were, but she slowly removed her SmartShades—though her retinal shields were up and ready to tackle anything Payden or anyone else might want to throw her way. Case continued wearing his eye protection.

"Christ," Payden said, peering at her. "What the fuck happened to you?"

"I could ask you the same damn thing."

Payden grinned, exposing the shiny platinum dental work, which he had gotten somewhere in China after losing his bottom jaw to frostbite in Tibet years ago—at least according to the dossier the CIA kept on him.

"So, it's true then," he said.

"What is?"

"You were there in Greenland…when it went off."

Rachel just stared at him.

"Well," he added at her silence. "For what it's worth, you still have those pretty eyes and that beautiful skin."

"These eyes wouldn't mind locking your ass in hell and throwing away the key."

"Ah, but you see, we already *are* in hell—a *cold* fucking hell—and there isn't a damned thing anyone can do about it. You shouldn't have dismissed Henrik's work so quickly. Now deal with the consequences of pissing off his son."

Rachel made a face. "For the record, Jimmy, Europe being cold has *nothing* to do with Kiersted's theory but with the actions of his fucking nut of a son."

"And yet, here we are. You willingly crossed into this frozen netherworld seeking my assistance." He removed his hat and offered it to Rachel while adding, "Here, see if it still fits. Then you can ride me like in the old days."

"Let's cut through the bullshit, Payden," Case interjected. "Your funds have dried up and you're no longer viewed in the best light by your former employers, especially Kiersted, who thinks you fucked him over. We are your best option. You get a deal by cooperating. Now, what do you know about Kiersted's whereabouts?"

Payden's eyes remained locked with Rachel's as he put his hat back on and said, "Keep your pit bull on a leash, Brown Sugar, or this meeting's over."

"Stop calling me that."

"You didn't mind it so much when I was fucking you."

Case leaned forward and was about to stand when Rachel put a hand on his forearm.

The CIA operative paused in mid stand, exhaled heavily, and slowly settled back in his seat.

"Good boy," Payden said, grinning again, the lavender overheads reflecting off the smooth platinum behind his lips.

"I wouldn't antagonize him, Jimmy. He could break that little neck of yours before any of those bouncers can react."

"Sure," he said, tipping the hat toward Case. "Assuming, of course, that I was stupid enough to agree to this meet without bringing some protection of my own. Just because you can't see it doesn't mean it isn't here."

"Fair enough," Rachel said after a moment of silence and staring. "So, how about it, Jimmy? We're here in good faith, and we can really help each other out."

"And how exactly you think you can help me?"

"Like Case said, Kiersted thinks you crossed him, which makes you as good as dead."

"But you can protect me?"

She nodded.

"How exactly?" he asked. "You couldn't even protect yourself."

"Don't kid yourself, Jimmy. They're coming for you."

Payden leaned back and briefly closed his eyes while pressing the tips of his thumb and index finger against them.

"You can't run forever," she added. "Not from him."

"Good old Billy," Payden said while staring at the Kirin, before taking another sip. "Why bother nuking a city when you can drown the world *and* freeze Europe?"

"Bastard escaped," said Rachel with a heavy sigh, to this day still unsure how the terrorist could have survived the onslaught of explosive rounds the Navy SEAL team had scored on him before the blizzard struck. "Won't happen again."

Payden shrugged. "Billy was always nuts, even before Henrik killed himself. And after Greenland, he's gone bat-shit crazy. Word I got was the man's now only half human, madder than hell, and more paranoid than ever. You should have never let that wounded animal escape."

"Yeah, too bad he blames you for it," Case said. "Wounded animal's now coming after your sorry ass."

Payden's eyes regarded Case with indifference, then shifted back to Rachel. "Like I told you when you first contacted me, I just highlighted to Billy the weak point in the glacier, which any glaciologist could have done. I wasn't a part of any operation, but I got the blame as the only outsider to his network."

"And now he wants you dead," said Rachel. "And that makes us your new best friends."

"Fucking half-human nut job," Payden hissed to no one in particular. "Should have died in Greenland."

"We can help you, Jimmy, but you need to help us first. Where is he now?"

"First the pardon," he replied, touching the brim of his hat with a forefinger. "It's going to take much more than your pretty eyes, new c-cups, fuck-me lips, and that brown sugar skin for me to tell you what I know. Though I have to say, you're still packing it quite well considering you got nuked and are turning the big four oh today. Maybe your government can throw in a round with you on this deal?"

"Asshole," Rachel said, looking away.

Case reached across the table, grabbed Payden by the lapel with his right hand, and pulled his upper body over the table towards him. The informant placed both hands on Payden's forearm but it was evident he would not be able to break the CIA officer's vice-like grip.

"Apologize to the lady," Case ordered.

"Fuck…you," Payden mumbled.

Case released his grip on the lapel, grabbed his neck, and squeezed. Payden's eyes bulged.

"I said, *apologize*."

In the same instant, the bathroom doors swung open and two large Asians in business suits stepped out and moved towards them.

"Let him go," Rachel said.

"First, he apologizes," Case insisted, keeping his clutch on the cowboy, turning Payden's face red now.

The Asian bodyguards were almost on top of them.

Rachel put a hand on Case's shoulder. "Please. We need the intel, and he needs our help even though he's too stupid to know it."

Case sighed and shoved Payden back in his chair.

The informant coughed and swallowed while raising his right hand and staring at Case, an action that made his bodyguards halt their advance. But they still settled behind their principal, their eyes glaring at the CIA officer, who sat back and crossed his arms.

"I wouldn't do that again," said Payden, adjusting his hat, inhaling deeply.

"I wouldn't insult her again."

Payden just sat there for a moment, then asked, "So, are we doing business or not?"

Rachel and Case exchanged another glance, before he produced a letter from a coat pocket, tossing it across the table.

Payden tore through the presidential seal and unfolded a single sheet of paper, reading it before producing a small FlexScreen, which he used to scan the holographic presidential seal at the bottom of the sheet.

"All right," he said. "It's real. Now the money."

Case looked at Rachel, who nodded, before tapping a finger against the side of a CIA card, transferring the agreed-upon funds.

"You get half now and half if the intel leads us to him," said Case. "And if it does, you also get WitPro. But if you *lie* to us, the deal is off and we come after you."

"My information's solid," said Payden.

Case leaned forward placed both forearms on the table, an action that made Payden lean back. "I just want you to know that if you *fuck* with us, we *will* hunt you down. Kiersted will be the *least* of your damned problems."

Salsa music continued to reverberate across the dark establishment, along with the howls from customers and moans from the holographs.

Payden nodded as he verified the transaction in his FlexScreen. He handed the letter to one of his bodyguards and the FlexScreen to another.

"Where is he, Jimmy?"

"Siberia," replied Payden with a grin, the platinum dental work gleaming.

"What's he doing there?" asked Case, leaning forward.

"He's going after the permafrost."

Rachel also leaned forward. "The perma—"

"Crazy motherfucker wants to set the world on fire."

"How, Jimmy? How is he—"

A blinding flash and an ear-piercing blast preceded a fireball expanding behind his bodyguards, who instinctively jumped over their principal, shielding Payden.

Before she could react, Case threw himself over her, pulling her down to the floor.

Almost in slow motion, a sheet of fire projected above them.

Then everything went black.

CHAPTER THREE
BAD AIR

"A child dying from malaria every 30 seconds is completely unacceptable when we have effective and affordable ways to help children and adults avoid infection. Incredibly, one out of four child deaths in Africa are due to it."
—Dr. Carol Bellamy, Executive Director, UNICEF

FURTWÄNGLER GLACIER. NEAR THE SUMMIT OF MOUNT KILIMANJARO. TANZANIA. JULY 7, 2029.

Dawn.

A stabbing pain in his stomach awoke him.

Dr. Konrad Malone stirred and sat up in his cot in the half-light stillness of a tent pitched near the downhill edge of the shrinking ice sheet blanketing the sloping rock, several hundred yards from the main camp.

He had come here three months ago to record the final moments of one of the world's last tropical glaciers. Malone believed that the death of these equatorial ice sheets coincided with the thawing permafrost as they were both formed at the end of the last ice age. His data suggested that the glaciers near the equator were the Earth's early warning system for the release of the billions of tons of methane trapped beneath the permafrost in the northern hemis—

Another pain stung his gut, and he cringed.

What the fuck?

His mouth dry and pasty, Malone parted the mosquito net draped over his cot and stood. He collected his three-month-old long blond hair behind his neck and slid a rubber band over it, turning it into a short ponytail to keep it out of his way.

He glanced over to his desk opposite the cot, where a large FlexScreen housed the color images from the cores he had collected since arriving here.

Slipping into a pair of faded jeans, a sweatshirt, and snow boots, he stumbled towards the desk, feeling nauseated and sore.

But from what?

Not only was he in great shape from a lifetime of hiking and living outdoors, but after three months of daily treks on the ice hauling heavy gear to drill for core samples, his forty-three-year-old body was slim, firm.

Food poisoning, maybe?

He took a moment to go over last night's meal, which had consisted of a can of tuna, dry toast, and canned peaches.

Sighing while grimacing, he powered up the 30-inch polymer FlexScreen lying flat on the desk's surface. The system came alive with the IARC logo, before facial-recognition software scanned his features, unlocking the device and displaying a collection of color images from recent ice cores. He noticed a small image of Natasha on the top right hand side of the screen, signaling she had sent him a video from the shores of Shirukak Lake. A V-shaped pale face sporting a handful of fine lines around hazel eyes stared back at him beneath blonde hair pulled back in a ponytail, much like his own.

He opened it and the satellite stream stored in the flash drive of the FlexScreen came alive.

"Dear Koni," she began in her very unique and even cute British-Ukrainian accent from her years at Cambridge, where she earned her bachelor's in climatology before heading back to the University of Kiev for her PhD. It was there she fell for one of her professors, the eminent but much older Dr. Sergei Shakhiva. Malone had first met the climatology couple at the turn of the millennium at a British Arctic Survey dinner in London.

Malone chuckled, remembering how he had first thought Natasha was the man's daughter. But he had been able to contain his surprise, and over the course of the dinner and the subsequent conference, he made a connection with the passionate scientists, forging a life-long friendship.

"The bloody Pentagon arrived early this morning, *finally*, to get an update on the tunnel project in preparation for a briefing to the president before his address to the nation on climate change next month. I'll be taking them down tomorrow morning as they missed the window for today. Methane readings continue to increase in magnitude and frequency. I'm afraid there's a correlation to your work in Africa, which means your glacier must be growing more unstable. Be careful Koni, Furtwängler can go at any moment, with you on it. Please drink lots of fluids, keep taking your malaria medicine, and get enough sleep. I just returned from three days hiking in Brooks. I missed you terribly and hope to see you soon. With all my love. Tash."

The transmission ended and was replaced by the IARC logo.

Malone looked away while frowning. He had been the one who broke the news to her about her husband's death. Sergei Shakhiva had died in his arms in a remote clinic in New Zealand and Malone had brought his ashes home for her to bury. He had given her the space to mourn but also kept checking in on her from time to time, unable to get the feisty scientist with the captivating hazel eyes out of his mind. During the ESS cruise last year, he had convinced her to join his cause—and his life.

The Ukrainian scientist had begged him not to go to Africa, but Malone had convinced her.

"The tropical glaciers in South America have already disappeared, Tash," he had told her. "Once the one atop Mount Kilimanjaro vanishes, I fear the thawing soil will not be able to contain the monster. I must go and monitor them and drill the final cores."

Malone had left the IARC base camp at Shirukak Lake—and the side of the woman he loved—to hop on jetliners and travel a half world away to witness the death of the last tropical glacier on the planet.

His job consisted primarily of collecting ice cores using automatic ice-drilling equipment flown here via helicopter. Then digitally scanning the ice cores before packaging them for their long trip to UAF via the same helicopter that brought them their supplies.

In the process, Malone also had to deal with local authorities and pay for endless permits and handlers to be allowed to camp near the unstable ice sheet in this closed section of Kilimanjaro National Park to remove the final samples from a glacier doomed into extinction.

Of all the ice sheets that had once crowned this mountain, only Furtwängler remained. Named after Walter Furtwängler, the fourth person to ascend to the summit on

Kilimanjaro in 1912, the glacier had lost over 80% of its ice by the year 2000. In 2006, scientists discovered a large hole in the middle of the glacier, which continued to grow over the course of several months, finally splitting the glacier in two, accelerating the shrinking process. More meltwater continued to slip beneath the ice, acting as a lubricant over the inclined bedrock, creating a glacier hazard that Natasha believed could send the final section of ice—a half square mile and nearly twenty feet thick—tumbling down the side of Mount Kilimanjaro in another month or two. Similar events had already taken place around the planet as the ice thawed, like the 2002 headwall collapse and slide of Kolka Glacier in Russia, which killed 120 people in the village of Karmadon; or the sliding glaciers in Peru in 2017 that nearly killed their colleague, Mario Escobar, and which resulted in over a thousand deaths and tens of thousands homeless in downhill towns.

I have to go, Tash. Furtwängler is an indicator of things to come in Alaska. It's the canary in the coalmine.

Be careful, Koni. Furtwängler can go at any moment with you on it.

Malone reached for the small espresso maker next to the FlexScreen, powered by the same solar energy. He filled the water dispenser with crushed 5000-year-old ice from an ice chest beneath the table and waited a minute for the system to warm up and melt it before placing his stained coffee mug beneath the dispenser. He pressed the red button in front of the machine three times, giving himself a triple dose of finely-ground Kenyan beans, which he drank without any cream or sugar, letting the brew do its mystical work.

And to make matters even riskier, last night a beautiful full moon had allowed him to stay up very late drilling, and he had lacked the energy to walk back to the safety zone. So, he had opted to spend the night in the operations tent and rely on the slide-rate monitors--pressure stakes deployed in front of the ice sheet--to trigger an evacuation alarm should the ice decide to accelerate

He exhaled heavily, knowing very well the risk he took. If his calculations were wrong, an avalanching wall of prehistoric ice would crush him with little warning, as even his alarms might not give him enough time to reach the safety camp several hundred yards to the east.

In addition, even his designated safety zone could be endangered should the ice sheet shift while breaking up, placing his local guides in jeopardy. Malone had had an honest discussion with them two weeks ago concerning the higher risk of the safety camp's location adjacent to the unstable glacier. Only two decided to remain with him. The rest had headed back down to take their chances with the civil strife that had plagued Tanzania in recent--

He tensed as another cramp raked his intestines like a hot claw.

Dammit.

Pressing a hand against the offending spot, he breathed in, exhaling slowly, and breathing in again as the sting slowly passed. His current state of misery for a moment made him question his commitment for being here, in the middle of a dying continent to seek answers he hoped would be trapped in the thawing glacier.

Africa was considered the cradle of civilization and this glacier contained atmospheric history spanning many thousands of years of humankind.

In spite of the pain, he knew he had to gut it out.

When we lose the ice, we lose the history.

But that still didn't justify putting those two remaining local guides—Gideon and Lashi—in danger by keeping them so close to the unstable glacier.

They both had families.

But I have no choice.

In addition to his belief that the timing of this melting glacier was connected to the potential global release of methane, Malone needed to collect as much surface area from ice formed 4000 years ago to search for clues trapped by the frozen layer that might help prepare the world for even worse upcoming global events. The ice in question resided ten feet above the bottom of the sliding ice sheet, which he drilled relentlessly to collect as much of it as he possibly could.

Frozen in time in Furtwängler was an inch-thick dust band that captured a dramatic climate event across Africa when millions of square miles of fertile ground turned into what was now the Sahara Desert. The samples Malone collected foretold a story of extreme drought that plagued ancient Egypt and threatened the rule of the pharaohs. The episode, which coincided with a drastic shift in weather patterns that lasted around 300 years, pushed the world to the brink of a second Permian-Triassic extinction event. But somehow, the Earth pulled back from the abyss, allowing modern civilization to flourish.

Somehow.

And I need to understand it in order to—

A cramp doubled him over, and Malone dropped to the side, collapsing on the floor in a fetal position.

Fuck me.

His vision blurring, Malone reached for the two-way radio to alert his guides sleeping in the safety zone, but a seizure gripped him with savage force.

Hanging on to the radio, he managed to thumb the transmitter button three times fast, three slow, and three fast, telegraphing an *SOS*, and repeating the sequence until he could no longer hold it.

Trembling uncontrollably, he just hugged himself—his body feeling on fire, a headache flaring, his vision tunneling, his ears ringing as a fever spiked.

Malone wasn't sure how much time elapsed as the convulsions intensified, as chills rushed through his system followed by hot flashes. But somewhere in the distance, he finally heard voices, saw shadows shifting in the dim orange glow.

"Koni-man?" said Gideon, as he entered the tent followed by Lashi, Gideon's younger assistant. "Are you all right?"

"I...my head...my stomach," Malone whispered as Gideon leaned down, placing a palm on his sweaty forehead.

"You are burning up, my friend," Gideon said in his thick accent, which made it sound as if he was singing his words.

"No shit," Malone replied, his convulsions intensifying. "Tell me something...I don't fucking know."

"You have malaria," Gideon replied, before adding, "Lashi, get the medicine kit."

Malaria?

"No...I can't...not again..." he mumbled.

"Yes, my friend," Gideon insisted. "You have the symptoms. You need medicine immediately or you will die. There is no time to lose."

Impossible, Malone thought. The extreme trembling prevented him from explaining to them that for the past months, at the insistence of Natasha, he had been taking chloroquine, a preventive antimalarial pill, even though the altitude alone should have been enough to keep the anopheles mosquitoes plaguing the plains below from reaching him.

She even made me...promise I would sleep...inside a goddamned mosquito net...

In fact, since this was a UAF-funded expedition, everyone had to use the nets, even the local guides, handlers, and porters.

Malone suddenly got very cold, then hot again—boiling hot—his ears ringing, his eyes feeling like they would burn off his face. It reminded him of New Zealand, of the week-long bout he fought with the cruel disease three years ago.

He closed his eyes, shutting everything out, praying he would pass out.

Someone peeled one of his arms away from his quivering body, and Malone felt the jab of a hypodermic as his guides hooked him up to an IV to feed him the newest malaria cure Natasha had forced him to take along on his trip. Based on an old Chinese herbal medicine, the cocktail called artemisinin, as powerful as quinine, should kill the parasites that had ambushed his body. That's assuming, of course, Gideon was correct and Malone had indeed once more caught the pandemic disease that was responsible for one in every two deaths since the beginning of civilization.

He had to play it safe when it came to malaria. He had to assume he had the disease and get immediate treatment. If he didn't have it, then he would have just wasted good medicine. But if he did and didn't get treatment, the parasites would migrate to his brain, turning the infection into the often fatal cerebral malaria.

Like Sergei, he thought, remembering how even the strongest antimalarial medicine failed to save him.

But how the hell did I catch it up here?

He understood why he'd contracted the disease in hot and humid New Zealand.

But here?

At this altitude?

He had arrived at the Kilimanjaro International Airport and immediately transferred to a helicopter that took him to an altitude traditionally high enough to keep him above the mosquito layer.

Meaning, there was only one answer.

Tash was right.

He felt a stab in his other arm, followed by warmth spreading up his forearm. Almost immediately, the pain started to recede. Gideon had just administered a sedative to take the edge off.

"This should help you rest, Koni-man. We'll get you help, my friend. We'll get you help soon."

"The ice...Gideon," Malone mumbled. "Monitor the slide...rate..."

A fog soon enveloped him, pulling him away from the burning fever, cramps, and convulsions of a disease he should not have gotten so close to the summit.

Tash has to be right.

The same warming trend that decimated the vast ice-cap that had once crowned Mount Kilimanjaro was also allowing mosquitoes to colonize previously inhospitable highlands.

As he felt his guides carrying him back to the cot and draping the mosquito net over him, the fever propelled his thoughts to the periphery of his consciousness.

Malone began to drift away, departing the misery of his situation, floating far away from Mount Kilimanjaro, from Tanzania, from Africa. In his chemically-induced dream, Malone headed northwest, across the Atlantic, to the place he suddenly longed to be, to his home state.

Alaska.

And Natasha Shakhiva.

Malone continued to tremble, but he no longer felt the stabbing pains, the fever or aches. The powerful sedative rescued him from this reality while the artemisinin cocktail worked its magic, tackling the reproductive ability of the parasites while also methodically exterminating them.

He kept his eyes closed, but in his mind he saw the glaciers. He saw fingers of meltwater staining the pristine ice sheet.

The glaciologist saw the shores of Shirukak Lake, and he also saw her hazel stare as he had boarded that flight in Fairbanks three months ago.

Be careful, Koni. Furtwängler can go at any moment with you on it.

CHAPTER FOUR
ACTS OF MEN

"As parliamentarians, we have to stand on platforms around the planet and explain to electors why the forest is burning, the cattle are dying, why there is surf in the High Street. To explain…that these are not Acts of God, but Acts of Men."
—Tom Spencer, Member of the European Parliament

NORTH SLOPE BOROUGH. ALASKA.
JULY 7, 2029.

The circular tunnel, twenty feet in diameter, projected at a shallow angle deep into the permafrost.

Built by the U.S. Army Corps of Engineers, it included tracks upon which Natasha rode inside a battery-powered vehicle accompanied by U.S. Army Colonel Marcus Stone. He was the newly appointed chief of the National Climate Defense Alliance, a recent and much-overdue partnership between environmental scientists and the U.S. defense and intelligence communities.

Sitting in the left-front seat of the six-person, air-tight tunnel transport system, referred to as the "Pod" by the IARC team, Natasha reached for the control lever. It resembled an oversized videogame joystick mounted in the center console separating her from her single passenger.

Wearing a pair of faded jeans, hiking boots, and a gray UAF sweatshirt, her shoulder-length hair pulled back in a ponytail to get it off her face while she worked, Natasha curled her fingers around the lever and inched it forward.

The Pod started its slow descent down the shaft in a silence broken only by the steady hum of the refrigeration units on the surface keeping the tunnel's entrance below freezing to protect the exposed permafrost down the mile-long pipe.

Daylight receded behind them, replaced by glowing Xenon lights evenly spaced on dark-grey walls made of wind-blown silt mixed with ice that filled up this valley during the last ice age. Above and below them, glass wedges, formed when surface water drained below and froze, reflected the Xenon's steady glow.

It didn't matter how many times she made this trip, Natasha always felt as if the Pod was transporting her through a journey back in time. Glistening walls of ice and soil from another era surrounded her, layers of history dating back to prehistoric times.

But her scientific eyes saw beyond pristine crystal formations sculpted by nature's formidable hand, by millennia of pressure and cold that preceded human life on this planet.

The vehicle carried them deeper into the layer of permafrost at a forward speed of twenty miles per hour, reaching a depth of seventy feet in a couple of minutes.

Natasha eased off on the throttle, gently slowing them down to a halt.

She read the shaft's air quality data on the twenty-inch color screen in front of the center console, confirming the absence of methane. As added insurance, she glanced at the methane-detectors located every fifty feet and hanging from the roof of the tunnel. They were all green.

"No methane today, Colonel," she replied. "Air's good."

"So, we do have bad air quality days down here?" Stone asked, frowning, the freckles on his square face shifting beneath a full head of closely-cropped orange hair. The colonel wore the new generation Army Combat Uniform, or ACU-NG, sporting a digital camouflage pattern that suggested shapes and colors without actually being shapes and colors, resembling more green-black-and-grey noise. Even the U.S. flag on his shoulder had been digitized into mutated greens and blacks. The tightly-fitting ACU suggested a body as hard as Stone's cold-blue stare.

For an instant, Natasha wondered if the rugged colonel, who appeared to be in his early-forties, about the same age as Malone, ate stones in his morning cereal.

She nodded while pressing a button on the side of the control lever, and the glass canopy slid back, an action that automatically shut off the Pod's compressed-air system. "Eleven days so far this summer at this depth with a reading above five percent, enough to ignite the air—and we're only halfway through July. But most of the activity has taken place in the middle of the afternoon, when the surface permafrost is at its warmest."

She glanced at her watch as she stepped onto an observation platform that ran for ten yards down the right side of the shaft. Stone followed her.

"It's only nine am," she said. We're okay for at least a couple of hours."

"Then what?"

"Then we leave and seal the entrance to extract any methane through the ventilation system and into a surface storage tank."

"What do you do with the methane?"

"Power the camp's generators. The IARC base is environmentally friendly."

"Of course, it is," he said, then asked, "Doctor, do you have any data to compare this year to prior years?"

She frowned. "We lack a pure baseline because this tunnel didn't exist last summer. But we have data from the Barstow tunnel and from the hundreds of bore holes drilled by prior IARC teams over the years across this region. Our best estimate is that ten years ago there were zero methane readings this deep at ignition concentrations. Historical IARC data shows the first reading above five percent four years ago, at the beginning of August. Last year we had three ignition-level events the entire summer. Today the number is eleven, six of which have occurred in the last ten days, and we still have another six weeks of heat. None of the events resulted in measurable surface-level methane release."

"So, it's still contained...but increasing."

"I'm afraid it's worse, Colonel."

Stone blinked. "Please explain."

"The problem is the feedback loop." She pulled a laser pointer from a pocket and directed the red dot towards a soil and ice formation just above them. It glistened more than others in this section.

"Looks wet," Stone observed, a hand on his chin, lips pursed.

"It's thawing," Natasha corrected. "Mind you that we are seventy feet below the surface, and by our estimates around five hundred feet above a massive pocket of trapped methane."

"But, I thought that at this depth the temperature remained well below freezing all year around," Stone replied. "How can it be thawing? Is it the tunnel lights, or maybe because this tunnel is connected to the outside world?"

"The tunnel has nothing to do with it. At the moment, surface temperatures are close to sixty degrees, which is around eight degrees warmer than ten years ago. Back in those days, the temperature dropped very fast during the first five feet to just below freezing, and dropped maybe another degree by this depth. So, most of the temperature change occurred near the surface. Today, that constant temperature level starts deeper, closer to fifteen feet, and it remains at or just above freezing all the way down here. That's why the walls are starting to bleed."

Colonel Stone, a civil engineer who worked for the Army Corps of Engineers for many years before being appointed by the president to lead the National Climate Defense Alliance a month ago, stared at the tunnel's inner walls for a moment and asked, "Will that be a problem for the structure of this shaft?"

Natasha shook her head. "Not for a while. What's of more immediate concern is the effect the rise in temperature has on the permafrost's CH_4 transport ability—or what we call the permafrost's *methane flux*—to the atmosphere. An increase in five degrees at a depth of just two feet increases the methane flux by nearly 120 percent. And today at that depth, we are over eight degrees warmer than ten years ago, which increases the methane flux by over 200 percent, because the rate is also exponential. Said another way, the warming trend is rapidly decreasing the permafrost's ability to contain the methane deposits trapped below us since the end of the last ice age."

"And that correlates to the increased number of methane events," said Colonel Stone with a heavy sigh, arms crossed while staring at the glistening ice outcrop.

Natasha solemnly nodded, glad this military man was getting a good perspective of the magnitude of the problem facing them.

"This is why we also didn't go any deeper," she finally said. "The crystal lattice of the semi-frozen permafrost is too sensitive to oscillations, which could result in a dramatic increase in methane flux."

"Oscillations?"

"Any structure, whether man-made or natural, such as a stack of soil layers or tectonic plates—or a bridge or tunnel—has an oscillation frequency, or resonant frequency, which is the frequency at which the structure freely vibrates according to its physical parameters. External vibrations, like the drilling equipment to dig this tunnel, produce such oscillations. When that external frequency source matches the resonant frequency of the structure, the oscillation amplitude increases in a positive loop, usually leading to the collapse of the structure. This resonant frequency principle is the reason why hanging bridges would sometimes collapse under heavy winds."

He nodded and said, "That's civil engineering 101. It isn't the sheer strength of the wind that makes the bridge collapse but whether the wind direction and intensity trigger a destructive positive loop in the structure."

Natasha liked this man a little more. "That's correct. And in the case of this tunnel, the drilling equipment was injecting oscillations into the soil that my team deemed too dangerous beyond this depth."

"Makes sense," he replied. "Now, this sensitive permafrost region covers most of the upper portion of the northern hemisphere, right?"

Natasha nodded while smiling politely. Colonel Stone apparently had read some of the literature she had forwarded to him when he took office a month ago. "It basically covers most of Canada and Alaska as well as Siberia. By our calculations, the amount of methane stored in gas-hydrates beneath the permafrost and the onshore permafrost reservoir is roughly estimated to be around two thousand Gigatons. A gigatons is—"

"A billion metric tons."

She paused and nodded. "To put it in perspective, a sudden release of just fifty Gigatons would increase the amount of methane in our atmosphere by a factor of *twelve*. This is why a small disturbance of these trapped gas hydrates could cause catastrophic consequences in a very short time."

The freckles on his cheeks shifted again as his face tightened.

"And this is where the positive cycles increase the risk," she continued, letting him absorb the full effect of the problem. "As methane is released through the permafrost, it will get trapped in the atmosphere, bootstrapping the greenhouse effect and resulting in warmer temperatures, which will increase the rate of polar ice melting, which will release the methane gas trapped in ice—in addition to the accompanying rise in sea levels. On top of the resulting floods, this rise in sea level will cause warmer ocean water to extend over existing permafrost regions, disturbing these massive methane pockets formed before the Holocene flooding 10,000 years ago. We saw these methane plumes erupt in the waters of the East Siberian Sea last year during the fifth U.S.-Russian joint cruise. These are some of the ways ancient methane enters the modern chemical cycle. By the way, the event in Greenland two years ago has elevated sea levels by almost two feet, accelerating this methane-release process."

They returned to the Pod and continued in silence down the shaft to its maximum depth of two hundred feet, which was designed by Natasha to allow them not just to study the permafrost but also to create the ultimate early-warning system. The moment the pockets of methane gas four hundred feet below them pierced through, invading the tunnel in large enough quantities, Natasha knew it would be time to pull the fire alarm with the National Climate Protection Alliance.

"So, this is in essence our canary in the coalmine," observed Stone.

"One of them, anyway, Colonel. We have others," she said, and then explained Malone's theory correlating the melting tropical glaciers with the thawing of the permafrost.

"Well," he said, crossing his huge arms and glancing about the tunnel. "At least when coal miners saw the dead birds they immediately left the mine. We live in the fucking mine—pardon my French, Doctor."

"No worries, and you're spot on. There's no place to run. We'll be basically quite…well, *fucked*, Colonel."

Stone grinned, then said, "It's Marcus, please."

"And I'm Tash."

They stood there in silence for a minute or so on a spot that made them the closest humans to flammable gas in large enough quantities to incinerate entire societies.

Natasha checked her watch.

Ten o'clock.

One more hour before we seal the tunnel for the day and—

The high-pitch klaxon of a methane detector echoed inside the tunnel, its sound amplified by the enclosure. The lights hanging from the tunnel's ceiling all turned yellow.

"Methane event," she said, returning to the Pod and inspecting the screen above the center console. "Two point eight percent. Not enough to ignite, but unprecedented at this time of the day and depth nevertheless."

She looked up from inside the Pod at the colonel standing tall and strong on the platform. "That would be our cue to leave."

"I don't smell anything," Stone said, getting in the Pod before the canopy slid forward.

"Methane, like carbon dioxide, is odorless to us, and in these concentrations not harmful to humans in short exposures."

She placed the control lever in reverse and the Pod began its long and inclined ascent to the surface.

"Methane is now reaching the tunnel four hours before any previous recorded time of the day, adding to the exponential nature of the positive cycle."

"I'm calling the Pentagon ASAP," he said.

She nodded, glad the man was getting it, but nonetheless feeling as if she were sitting atop a time bomb the size of which humanity had never known.

Maybe with the exception of the poor bloody bastards in ancient Egypt.

Every time she came down here she always got the feeling of being on the cusp of the beginning of a very different era, just like what that ancient civilization experienced 4000 years ago. But as bad as that was, humanity had actually dodged the big bullet then.

Which is what Koni's trying to understand with those ice cores in Africa.

Natasha stared at the walls of trapped time surrounding her as her mind traveled much farther back in time, to the Permian-Triassic Extinction Event.

The big bloody bullet.

And which the evidence at hand suggested could become reality again.

An event of a magnitude the world had not yet grasped.

CHAPTER FIVE
THE ENEMY OF MY ENEMY

"The enemy of my enemy is my friend."
—Ancient Indian Proverb

PARIS, FRANCE. JULY 7, 2029.

The smell of cordite assaulted her nostrils.

Rachel Daly opened her eyes and watched the glow from emergency lights diffusing through the smoke, dancing in the thickening haze that veiled the cries and screams mixing with the ringing in her ears.

Case Patterson lay partly on top of her caked in white dust. He was no longer wearing the SmartShades, his face on her chest, wincing in obvious pain as he came around, an arm still around her back.

She remembered now.

The blast; the pressure; Case using his body to shield her, embracing her while taking the brunt of the impact.

Behind them, yellowish flames crawled up the walls and across the ceiling of the club, flickering through the smoke.

"Case!" she shouted above the billowing fire and the cries of patrons. Shadows stumbled in the descending inky cloud, scrambling towards the front of the building and away from the inferno sealing the rear emergency exit.

"CASE!"

The CIA operative blinked, coming around as she shook him, grabbing the sides of his face with her gloved hands.

A sense of relief that went beyond professional courtesy washed over her when he opened his eyes and stared at her.

"Hey," he mumbled, blinking, his face inches from hers. "You good?"

Seriously?

The man had just used his own body to shield her, and in her book, such reaction spoke volumes about the kind of person he was. And on top of that he was now asking if *she* was okay.

"Peachy, thanks to you."

"I have...my moments," he replied with effort, pressing an elbow against the floor to prop himself off of her.

"We need to get the hell out of here," she said, sitting up, feeling the heat on the back of her neck, the roar of whooshing flames drowning out most other sounds.

He turned around to check the nearing inferno.

"Case...your back."

The blast had shredded his jacket and peppered the skin between his shoulder blades with what looked like flesh wounds.

"Had worse," he said, grimacing while still getting his bearings. "Where's Payden?"

Squinting, the smoke stinging her even with the protection of her SmartLenses, Rachel gazed around the bar, pressing the sleeve of her shirt against her mouth, breathing through it.

The ocular software kicked in, filtering the inky particles obscuring the place, cleaning the scene as she probed her darkening surroundings, searching for the shape of —

There!

Payden shifted under the weight of his inert bodyguards a dozen feet away, blood oozing from their ears, their backs charred, smoke coiling to join the boiling layer accumulating against the ceiling. They had shielded their principal, absorbing the force of the blast.

But the bodyguards had been closer to the explosion. In addition, Rachel realized they had also shielded Case and her with their towering bulks by standing behind Payden when the bomb detonated.

Lucky for me.

Not so for Jimmy.

But your luck won't last long in here.

The blaring inferno swallowing the rear of the building leaped towards them, hungry, seeking fuel, reaching the bodyguards on top of Payden.

"Jimmy!" she screamed, crawling over to him, clambering on hands and knees, grabbing his wrists, tugging hard to free him from beneath the bodyguards.

Payden flinched, coughing blood, grunting as she pulled hard.

She remained as low as she could, dragging the renegade scientist out from under his dead bodyguards and towards where Case knelt.

Through the smoke, Rachel saw the burns across Payden's legs and back, the smell of charred skin and singed hair filling her nostrils, nauseating her, blending with the swirling cloud threatening to swallow—

The blaring reports of gunfire thundered inside the structure. Sparks exploded to her right as rounds struck the stained concrete floor, the sound mixing with the swelling flames. She released Payden while reaching for her 9mm Beretta 92FS, the same gun she had learned to shoot in the Navy.

Case grabbed the heavy metal table where they had sat and flipped it on its side with his left hand, momentarily shielding them from their assailants. He then reached for his own pistol, a Sig Sauer.

Rachel laid sideways on the floor, exposing her upper torso around her side of the table, her Beretta clutched in both hands, her SmartLenses probing deeper. The ocular software resolved two figures shifting in the smoke clutching automatic weapons.

"Got them?" Case asked, mimicking her posture on the other side.

"Yep," she replied, aligning the incoming threat in the sights of her weapon. "Take the left one. I got the right one. Ready when you are."

They fired in unison, the reports cracking above the inferno.

One assassin arched back on impact while trying to return the fire, his bullets ripping through the scorched ceiling above Rachel and Case. The second assassin was able to dive out of sight.

Red-hot cinders and smoking debris rained on them as they instinctively rolled to shake off the smoldering rubble.

"Did we get the second one?" she asked, dropping behind the table alongside Case while also kicking the smoking plaster away from them and Payden, who kept moaning while coughing up more blood.

"Don't think so," Case replied, his weapon trained on the spot where the mark had vanished.

Adrenaline searing her senses, she scanned for more threats as the heat continued to rise, and the flames behind them threatened to set their backs ablaze.

"He's waiting for the fire to flush us out," she finally said, realizing the assassin's tactic, her eyes starting to burn even with the protection of the SmartLenses.

"Yep," Case replied.

"Time's on his side," she added over the rumbling fire.

"See anyone else?"

"Nope." Her SmartLenses found only patrons stumbling through the smoke towards the front exit.

"Meaning it's just him against us."

"What do you have in mind?"

"The assassin who died," Case replied, narrowing his eyes. "Gave me an idea. Be ready to shoot the moment he gets up."

Case pointed his Sig at the smoldering ceiling exactly above where the assassin had vanished. He discharged his entire load in ear-shattering crescendo. Reloading, he did it again on the same spot, carving a circle in it.

Fire rained a dozen feet from them, like a flaming hail shower, followed by a scream and a dark silhouette rising through the glowering debris.

Sweating profusely and feeling lightheaded from the debilitating heat, Rachel fired again and again, spent casings flying off to the right. She ignored the heat and the near-blinding smoke, her SmartLenses tracking the shadow leaping across her field of view.

The assassin clutched his chest, dropping from sight as he fired at nothing, the reports from his weapon vanishing just as he did.

"Now!" Case said, surging to his feet while grabbing Payden by the right shoulder. Half conscious, the informant moaned as Rachel ran her free arm under the other shoulder, hoisting him to his feet.

They moved swiftly towards the exit in a deep crouch, dragging Payden as the fire consumed the bar.

Her skin protested the heat just as her lungs rebelled from the scorching wind she sucked in while shielding her mouth with the sleeve of her shooting hand, trying to breathe through it.

Sirens in the distance signaled nearing emergency vehicles, their sound mixing with their clicking footsteps and the grumbling fire.

Help's on the way.

But not for us.

They were CIA, supposed to be invisible. They could not afford to be questioned by local authorities.

Tears veiled the exit thirty feet away, her throat seared by hot smoke, choking her as a huge burning beam broke loose from the ceiling above the bar to their left. It crashed over the stage with a deafening sound that shook the entire structure. The impact kicked up a cloud of sparks and flaming debris, dancing ahead of them like a million fireflies.

Shielding their faces while dashing through it and across the final dozen feet, they reached the exit, the street. Safety.

Rachel took a deep breath as dark smoke thinned, unveiling a night stained by the red and yellow lights of arriving emergency vehicles. A large crowd of onlookers formed a semicircle a respectful distance from the entrance.

Case and Rachel concealed their weapons and cut left with Payden in tow, remaining at the edge where the smoke cleared, using it to shroud them from a potential second team positioned at a vantage point across the street or from converging U.N. security forces.

They reached the crowd and pressed on, going through a cordon of onlookers more interested in watching the burning building than in the departing trio.

"He won't last long," said Rachel, her hair soaked with perspiration and stuck to the sides of her head as they continued dragging Payden.

They turned right at the corner, and left at the next, reaching a dark alley away from the chaos on Boulevard de Clichy.

They hid in between two dumpsters and carefully set Payden down. Rachel knelt on one side and Case on the other.

"Jimmy. Can you hear me?"

Breathing in short raspy gasps, Payden slowly opened his eyes, coughing blood, before nodding, then smiling and whispering, "Thanks…Brown…Sugar."

"Who did this, Jimmy?"

"Billy…has to be," he whispered. "Bastard…tracked me down…somehow…"

Rachel glanced at Case, who motioned her to continue.

"How do I find him?"

Payden coughed more blood, his eyes losing focus. He was going into shock.

Rachel leaned closer, cupping his face with her hands, forcing him to stare at her.

"Jimmy! Tell me how to find him."

"Missed…those eyes."

"Jimmy! Dammit!"

Payden's stare locked with hers, and breathing deeply, he said, "Vorota…" his breath pungent with beer and the coppery smell of blood, his mouth a mess of shiny platinum and red. In a strange way, he looked almost robotic. "Andrei…Vorota."

"Who's he?"

"Arms dealer…"

Case was already checking his FlexScreen, producing a moment later a photo of the Russian dealer taken a year ago according to the encrypted CIA dossier.

He showed the screen to Payden. "This him?"

Payden's breathing became more erratic, with the gurgling sob that signaled internal bleeding. He was slowly drowning in his own blood. Still, the informant managed to stare at the digital image for long enough to nod ever so slightly before going into quietus spasms.

Rachel held him for a final minute, until all movement ceased.

"Come," said Case, already standing. "We need to reach the embassy and get to the airport ASAP. I'm going to request an Agency jet."

"Case, your back. You need—"

"I know. But we need to get out of here."

"Thank you," she said, placing a hand on the back of his head and wiping off the layer of ashes.

"Anytime," he replied with a slight grin. "Let's roll."

They walked to the opposite end of the alley with the sound of fire engines and police vehicles resonating in the background.

She looked back just as they turned the corner. For one final instant, Rachel stared at the forever stilled figure of someone whom she had once cared for.

As much as she hated James Payden for the choices he had made in his life, for betraying her as well as the global climate community, for selling his intellect to the dark side—for showing Kiersted where to plant his suitcase nuke, and nuking her in the process—he had been the only person on the planet who knew that today was her birthday. Her parents had died long ago and all of her adult relations had been short-lived due to the demands of her job, requiring her to travel the world in search of potential climate threat. Even the place she called home, the Global Climate Counterterrorism Unit, amounted to little more than a handful of acquaintances plus an impersonal cubicle lost in a sea of government offices in Washington, D.C.

So, Rachel Daly, forty years old, had no one to share this milestone in her life, no one to celebrate her birthday because no one knew or gave a damn.

Except for James Payden, a man who had insulted her in that bar, and who was now dead, though in her mind he'd died long ago. And the thought of death made her think of her very dark medical prognosis.

Happy fucking birthday to me, indeed.

She walked next to Case towards the American Embassy on the Champs-Elysées, near the Place de la Concorde.

And did so in silence.

CHAPTER SIX
CLIMATE DISSIDENTS

"Those who are absolutely certain that the rise in temperatures is due solely to carbon dioxide have no scientific justification. It's pure guesswork."
—Henrik Svensmark, Director of the Centre for Sun-Climate Research, Danish National Space Centre

NORTH OF KANGERLUSSUAQ. GREENLAND'S NORTHWEST COAST. JULY 7, 2029.

The distant gunshot cracked across the vast expanse of tundra, echoing against the rocky hills surrounding it.

Standing at the edge of an overhang above a coastal valley once permanently covered with ice, William Kiersted observed the carnage below.

Villagers had gathered most of their sled dogs and were shooting them.

You never really know what you're capable of.

Dogs in Arctic communities such as the one below were working animals, used to travel to other villages or to hunt the whales and seals that often got trapped in frozen bays. The retreating Greenland ice shelf had robbed them of their work, and lacking any seal scraps to feed them, their owners had no choice but to put them down.

Mosquitoes buzzing about him—another result of the warming trend—William stared at the four-by-four Toyota trucks fitted with oversized tires parked along the east end of the sea-side village. They were the locals' new mode of transportation through the thawed tundra and the trails and unpaved roads leading to nearby towns and seaports.

Another shot whipped across the valley, followed by a high-pitched yelp as a villager's bullet failed to kill a large grey and white Alaskan husky. The doomed animal thrashed and yelped on the grassy meadow amidst the barks and howls from other condemned dogs and the cries of the villagers.

These people love their damn dogs.

Another villager put the animal out of its misery with a well-placed round to the head.

The yelping ceased, but the barking continued from a dozen chained huskies as two men picked up the carcass by its legs and carried it to a nearby pile, which they doused with kerosene before setting it ablaze.

William stared at the inky smoke coiling to the blue skies as more shots echoed across the field, before walking away from the edge and towards the large Cessna Caravan turboprop being refueled at the hilltop airstrip.

Once used heavily by glacier-tour groups, the strip remained in operation primarily to serve general aviation aircraft traveling between America and Europe for a variety of reasons, including ferry pilots performing aircraft deliveries, corporate jets on business trips, and research teams such as the one William and his small team pretended to be.

He stared at the red and blue emblem painted on the sides of the 12-passenger Caravan from the European

Arctic Research Agency, a front company William had founded to allow him easy access to countries in the region. His credentials had been good enough to fool the two part-time customs officials smoking by the terminal across the tarmac—at least enough for them not to question the strange machinery stored in the plane's rear cargo compartment.

Or to spot the weapons we're carrying in a secret compartment beneath the floor.

The sturdy Caravan stood tall atop a pair of Wipline 8000 amphibian floats that sported retractable wheels beneath them, turning the venerable Cessna turboprop into a truly versatile machine. And making it the largest single-engine plane on floats commercially available today.

As more reports reached the airstrip, William paused to admire the slim silhouette of Lian supervising the fueling process.

Two mechanics on ladders huddled over the open engine cowling while a ground attendant, also on a ladder, finished fueling the tank in the Cessna's left wing before shifting over to the right one.

After discussing something with the mechanics, who headed back to the terminal, Lian used the ground crew's twenty-foot-tall fueling ladder to inspect the level of the right tank with a dip stick. He knew enough about pre-flight checklists to be aware that she wanted to make sure the crew had pumped the correct amount. Climbing down and walking under the same wing, she used a clear sampler cup to collect small amounts of fuel from multiple drain points, checking for water and other contaminants.

Apparently satisfied, she moved the ladder to the left wing to repeat the process.

William admired the fluidity and precision in her movements as she performed a preflight check, making her way around the plane. She was a pro and an asset to his mission. Lian could fly the Caravan at tree-top level for hours and take-off and land on any body of water or virtually anywhere on land flat enough and in pretty much any weather. She had incredible physical and mental endurance, spoke Mandarin, English, and good-enough Russian, and could also handle most firearms with expert ease.

It was Lian who had dragged his half-dead body after taking multiple bullets and shoved him into their getaway helicopter when American commandoes surrounded his team in Jakobshavn's tongue.

It was Lian's superb flying skills that had allowed her to take-off in zero visibility just minutes before the Americans overran their position.

It was Lian who had fooled the aircraft dispatched to intercept their escape, flying in a blizzard through mountainous terrain.

It was Lian who had kept him alive in a remote hospital north of Beijing in the midst of the world's largest manhunt.

And it was Lian who had secured the services of the world's best surgeons to make him whole again.

Wearing skin-tight blue jeans, boots, and a black sweater, Lian looked up to inspect the underside of the Caravan's nose, beneath the engine, aiming the beam of the LED flashlight she held in her right hand.

William approached her from behind as she leaned down to inspect something on the ground. In doing so, she revealed a small red lotus tattoo on an exposed inch of skin between her jeans and sweater, just above her buttocks.

She continued to inspect what looked like a small puddle of oil as she said, "Enjoying the view, yes?"

William smiled. "Enjoyed it all last night."

She straightened and turned around, her dark hair framing the smooth skin of her narrow face, her fine features tightening. She looked more Indonesian than Chinese, her light olive skin glistening in the morning sun.

She put a hand on her child-thin waistline while compressing her crimson lips into a frown.

"What?" he asked.

"Minor leak." She trained the beam of her flashlight on a dark circle on the tarmac directly under the engine.

William shrugged. "Fine. Fix it."

She shook her head and looked toward the terminal. "Need to show them how. They went to get tools. Ten more minutes."

William nodded. Like all top-notch military pilots, Lian knew her aircraft's systems well, and dealt with equipment issues with calm pragmatism.

He returned to the edge of the field and regarded the sea beyond the abyss, confident she had her end of this mission covered.

The strip stretched for nearly a mile on this wide plateau, once blanketed with ice except for the air field. But the ice no longer returned to these coastal regions during the winter months. In its place a rising sea in the past two years had swallowed many seaside villages, and those which survived, like the one below, were forced into a very different form of existence.

William lost track of time as he stared at the product of his handy work on the glacier's tongue.

They should have listened to my father.

They should have treated him with the respect he deserved.

And now they'll pay again for what they did to him and mom.

They'll pay for what they did to me.

The world will die in two days and—

"Talking to yourself again, Billy?"

William turned around and stared at Lian, arms crossed and head cocked to the right, a shrewd smile on her face while regarding him with dark amusement.

As he was about to reply, another gunshot cracked in the valley as the column of smoke and a pungent smell of burnt flesh and singed hair continued to rise, pushed inland by the sea breeze.

"Finished?" he asked.

"Of course," she replied.

He nodded at the self-assurance exuding from this woman.

They walked side by side to the Caravan, entering through the retractable step ladder, which William pulled up behind him, locking the hatch.

She blew him a kiss before heading towards the cockpit while he turned aft, beyond the sleeping fig-ure of Hans-Jorgen, the only other surviving member of the Greenland strike, and who had been instrumental in staunching the bleeding while Lian flew the helicop-ter in the blizzard. Behind Hans-Jorgen sat Doctor Yuri Gerchenko, the elder Russian mechanical engineer in charge of their precious equipment safely secured in the cargo area behind the lavatory.

And that formed this team, this cell of his global cli-mate organization—small, nimble, and operating com-pletely autonomously from his other cells.

William took his seat next to the snoring Danish war-rior, whose bulk dwarfed even the wide leather seat of the executive seating configuration of this Cessna Caravan, which William had received as payment for success-fully handling a weapons deal for the Russian Mafia six months ago. Lian had personally chosen the options on the brand-new aircraft normally configured to carry 12 to 15 passengers. Instead, she customized it as a long-range cruiser with four executive seats in the main cabin, a gener-ous lavatory, and plenty of utility capability for the various cargoes they would be hauling.

The turboprop came alive and Lian taxied to the end of the runway before turning into the wind.

As expected, the former Chinese military pilot treated them to a smooth takeoff before steering the nose toward their new target.

This time they will not hurt me, he thought, flexing his right forearm muscles, whose nerve endings controlled the third generation iLimb prosthetic hand and wrist medical specialists in Beijing had surgically fitted to his maimed forearm. To interface it, William had been injected with hundreds of myoelectric sensors, which detected his muscle activity before transmitting commands to the artificial hand through a web of fiber optic connectors. Power came from a hydrogen peroxide pneumatic system that had replaced the bulky and slow electric motors of prior-generation units. The hydrogen peroxide reacted with an iridium catalyst to drive the hand's movements. William simply replaced a small capsule of hydrogen peroxide every month in a com-partment near the base of the thumb, and he changed the even smaller iridium catalyst unit next to it once per year to keep his hand fully operational.

He watched as his fingers stretched before slowly curl-ing into a tight fist. It had taken three frustrating months of therapy to control finger movement with enough dexterity to tie his own shoe laces, type on a computer, and even handle a knife or firearm as expertly as he could with his right hand. Plus, the iLimb included a rotating thumb, which allowed him more freedom of movement than his real hand and a stronger grip. And to top it all off, the iLimb looked as real as his biological hand, down to the flesh color, veins, hair, and fingernails.

But it was the fingers of his right hand that William used to feel the scar tissue on his abdomen, just below the sternum, where American bullets had ripped it open, filling his stomach and intestines with lead. William could no longer eat like a normal human being after Chinese surgeons removed large sections of his damaged digestive system, leaving him with little ability to process many foods. Nourishment now came primarily in the form of easily digested liquids, an occasional IV, and various types of baby food.

William lowered his only natural limb to touch his artificial legs, amputated above the knees after gangrene set in before Lian could reach the hospital in China. The third-generation prosthetics, also from iLimb, operated on the same principle as his artificial hand, detecting the movement of his remaining thigh muscles for control and also powered by hydrogen peroxide capsules and iridium catalysts.

But it was his face that bothered him the most. He had lost his right cheek, right eye, and part of his jaw to a bullet, forcing him to wear a flesh-colored carbon fiber mask, fake hair, and a third-generation lens that wasn't quite as sharp as his undamaged eye, but provided him with the peripheral vision and depth perception he had lost on Jakobshavn's Isbrae.

William looked at his reflection on the Cessna's oval side window, cringing in an anger he seldom showed. Plastic surgeons had done what they could to mold the carbon fiber and transplanted tissues to match the left side of his face, but the overall effect was more android-like than human.

He closed his eyes in silent fury at the world for the loss of his parents.

And for robbing me of my humanity.

As Lian reached their cruising altitude high above a layer of broken clouds, William opened his eyes and stared into the distance. Somewhere beyond the horizon lay millions of square miles of permafrost. And the fifty-year-old Soviet technology monopolizing the cargo compartment was just what the thawing soil needed to unleash the monster and give the planet a fresh beginning.

CHAPTER SEVEN
THE FIST OF GOD

"And there was lightning, and voices, and thundering, and an earthquake, and great hail."
—Revelations 8:12

FURTWÄNGLER GLACIER. NEAR THE SUMMIT OF MOUNT KILIMANJARO. TANZANIA. JULY 8, 2029.

It happened suddenly.

The crystal lattice formed 11,000 years ago cracked along the eastern rim of the towering headwall.

Multiple fissures channeled surface meltwater down to the base of the ice sheet, lubricating its contact with the bedrock, allowing the gravitational pull to exceed the opposing surface friction.

The moulin—the widening cleft in the ice—swallowed blue streams of water in a cascading rush at the heart of Furtwängler's rapidly expanding ablation zone.

Decades of relentless warming and decreased sun-blocking snow tore through the heart of the last ice sheet in Africa. The final pocket of white atop Mount Kilimanjaro trembled as molecular bonds disintegrated by the trillions, turning ice into slush, and slush into rivers gushing out from beneath the hydroplaning glacier.

And the moulin widened.

Resembling sheet lightning in slow motion, rifts propagated across the ice, devouring foaming torrents of deep-blue water across the icescape while spreading jagged tentacles in all directions, fracturing the surface like a collapsing windshield; and going deeper, to the base of the glacier.

Yielding to heat and gravity, Furtwängler shuddered, struggling to remain whole, resisting the forces ripping it apart, rapidly losing its grip on the inclined bedrock as the deluge flowing from the surface released its brakes.

* * *

The soul-numbing crash rattled Dr. Konrad Malone from his malaria-induced sleep.

The ice, Gideon…monitor the—

The loud explosion that followed tipped his cot, the sound reverberating inside his tent, pounding his eardrums.

Malone tumbled to the ground, skinning both palms as he broke the fall. He tried to stand but fell again as another explosion shook the rocky terrain beneath him.

Sweet Mother of—

The ensuing shockwave ripped through the canvas, exposing the surreal sight outside while pushing him back with animal strength, as if the Fist of God had punched him squarely in the chest. The blow knocked the wind out of him, striking him down, leaving him gasping for breath curled up on the gravel floor.

Beyond the shredded canopy a thick column of ice three stories high broke away from the collapsing head-wall, striking a rock formation a hundred feet from him. Roaring while breaking up on impact in a deadly avalanche of car-size blocks, it careened down the steep mountain-side, accelerated by a deafening wave of icy water shooting out from beneath the glacier, shattering into smaller chunks amidst clouds of white foam.

Stumbling to his feet, Malone struggled to clear his mind. He needed to get out, had to exit the tent, gain perspective, define an escape path.

He looked about him, realizing he wasn't in the operations tent in front of the glacier anymore.

Gideon and Lashi must have carried me to—

Gideon and Lashi! Where are—

A massive sheet of ice tore away from the glacier's sidewall with a high-pitch shriek, almost as if crying out to the heavens in a final moment of agony, briefly looming over him just as Furtwängler shifted.

Fuck me.

Malone stared at it with frozen terror, the sheer magnitude and proximity of the tilting wall of ice gripping his senses, humbling him as he momentarily recognized his tiny reflection standing in the middle of the collapsed tent facing this glistening monster.

Instead of leaning downhill, the colliding forces of the glacier pushed the seceding ice wall towards the safety camp.

Towards the stunned glaciologist.

He scrambled away as the blast shook the bedrock beneath his bare feet. The exploding frozen barrage swallowed the tent seconds later in a cloud of glacial shrapnel.

Malone ran, ignoring the gravel stinging his soles and the shards of ice scouring the terrain just behind him with the power of a hundred whips. He had to get away; had to—

The shockwave kicked him in the back, bending him like a bow, lifting him off his feet, and flinging him into the larger dining tent, which collapsed on impact.

More ice separated from the headwall as it gathered speed, breaking up in motion while following the steep contour of Mount Kilimanjaro. Its sheer mass set off a gust of wind that lifted the canvas where he lay dazed, confused, catapulting him across what remained of the dining tent.

Malone looked about him as the exploding glacier, the sky, and the flapping canvas below him changed places in a nauseating whirl until he struck something soft, briefly cushioning his fall.

Fighting the sudden urge to vomit, he staggered once more to his feet in the middle of the dining tent, clambering away from the wintry onslaught behind him.

The incessant frigid volleys from the collapsing ice sheet, like a bombardment of hand grenades detonating in uncontrolled fashion all around him, pounded his eardrums.

But he persisted, ignoring it all—the blasts, the avalanches, the scraping gravel, the roaring glacier. Through the insane blur of a world collapsing around him, mixed with his growing dizziness, Natasha's words echoed in his mind.

Be careful, Koni. Furtwängler can go at any moment with you on—

More explosions rumbled across the safety camp, shredding tents and destroying equipment; the blinding-white hail-laden salvos battered him, smacked him, and pushed him into a small communications shack at the farthest edge of the camp.

Malone braced himself for impact as he flew sideways for a dozen feet, hands on his face to protect it from the flesh-rending ice. He sunk his right torso into the canvas, which wrapped around him, momentarily lessening the blow before a hard object rammed into his gut, bending him in half.

Coiled in a fetal position, quivering, gasping for air, his arms, chest, and back bruised, Malone watched through tears as the doomed glacier rushed downhill in a death spiral amidst ground-trembling bursts of silver and white beneath an African sky.

Scourged, his body whipped raw, no longer capable of running, he surrendered to nature and simply lay there as the avalanche lurched past him towards the valley thousands of feet below. Its ear-piercing roar steadily dwindled, receding into a distant low rumble, before vanishing altogether. It was replaced by the whistling wind sweeping over the wet rocky ledge where the glacier had lived since the end of the last ice age.

Dumbfounded, he stared at the naked bedrock in silence, breathing in and out, swallowing, the realization of what he had just witnessed overshadowed by the sheer disbelief he had actually survived it.

But where are Gideon and Lashi?

Malone didn't recall hearing them in the past two minutes, though the roaring ice would have drowned their cries.

We'll get you help, Koni-man. We'll get you help soon.

Malone remembered now.

He glanced at his watch, realizing he had been sleeping for nearly 24 hours.

Maybe they left to get help?

Malone could only hope they had. But whatever the answer, he recognized that although he had survived this, for the time being he was alone, and it was not clear when help would arrive.

But through the shock and the pain, through the intense discomfort of his throbbing abdomen and lacerated body, through the terrifying near-death experience, he had another realization: The secrets trapped in Furtwängler were safe; they were alive in the core samples he had taken in the past months.

And in them, forever frozen in time, lay the data he needed to understand how the world had come so close to the brink of another Permian-Triassic extinction event 4000 years ago.

But first you need to get to it.

He needed to reach the basement labs of the University of Alaska, Fairbanks, where the bulk of the ice he extracted from the vanished glacier resided.

Malone fought the dizziness invading his mind, the invisible force propelling his thoughts to the periphery of his consciousness.

Hidden in the layers of dust trapped by millennia of glacial activity was the proof he needed to convince and prepare the world for the apocalyptic events the planet could face very soon.

Even if humanity somehow managed to dodge the Permian-Triassic bullet again, the climate problems plaguing the world today would be child's play compared to the terrifying future it potentially faced.

His eyelids grew very heavy as he lay there staring at the blue skies a final moment.

Furtwängler really did a goddamned number of me. Kicked my ass.

And just before passing out, that thought somehow evoked images of the nightmare endured by Egypt's pharaohs.

CHAPTER EIGHT
DIVINE KINGSHIP

"Have the wisdom to abandon the values of a time that has passed and pick out the constituents of the future. An environment must be suited to the age and men to their environment."

—Ancient Egyptian proverb found in the temples of Luxor

MEMPHIS, EGYPT (CAPITAL OF THE OLD KINGDOM, 12 MILES SOUTH OF MODERN-DAY CAIRO). 2210 B.C.

The blood…it's everywhere.

Pepi II Neferkare had never seen so much innocent blood spilled in his forty years as pharaoh.

The crimson pool surrounding the altar coagulating in the mid-morning sun buzzed with flies.

The sacrifices began shortly before dawn, the coolest time of the day, before the scorching heat forced most to seek the shelter offered by the thick limestone walls of pyramids and temples.

One by one, slave girls furnished with fine linen, lapis beads, gold necklaces, and ivory and turquoise bracelets had been escorted in complete secrecy by his personal guards up the steps of the Temple of Ptah, the creator god of Memphis' holy triad.

The girls had been forced onto the smooth granite surface of the altar and held down amidst screams and cries for mercy. Before the chief priest carved out their beating hearts, which he offered to Ptah.

The middle-age pharaoh inhaled deeply.

It was here, at the terraced summit of the Djoser Complex of the necropolis of Saqqara, on the outskirts of Memphis, out of sight from his decimated people, where Neferkare carried on this extreme ritual.

The desperate measures of a desperate man.

He looked out into the distance at the meeting point of the Nile Valley and the Delta, as well as at the capital of the most powerful empire on Earth. It was erected hundreds of years ago by Min, the legendary first king of Egypt who unified the north and south kingdoms.

Now a force not from man but from the angered gods threatened to destroy centuries of prosperity.

But he couldn't understand their anger as he returned his stare to the slaughter before him. None of his priests, his scribes, his scientists—even his closest advisors—could conjure an explanation.

They're all clueless. Fucking useless to me.

Neferkare sighed.

Three of his wives had accompanied him this morning, and, so far two had left in shame. Iput II, his youngest consort and also his niece, had started vomiting and had to be escorted out. Neith, his half-sister wife had fainted at the sight of so much gore and was carried back to her chambers. Only Udjebten remained, the oldest of his wives, ten years his junior and a cousin, sitting still though quite pale, her crimson lips trembling, her eyes filled with tears.

Speaking of useless…

They're all weak, and their offspring are weak.

Neferkare ruled by divine kingship, seen by all in Egypt as the mediator between the gods and the people. And that meant everyone held him accountable for controlling the yearly floods of the Nile, enabling the agriculture that fed his nation.

The pharaoh and his family had to be strong for Egypt, especially in present times, when the Nile's yearly floods had shrunk significantly as clouds thinned and rainfall decreased. The result was less and less arable land and diminishing produce, triggering hunger—famine in some regions—and the quite predictable civil unrest.

The very source of life for Egypt was vanishing in front of his frustrated eyes, and all of his spells, all of his offerings, and all of his sacrifices would not appease Ptah.

The Nile floods would not stop receding season after season.

The rainfall would not increase.

The relentless heat would not stop, even in winter.

Fertile grounds turned into arid tundra and desert, spreading famine and disease.

And I'm surrounded by a family of goddamned weaklings.

His useless royals had grown fat and complacent and lacked the visceral fortitude to do what needed to be done.

It was at times like this that Neferkare longed for his mother, the legendary Ankhesenpepi II. Upon the death of her husband, Pharaoh Merenre, she had kept Egypt together by force and ruled as regent until Neferkare turned six years old. She then continued to advise him until her death twenty years later.

I miss you, mother, he thought, having spent most of his adult life searching for a worthy queen among his many beautiful but inadequate wives, who birthed him frail offspring.

Holding the crook and the flail as icons of royalty, Neferkare dropped his gaze to the thick bracelets hugging his wrists. They were made of gold from Nubia and sported lapis falcons symbolizing the god Horus inlaid with precious stones from the deserts of Egypt and neighboring countries. The crook in his left hand, a cane with a hooked handle, gold-plated and reinforced with blue copper bands, represented his control over Egypt, his right to rule. The flail in his right hand, a solid gold rod with three attached beaded strands of precious stones, represented his benevolence and wisdom. The crook and flail and the bracelets, along with an equally ornate and heavy necklace in the shape of a falcon with its wings spread, and his gold and copper headdress sporting a blue Horus above his forehead, telegraphed him as pharaoh of Egypt wherever he went.

And Neferkare had used this divine power his entire life to enforce the law in the name of Maat, the goddess of truth, morality, and justice.

Just as his mother had taught him.

He briefly closed his eyes.

Truth, morality, and justice for the benefit of my citizens.

And that's precisely what he did today, lifting the crook at each crying virgin dragged before him. Ignoring pleading eyes and yelps for mercy, he sentenced each to death for the greater good of Egypt.

He needed to placate Ptah and return the floods of the Nile. The army of male slaves dying by the thousands each month building ever-greater temples and pyramids to Ptah was apparently not enough, forcing him to resort to this dark ritual.

Truth, morality, and justice.

By his feet lay a young cheetah, a gift from Harkfuf, governor of the city of Aswan and his most trusted general and advisor, during one of his many expeditions into Nubia this past month. In fact, Harkfuf was charioting down to Nubia once again in search of more slaves.

The cheetah had been one of several brought back by Harkfuf and raised by Neferkare's personal handlers, who turned the wild beast into one of his favorite exotic pets. It accompanied him this blistering morning along with the two falcons perched on either side of his large throne.

The cheetah, the only female in the litter, stared at her master for a moment before growling at Udjebten, who, like the rest of his wives, was frightened by the beast. And that delighted Neferkare, who despised them all for failing to produce a suitable successor to the throne.

I should have them all killed and fed to her.

Neferkare raised his eyes as the guards escorted the next slave onto the terrace. Unlike those preceding her, this one did not attempt to fight back, holding her perfectly shaved head high. Her stance was proud, royal-like, and her strides elegant. She bowed gracefully when presented to him.

Neferkare hesitated a moment, sensing he had seen her before but failing to remember, finally raising the crook, condemning her just as he had every other virgin this morning.

The guards dragged her away, lifting her slender frame and slamming her against the flat surface of the altar.

But unlike the other slaves, she didn't utter a scream, a complaint, a plea, further intriguing the pharaoh.

As guards held her by the ankles and wrists, the high priest ripped open her linen garment, exposing her young breasts. Her dark-olive chest heaved as he loomed over her clutching a serrated copper blade.

She was beautiful indeed, probably not older than sixteen or seventeen but already a woman, with fine Nubian features, captivating light-brown eyes, and lips the color of rubies.

Truth, morality, and justice, my son.

The words echoed in his mind as the young woman's eyes, encased in heavy makeup, widened when the tip of the blade nicked the smooth bronzed flesh just below her left nipple. It was indeed a shame that such beauty had to perish by the sword, but Neferkare had to sacrifice the slaves for the benefit of the citizens, of the royals, of his armies.

Of my way of life.

But at that moment, just as the chief cleric raised the blade to make the initial cut, Neferkare recognized the skin paint on her exposed right shoulder. It was the seated figure of the goddess Hathor, placed only on Nubian royalty.

She made eye contact with Neferkare, who suddenly remembered her from Harkfuf's last campaign in northern Nubia a month ago. She had been the only daughter of the noble chief ruling the region.

A Nubian princess.

Royalty.

Neferkare raised the flail in his right hand, an action that immediately stopped the priest just as he started to press the tip of the blade on the spot he had marked, making her twitch on the stone.

His beliefs in truth, morality, and justice could not allow him to slaughter royalty, irrespective of it being Egyptian, Nubian, Syrian, or Arabian.

Slaves were dispensable, to be sacrificed to appease angered gods.

But royalty was royalty.

They did not die by the sword unless in battle defending their lands or if guilty of high crime or treason.

The pharaoh gestured for her to be deposited by his feet, next to the cheetah, earning him a curious glance from Udjebten sitting by his side. But the lavishly-dressed woman didn't dare speak.

Udjebten, in her thirty-fifth year of age, had birthed him four useless children; three insolent daughters whom Neferkare had finally gotten married by forcing three of his captains to do so or face castration. And then there was his son, too weak to serve in the military, too stupid to study the sciences, and lacking the sense and wisdom required to rule.

Fucking useless. All of them.

But maybe not this one.

The guards complied immediately, lifting her off the altar and placing her gently in front of the god-king.

A fine trickle of crimson running down the left side of her chest, the Nubian princess hugged his feet and kissed them. Then, raising her appreciative gaze to him, she placed a hand on the cheetah's head, stroking it gently, pleasantly surprising the pharaoh—and shocking Udjebten, who failed to suppress a gasp.

The high priest was momentarily confused, before understanding his terrible mistake and immediately dropping to his knees seeking forgiveness.

"My lord, my god," the Nubian princess said with a deep voice that belonged to a goddess. "I am prepared to die for you if my death can bring rain and prosperity to Egypt."

Albeit impressed, and immensely delighted for annoying Udjebten, Neferkare simply nodded. The Nubian wasn't afraid of death, and she certainly didn't fear the large cat and the massive fangs that could disembowel her in an instant.

Strength.

Neferkare saw it in her eyes and in her pose as she sat not like a slave, but like royalty.

Harkfuf had reported that her father had fought courageously during the two-week siege of the border city of Buhen, resisting with an intensity he had not seen in years. But the Buhen militia had been no match for Egypt's superior war machine, for Harkfuf's trained army. Her father and his militia had perished in the end, resulting in the capture of many slaves, which Neferkare used to build his monuments, to augment Memphis' power and beauty.

Power and beauty.

The Nubian princess, mistaken by the clergy as a slave—a crime carrying the punishment of death by dismemberment—certainly possessed both. And that meant that in addition to providing him with pleasure following days like today, she could also birth him strong and beautiful children, mixed royals who, albeit may never become pharaohs, could still ascend to positions of leadership in his government, in his armies, and whom his country would need to lead Egypt after his death. Such Nubian-Egyptian children could also prove valuable in future trade negotiations with Egypt's large neighbor to the south.

The high priest, still prostrated by Neferkare, Udjebten, and the princess, awaited his fate.

Neferkare decided to test the Nubian's royal acumen by pointing at the high priest while locking eyes with her.

She immediately placed her left hand over the small cut the priest had inflicted on her and her right hand over his right bracelet, which hand clutched the flail, signaling forgiveness.

Motioning the visibly relieved cleric to continue, Neferkare gestured the brave and merciful princess to watch as the guards dragged the next slave, also Nubian, onto the terrace.

This one was a bit older than the princess and quite feisty, like the ones he had ordered slaughtered through the morning, tugging and shoving to free herself from her captors.

Neferkare lifted the crook.

The guards slammed her onto the altar, her back and head crashing against the rock, blood immediately spurting from a gash on her skull, soaking her hair. The blow obviously stunned her as the priest tore off her tunic, exposing breasts larger than the princess', who had already draped the torn garment over her exposed skin, protecting her regency.

Still in a daze, the slave moved her bleeding head from side to side lethargically as the cleric brought the knife slowly over her. Pressing its serrated tip against her smooth skin, he pricked it, just as he had done with the princess, to mark the exact spot for the incision.

He glanced once toward Neferkare's right hand to make sure he was not making the same mistake twice. Failing to see his king raise the flail, the priest quickly sank the blade, blood jetting, arresting the slave from the head-crash-induced stupor.

Remembering where she was, realizing what was being done to her, the girl kicked and screamed, refusing to accept her fate, fingers tense as she tugged at the vice-like grips of the muscular guards. Her howls echoed across the altar as the priest cut deeper, blood splattering his tunic, staining her frayed garment.

Neferkare's eyes checked the princess, who maintained her composure, chin up, gaze steady on the altar just as she had been commanded by her lord. A hand slowly rubbed his feet while the other tenderly stroked the cheetah, which was now resting its large head on her lap, eyes closed.

Incredible, he thought. Not once in his life had he witnessed such display of sensuous courage by another woman besides his mother.

The priest cut deeper, pressing her back against the rock as blood and foam exploded through her mouth, through her nostrils, drowning her cries as she writhed and coughed.

Udjebten leaned forward and vomited before collapsing on her side sobbing and shaking. A pair of chamber maids rushed to her side.

Oh, please.

Neferkare rolled his eyes before shifting his gaze to the princess, who stoically continued to watch the carnage while the maids took Udjebten away.

The slave jerked a hand free, stretching it towards the princess. "Nitocris!" she somehow managed to cry out, before retching more blood. "My...princess! Mercy!"

A guard slapped her, grabbing her wrist, regaining control as the cleric hacked through the ribcage.

She coughed, crimson froth bursting through her lips.

Neferkare once more looked at the Nubian royal whom the slave had called Nitocris. He admired her composure, her supple strength as she continued stroking the cat; the control she exhibited in the face of the butchering of someone she apparently knew.

The slave tried to resist her fate one final time to no avail, chest heaving, taking in slurry breaths as she drowned in her own blood, as she became sluggish, surrendering to the sharp metal.

The priest sunk his free hand in the chest cavity while working the copper tool with the other, making the final cut, severing the heart.

Just as he had done dozens of times this morning, he plucked it out still pulsating from the serrated void, holding it over her dead eyes staring into the distance.

He first offered the throbbing organ to Neferkare before setting it by the foot of Ptah's marble statue, where it beat for a few silent moments.

As the guards dragged the body away, another girl slave was escorted onto the terraced summit.

Truth, morality, and justice.

The pharaoh hated being forced to reenact such a terrifying practice for the first time in a hundred years, to the point that he had forbidden its recording. He had dismissed the scribes and sculptors that always followed him to capture his daily ruling on papyrus and in stone for all posterity. Neferkare had decreed the worst form of death to anyone who ever spoke or recorded the events that had taken place this past week, the slaughter of hundreds of young slaves to appease a seemingly unappeasable god.

Sitting on a throne of carved wood inlaid with silver, gold, and an assortment of stones—amethysts, lapis lazuli, garnets and jaspers—beneath the shade of a bright-green linen canopy, and fanned by petrified Syrian female slaves, the god king contemplated the statue of Ptah, standing tall next to that of Ptah's wife, Sekhmet, goddess of war.

War.

Ptah was lucky to have by his side such a zealous and beautiful wife. Sekhmet was the icon of strength in a country that urgently needed firm and decisive leadership.

Neferkare stood, an action that forced many to their knees, heads against the stone floor, including the Nubian princess. His personal guards—ten of them—and the Syrian slaves holding large fans made of colorful peacock feathers remained standing by royal decree.

The heavily armed guards always shadowed Neferkare, ready to sacrifice their lives for the god-king. The female slaves followed Neferkare with orders to never stop cooling him. A breeze should always caress the skin of the chosen one.

Neferkare leaned down and touched the hand of the Nubian princess. "Come," he said. "Stand by my side."

"My lord," Nitocris replied, standing with grace, a hand keeping her tunic closed, the other held by Neferkare. She was as tall as him, with a swan-like neck, a triangular face, high cheekbones and a fine nose over lips that awakened something in the forty-six-year-old pharaoh.

He snapped his fingers once and two maids produced fresh linen garments and a carved-wood bowl filled with jewelry. Every soul on that terrace except for the two chamber maids looked away and froze as they removed Nitocris' shredded tunic, exposing her recently waxed body to him, devoid of any hair except for the fine eyebrows crowning her captivating eyes.

Neferkare held up a hand, prompting the maids to pause and also look away.

The pharaoh and the Nubian princess faced each other in the late-morning breeze, the world around them forbidden from gazing at them, and completely immobilized, as if time had stopped by his hand.

He touched the tip of his tongue with his index finger, wetting it before softly rubbing off the trickle of coagulated blood below her left breast.

She shuddered at his divine touch, for the first time displaying an emotion, her eyes filling as she said, "Thank you, my lord."

Neferkare would have her tonight, and the night after that, and the night after that, until she birthed him a worthy successor.

Satisfied, he gave his command to the maids, who dressed her wound and then robed her in a beautiful gold gown and matching sandals, bracelets, rings, and necklaces.

The effect magnified her regal presence, her deep bronze skin radiating a glow that challenged the sun as she offered him a brief smile.

Satisfied, Neferkare ordered time to continue on the terrace.

The priest began to slaughter the slave on the altar, the sawing and slicing of bones and muscle, the harrowing screams fading as he lost himself in Nitocris' captivating gaze.

Could this be the one, mother?

The god-king took a deep breath and held her hand as they walked towards two warriors kneeling by the edge of the terrace, messengers from Harkfuf, whom Neferkare had dispatched last week on another Nubian expedition to seize more slaves.

The warriors wore dark wrap-around kilts and reed sandals. Their chariot and weapons—copper swords, spears, daggers, bows and arrows—were parked in the Great Courtyard under the sizzling sun by the foot of the steps leading to the terrace. No one could approach Neferkare armed, except for his personal guards, whose loyalty was guaranteed through their families, their mothers, fathers, wives, and kids.

"Rise," Neferkare commanded, flanked by his guards while the Syrian slaves kept up their incessant fanning. It wasn't even noon and the heat had already grown unbearable in the shade.

The two warriors complied, standing.

"What news do you bring from Harkfuf?"

The oldest warrior produced a small papyrus scroll, which he unrolled and began to read.

Neferkare remained impassive as the messenger conveyed the general's report, which, to Neferkare's surprise didn't describe his Nubian slave-hunting campaign. Rather, the messenger talked about the severe drought in several regions north of Nubia which were forcing Nomarchs, regional representatives of Neferkare, to take control of their estates, assuming responsibility for maintaining order, and threatening to splinter Egypt into feudal states.

"General Harkfuf requests a reinforcement of chariots to quench the insurgency, my lord," the messenger concluded, rolling the scroll. "The Nomarchs are growing too strong in the south."

Neferkare maintained his stoic composure but internally he was enraged.

I need more fucking slaves!

The intense heat and lack of water was killing them faster than he could replenish them. And now Harkfuf was having difficulty reaching Nubia. His mission south had been interrupted by Neferkare's own Nomarchs—his own nobles whom he had personally empowered with lands, wealth, slaves, and militias to be his representatives in the outer reaches of the empire. Now those same Nomarchs were challenging his divine rule, slapping the very hand that had enabled them.

Such treachery, punishable by the worst kind of death for all perpetrators and their families, would be dealt with swiftly and publicly to set a much-needed example for all Nomarchs in the kingdom.

Neferkare ruled, dispatching a contingent of five hundred chariots and three thousand soldiers to the region to restore the peace and bring the offending Nomarchs and their families back to Memphis to face their nightmarish punishment.

But as he felt the infuriating heat against his tanned skin, as the high priest held up yet another beating heart to an unmerciful Ptah, as the fertile valleys bordering the Nile dwindled with each passing season, something told Neferkare that such punishment would not matter in the long run. Something told him such insurgencies would become the norm.

The hands of his priests were crimson from the spilled blood of incessant human sacrifice. The backs of his slaves were raw from hauling the stones of massive structures rising up to the heavens to pacify the gods. His people were starving. His armies grew restless. The Nomarchs were rebelling against Memphis.

His nation was slowly disintegrating.

And the clouds would not return, the rain would not fall, and the Nile would not swell over its banks.

His divine power could not return the floods.

The god-king of a dying empire stared into the distance, growing angry at the heavens, before doing the only thing he could do against an enemy that didn't fight with swords and chariots.

The final pharaoh of the Sixth Dynasty of Egypt's unified Old Kingdom signaled his priests to bring forth the next slave to the sacrificial altar.

CHAPTER NINE
REGRETS

"Day doth daily draw my sorrows longer, and night doth nightly make grief's length seem stronger."
—Sir William Shakespeare

31,000 FEET OVER GERMANY. JULY 8, 2029

"You up for this?" Case asked.

He lay shirtless on his belly on one of the sofas in the VIP-style seating of the main cabin. This Citation X had been customized as a VIP transport and airborne operations center. It came complete with dedicated satellite links and two operators in the rear of the cabin sitting at workstations working out the final preparations before landing in the Russian capital in an hour.

They had reached the embassy in Paris just past midnight, where a car had been waiting to take them straight to Charles de Gaulle International Airport while getting debriefed by Langley on the way. The CIA jet was now taking them to Moscow to work out a plan to capture arms dealer Andrei Vorota

"Me?" she said, sitting at the edge of the sofa armed with the first-aid kit she had snagged from the Embassy's nurse's station on their way out since there was no one there to work on him at that hour. "I could be asking you the same question. Your back's a mess."

"I've had worse," he replied, "as you can now see."

She used cotton balls and peroxide to clean cuts, scrapes, and minor burns. Though nothing compared to the scar tissue in between his shoulder blades, and along the right side of his torso disappearing below the waist. He also had a number of scars that almost looked as if someone had taken a metal claw and raked his shoulders raw. And before he lay down, she had gotten a glimpse of his equally scarred chest.

"You've lived hard," she said, working her way down the middle of his back, rubbing off the grime, before going through it again more carefully after getting a better view of the damage he had sustained while protecting her.

She sighed, staring at his muscular back, her dark fingers contrasting sharply with his pale skin as she worked each spot carefully. The man was strong alright, but he had also been banged up quite a bit.

"Ten years in the teams will do that to you," he said, referring to the Navy SEALs. "That's why I decided to take it easy and join the Agency."

She pressed a cotton ball hard into the worst scrape, trying to get at the dirt lining it. He moaned.

"This is your idea of easy?"

"I'm half naked and a gorgeous woman has her hands all over me. Maybe I'll find you a cowboy hat."

She dug her thumb into the largest bruise.

"Fuck!" he yelped as he squirmed. "What the hell?"

"Behave yourself."

Breathing heavily, he said, "Seriously, are you up for it?"

"No, I'm *not*," she replied, digging her thumb again.

"Dammit!" He flinched, then looked up over his right shoulder. "What are you—"

She slapped him on the back of his head. "I was only nineteen and drunk and—"

"Stop! I mean, are you up for what's coming in *Moscow*."

"Oh."

"Christ," he mumbled, resting his head back down.

As she considered the question, she opened a tube of antibiotic cream and applied it liberally to his flesh wounds. "Well, I thought I was ready in Paris, and also in Greenland. So…"

"Listen," he said, struggling to turn his head to look at her again. "You did everything right in Paris, and as far as Greenland goes, well sometimes the bastards just get lucky."

She thought about that while working the clear paste with the tips of her fingers into every spot. She then reached for a pack of oversized self-adhesive Band-Aids and placed them carefully over each area.

"That's the problem, Case. We need to get lucky *every fucking* time." She surveyed her work, making sure she had covered every wound properly. "The goddamned terrorists, on the other hand, only need to get lucky *once*."

She stood and added, "Good as new, Big Boy," and moved to a bucket seat facing the sofa while buttoning up the first-aid kit and sliding it under her seat.

He also stood and stretched, twisting his back, testing the bandages. "Good field dressing," he said, before slipping on a clean sweatshirt. "I owe you one."

"Seriously? Least I can do."

"Still, glad to know someone has my back, no pun intended."

She smiled, then turned serious. "I need you healthy to help me keep these bastards from fucking up the world any more than they already have."

He raised his eyebrows. "Yeah. Gotta try to leave some semblance of a world for the next generation."

The comment made her remember Case's dossier. He was divorced with children. "Two kids, right?"

He did a double take on her and made a peace sign. "Yep. Two. They're with the ex. Left me for a Rodeo Drive plastic surgeon. They all live in Malibu."

"I'm very, *very* sorry."

He momentarily avoided her stare. "It's all right. I wasn't a good husband...or father for that matter. Hard to be there for them when you're away for months at a time."

"How old are they?"

Case's face softened as he worked the FlexScreen and handed it to her. There was an image of a boy and a girl.

"Cameron's fifteen and Heather seventeen," he said. "I was supposed to spend two weeks with them this summer, but shit keeps coming up, and from the looks of it I doubt it's going to happen."

Rachel took in the picture. The boy looked like him, with well-defined facial features, a strong chin, full lips, and dark hair to complement his dark-brown eyes and thick eyebrows. The girl was a drop-dead gorgeous blonde with perfect hair, perfect skin, perfect features, and incredibly-blue eyes.

"Well, Cameron certainly looks like you. Very handsome."

Case smiled. "You hitting on me now?"

She shook her head. "Don't get any ideas. But Heather...how do you manage to keep the boys away?"

He dropped his gaze. "Like I said, I wasn't around enough to do any of that."

"Well, she's quite the prom queen." She returned the FlexScreen to him.

"That's her alright," he replied, staring at the image. "Spitting image of Molly, my ex, who used to be a New York model. To Molly, it's all about the looks, and unfortunately so it is for Heather thanks to my wife's influence and all of the free procedures they get from the new head of the household."

"But they're still your babies," she said.

He looked out the window. "There was a time when I used to say how my kids were the most important thing in my life, and I really meant it. But then the trips began, and I started missing things. A little league game here, a recital there, and before long, well…"

Case sighed as he rolled up the FlexScreen and put it away.

"When was your leave supposed to start before I crashed into your world?"

He chuckled. "Tomorrow. I was going to call them from the embassy and let them know, but…"

"Call them, Case."

"You mean now?"

She shrugged. "We're going to hit the ground running in Moscow, so, yeah. Better get it over with now."

"Fuck," he mumbled.

"I'll give you some space," she said, standing.

"Where are you going?"

"Gotta pee, if that's okay with you."

She left him working the FlexScreen, walked past the operators at their stations, and stepped into the small aft lavatory, closing and locking the door behind her.

Dropping her trousers and panties, she sat on the toilet, shivering when the cold metal touched the bottom of her thighs.

Here we go again, she thought, tensing while urinating. Another side effect from her bout with radiation sickness was dysuria, a mild but frequent burning sensation as a result of chronic cystitis, or lower urinary tract infection. Apparently, her plumbing also wasn't happy about getting nuked. Just like her malfunctioning salivary glands, things were drying up down there as well. But unlike her damaged uterus and breasts, she couldn't just rip them out. So, she made it a point to down a daily dose of cranberry pills, plus lots of water.

But it still hurts.

Every goddamned time.

She gripped the sides of the toilet seat and even broke a small sweat for the agonizing minute it took.

Finished, Rachel got dressed, splashed water on her face, and just stood in front of the small stainless steel sink staring at her reflection on the oval mirror above it.

She inhaled deeply as the pain receded, glaring at the gaunt image staring back at her.

My face is round, dammit, not rail-fucking-thin.

And then there was her skin. It used to be the color of dark honey, very smooth and uniform. But after Greenland, the area around her eyes had turned a dash darker than the rest, giving her a sort of raccoon-like look that became more pronounced when she didn't get enough sleep, as had been the case this past forty-eight hours.

And to add insult to injury, as she stared at the damage Kiersted had inflicted, Payden's words suddenly echoed in her mind.

Christ. What the fuck happened to you?

"Greenland, Jimmy," she whispered while staring into her father's light-green eyes. "That's what the fuck happened."

She splashed more water, dried off, and headed back to her seat.

Case was staring out the window, and his eyes looked up at her as she came up from the back of the plane.

"You okay?" he asked. "You look a little pale."

She frowned, before reaching for her bag on the seat next to her and producing a pack of AZO cranberry pills and another one of antibacterial pills. She downed two of each with a swig of water. "Lady issues," she finally said.

"Oh. Sorry. Molly had to take those sometimes. Especially after…"

"Yeah, well," she said, waving the pack of pills. "These are courtesy of William Kiersted. Still getting fucked by him."

"Rachel, I—"

She shrugged it off. "It is what it is. We all have our own crosses to bear. And speaking of that, did you get ahold of them?"

He nodded. "Wasn't pretty, and Molly was there, which never helps. But at least it was short."

"So very sorry."

"It's the life we chose."

"It is indeed," she replied, considering her own situation.

"How about you?" he asked. "Got anyone?"

She pointed a finger at her chest. "Me? Nah. Both parents died a while back, when I was in college. Of course, as you now know, there was Jimmy there for a little while, followed by a series of jerks in the Navy and the GCCU.

And after Greenland, well, no kids either, at least biologically. Kiersted really did a number on me."

"Well, you're here now," he said. "That has to count for something."

"I guess."

"And for what it's worth, any guy would be damned lucky to have you just as you are." As he said this, he leaned forward and touched her on the right shoulder, giving it a gentle squeeze.

She stared at him for a moment, and felt something stir inside of her—

"And happy belated birthday, Rach," he said, leaning back. "May I call you Rach?"

She tilted her head. "Well, Case, you now know about the cowboy hat, that I now live with these damned UTIs, have fake boobs and no uterus, and just turned forty. And on top of all that, the only reason my face doesn't look like fried bacon is because you used your body to shield me, which is far more than all of the assholes I ever dated did for me. So, sure. Rach will work. Better than Brown-fucking-Sugar."

He regarded her in a way that somehow made all of the above momentarily vanish. Then he said, "Maybe you'll let me buy you a drink when this is over?"

As she considered that, the pilot announced the start of their decent into Moscow.

CHAPTER TEN
OUR GREATEST CHALLENGE

"Climate change should be seen as the greatest challenge to face man and treated as a much bigger priority in the United Kingdom."
—Prince Charles

NORTH SLOPE BOROUGH. ALASKA.
JULY 8, 2029.

"Loosely defined," Natasha Shakhiva said, sitting across from Colonel Marcus Stone in the mess tent of the IARC camp, "Radiative forcing is the net result between the incoming radiation energy from the sun and the outgoing radiation energy reflected back into space. These are the primary forces modulating global temperature change."

Stone bit into a turkey sandwich, chewing quickly, swallowing, then asking, "I read about that in your report. A sort of tug-of-war between positive and negative forces steering the direction of temperature change on the planet, right?"

Natasha had to continue to give the man credit. There seemed to be a brain behind the uniform.

"Correct," she said, toying with her salad with a plastic fork. They sat alone late in the evening trying to eat

126

something even though she didn't feel like eating. They had visited the tunnel again today, and this time they had to evacuate it even earlier that yesterday. The day had ended with so many methane events in the tunnel that their storage tanks were filled by midafternoon, requiring the excess gas be channeled to the burn-off vent. Similar to those in oil refineries, it released a roaring plume of orange fire atop a fifty-foot-tall chute. Even at this late hour the burn-off unit continued to consume the excess methane, casting a novel flickering glow across the camp, which Natasha saw as an omen of things to come.

Pointing at the fire beyond the screened window with her white fork, she added, "That's one of the positive forces, along with CO_2 and ozone, which absorbs some of the infrared energy emitted by the sun, preventing it from being reflected back into space."

"I thought there were others."

She nodded. "But not as significant. There's nitrous oxide, halocarbons, jet contrails, and even energy particles from interstellar media, like supernova explosions."

Stone's freckles shifted on his face beneath the orange hair while he held the sandwich with both hands. "I thought that last one was the theory of that Danish scientist who was discredited some years ago, and whose terrorist son was responsible for Greenland."

"Henrik Kiersted," she replied, frowning. "There's actually an element of truth in his research, but it's quite negligible, which caused his work to be dismissed."

Stone chewed another mouthful before asking, "What are the negative radiative forces?"

"Primarily sulphate aerosols and white smoke, both of which reflect sunlight. And then there's the terrestrial albedo effect, whose total contribution to climate change is difficult to calculate with any real precision."

Stone lowered his sandwich and gave her a puzzled look. Since arriving here yesterday, the good colonel had been picking her brains, trying to absorb as much global climate intelligence as possible before heading back to Washington to brief the president and officially start his new job. But what amazed her was the fact that Stone didn't write anything down, yet he seemed to retain the relevant information, the building blocks of climatology and glaciology.

"Albedo effect?"

"Alright, Marcus," she said, leaning forward. "Take the albedo of snow, for example. It's about 90%, meaning it reflects 90% of the solar energy it receives back into space while only absorbing 10%. At the other end of the spectrum is the albedo of fresh asphalt, the darkest surface on the planet, at 4%, meaning it absorbs 96% of the sun's heat and injects it straight into the Earth. Human activity has changed the Earth's albedo due to forest clearance, roads, parking lots, buildings, and farming. On average, the data suggests we're worse than we were a few decades ago."

Stone finished his sandwich and crumpled the plastic wrap and napkin into a tight little ball before stretching a thumb at the column of fire burning high above the camp. "Hey, Tash," he said, "that can't be a good thing."

"Nope. The concentration of methane relative to CO_2 is quite small today, averaging less than 3%, but because it is such an effective greenhouse gas—far more effective than CO_2—its radiative force is about a third of that of CO_2. So even though methane today takes a second place to CO_2, it does so with a very small amount of the gas present in the atmosphere relative to CO_2. And this is why the fire outside is the bearer of such terrible news. It's telling us that the permafrost shield is vaporizing in front of our eyes and no less than two thousand gigatons of methane could be released into the atmosphere. That amount represents nearly a million times more methane than exists today, and given its amazing efficiency as a greenhouse gas, it will cause a major inflection point in the world's climate."

"Meaning it'll vastly accelerate the warming process?"

She nodded. "What our current models project taking decades or even centuries to happen, like sea-level rises, the melting of ice sheets, and the probable creation of new ecosystems—such as the mini ice age in Europe today—could take place in a matter of a few years. And that doesn't take into consideration the drastic reduction of oxygen in the atmosphere as it gets replaced by methane. Under the best scenario, we would be getting at least a repeat of what Egyptians experienced four thousand years ago, when their civilization almost ended during a period of extreme drought that lasted a few hundred years."

"And what's the worst-case scenario?"

"Well, Marcus," she said leaning back and crossing her arms. "That would be a repeat of the Permian-Triassic extinction event."

"Tash, I read in your brief that you and Doctor Malone believe it was a global methane release that triggered the Permian-Triassic extinction event and not an asteroid?"

"Yes. An asteroid killed the dinosaurs over 180 million years *later*. The Permian-Triassic event is marked by many clues pointing to a global release of methane gas."

She reached for her handheld FlexScreen, unfolded it, and entered a few commands, bringing up the picture of a large tiger-like creature with long saber teeth fighting against a dimetrodon, a large beast sporting a sail-like dorsal fin. She showed it to Stone. "Here are a couple of the most memorable creatures from that time. Paleontologists have recovered many of their bones, as well as from other specimens of the same time period, and they all show high methane readings. These creatures were exposed to excessive levels of methane in the atmosphere around 250 million years ago, at the end of the Permian period."

"I recognize the dimetrodon from my son's books," Stone said, peering at the color screen while chewing.

Natasha smiled. "How old?"

"Just turned nine."

"And his name?"

"Marcus Junior." He grinned, unrolling a small FlexScreen and showing it to her. It depicted a petite brunette of around thirty holding the hand of an orange-haired kid with freckles.

"No DNA testing for that little one."

"Nope," he said.

"Beautiful family, Marcus."

"Thanks. It's why I took the job. To try to leave some semblance of a world for him to live in—and his kids." He rolled up the unit and raised his brows.

Natasha blinked. There was deep-rooted passion in addition to a brain behind the pixelated uniform.

Before she could reply, Stone pointed an index finger at her FlexScreen. "The creature next to the Dimetrodon looks like a saber-tooth tiger. I thought they roamed the Earth much later, after the dinosaurs."

"That's correct. Saber-tooth tigers were warm-blooded mammals that lived from several million years ago up to around nine thousand years ago, but certainly not hundreds of millions of years ago. The last species, called the Smilodon, is the one most people think about when they hear the words—" she threw air quotes, "*saber-tooth tiger.*" Pausing for effect she added, "And it shared the world with Neanderthals and later with Homo sapiens. This one from the Permian period is called a Gorgonopsian, or Gorgo for short, and it was the top predator back in its day, when the continents were all joined into a supercontinent called Pangaea. We believe Gorgos became extinct when the herbivores they preyed on died away as methane releases and subsequent fires consumed most of the Earth's vegetation, killing their food supply."

"I never knew there were mammals that far back."

Natasha pushed her salad aside and leaned forward, planting her elbows on the table. "Technically, Gorgos weren't mammals, but they were the predecessors who never got a chance to continue evolving because of the methane. Now, here's an interesting thing to think about, Marcus. What would have happened to our world if the Permian-Triassic extinction event never occurred?"

Stone made a face. "I don't follow."

"Two hundred and fifty million years ago, the first mammal-like creatures, like the Gorgos, began to roam the Earth, just like a few million years ago the early versions of mammals, like the saber-tooth, showed up on Earth, to be followed by more developed mammals, including Neanderthals and then Homo Sapiens—us. Unfortunately, life as it was developing on Earth back in the Permian period came to a crashing end, killing any possibility of further evolution, including men. The slate was wiped clean and the dinosaurs took it over starting in the early Triassic Period, until the Cretaceous-Paleogene extinction event 66 million years ago, when it was wiped clean once more, but this time by an asteroid, kicking off the evolutionary process that resulted in the current species. Imagine the possibilities, Marcus. What if the Permian Period would have continued evolving? Mammal-like creatures would have continued to advance, perhaps into actual mammals, dominating the Earth, potentially giving the human race well over a couple hundred million years' head start. Wrap your head around that. It took us just ten thousand years to develop modern civilization, and you can argue that true progress really happened in the last few hundred years."

Stone paused, his narrowing stare apparently considering that. "If only," he finally said, before looking over his shoulder and asking, "And that fire outside is our early-warning signal that history is about to repeat itself?"

Natasha looked away. "I hope to God I'm wrong."

"Ah," Marcus said. "A scientist who believes in God?"

She shrugged. "I like to cover all my bases."

He nodded, then asked, "Is this camp still safe?"

She looked away. She had discussed that very question with Mario Escobar earlier in the afternoon, soon after the burn-off started. They had arrived to the same conclusion.

"This year, yes," she finally replied. "The permafrost's methane flux is low enough to keep most of the trapped gas contained. But I can't say with certainty next year, or the year after that as the Earth gets progressively warmer. The sensors in the tunnel indicate that most of the flux is taking place at a depth of 140 feet or deeper with a concentration as high as 16%, which explains the steady burn. We think that will continue at least through September. After that, winter will shut off the flux until the following summer. But next year we will get just a dash warmer, meaning the permafrost will get incrementally softer and the flux will increase."

"Hold on, Tash, what about the colder temperatures in Europe? Isn't that going to help reduce the warming trend?"

"I wish. Europe is a localized anomaly because of the reduction in oceanic currents in the North Atlantic. And while the overall albedo effect will improve because of the snow coverage, it's still very minor compared to the global positive radiative forces preventing heat from being reflected back into space. And the moment methane enters the equation in high concentrations all bets are off. And that's the million-dollar question, Marcus: when will it reach the surface, and also, will it do so evenly across the global permafrost regions?"

"That would depend on the actual depth of the pockets, right?"

She continued to be increasingly—and pleasantly—surprised by this man. "Yes, in part. But also, it will depend on the corresponding rise in sea levels, which would cover some of the methane hydrates formed beneath the soil in coastal regions. These are ice formations that encapsulate the gas molecules and are scattered several hundred meters deep and in fact are being mined today as a source of clean-burning energy. When sea levels rise and cover the soil, the water will warm it and melt the crystals, releasing the methane in unpredictable ways, compounding the problem."

"So, the Greenland event certainly isn't helping."

"Correct," she replied.

"Sounds like it's only a matter of time before—"

"Correct again."

Stone nodded solemnly, crossed his arms, and contemplated the glowing fire casting a somewhat magical aura on the camp.

Natasha also stared at the blazing radiance outside. For reasons she could not explain, the soft glow carried with it an image of Konrad Malone, standing tall with his blond closely-cropped beard, ponytail, and mirror-tint sunglasses basking in the bright sun of an Alaskan summer.

She closed her eyes, wishing they were alone somewhere in the Brooks Mountain Range sharing a sleeping bag, him holding her tight as the world slowly closed in on them.

Dammit, Koni. When will I see you again?

"You okay there, Tash?"

Before she could stop herself, she said, "No, Marcus, I'm pretty bloody far from okay. I'm missing someone." She regretted saying that the moment it came out.

Stone dropped his bushy orange brows over his eyes. "So, there's more to the sadness I've noticed in those beautiful hazel eyes since I got here yesterday. I thought it was because of that." He extended a finger at the plume of fire atop the burn-off tower. "So, who's the lucky fellow?"

"Excuse me?"

A smile cracked the colonel's stoic face as he said, "Who's the lucky fellow who stole your heart?"

Annoyed at herself, Natasha considered her reply when Mario Escobar stormed into the mess tent. Wearing khaki cargo pants, an IARC pullover sweater, and sneakers, he held a twenty-inch FlexScreen like a long scroll.

"Mario? What's the matter?"

The middle-aged glaciologist and bush pilot, visibly agitated, set the unit on the table in between Natasha and Stone, and unrolled the screen. It depicted the still image of a bare mountain peak, which Natasha recognized immediately.

"Oh, no," she said, her throat suddenly going dry. "When did it happen?"

"What is it?" asked Stone, shifting his gaze between the high-resolution image and the Ukrainian scientist.

"It's…Furtwängler," she replied, controlling her emotions. "The last tropical glacier on the planet, located atop Mount Kilimanjaro. It has collapsed."

Natasha slowly turned to Escobar and asked, "What about Koni?"

Instead of replying, the Bolivian scientist shifted his gaze to the screen while pressing the **REWIND** button, which caused the image to come alive showing a video in fast reverse, depicting an avalanche of crumbling ice looming at the bottom of the screen while making its way up the peak, covering it. "That's what I wanted to show you," he finally said, stopping the image and pressing the **PLAY** button on the screen. "Here are the final moments of the glacier as recorded live by our satellites."

Her vision tunneling, her heartbeat pounding against her temples, Natasha forced herself to watch as rifts streaked across the ice sheet. Its headwall finally crumbled in starbursts of white before tumbling downhill.

Escobar panned to the right side of the screen while zooming in, nearly filling the display with an aerial view of the safety camp, a dozen tents and carts of equipment scattered across a bare rock clearing next to the right end of the ice sheet.

What followed was nearly impossible to believe: a lone figure racing from the collapsing glacier, which shifted while breaking up, causing massive boulders to crash by the rocky slope on the outskirts of the camp, avalanching over tents and equipment. The figure disappeared in the resulting haze before emerging again, scrambling in obvious frantic haste, getting tossed about by resulting shockwaves, only to get up again and again, until finally crashing into a tent on the opposite end of the camp as the ice sheet disappeared from view.

"Has to be Koni," Natasha said with certainty. "Has to—"

"Who's Koni?" interrupted Stone.

"Doctor Konrad Malone," explained Escobar while Natasha felt as if she were having an out-of-body experience, the feeling reminiscent of getting the news about Sergei three years before.

This isn't bloody happening!

Not again!

"How can you be so certain?" asked Escobar while Stone watched her closely, his eyes glinting concern.

Taking a deep breath, her voice beginning to crack, she said, "Only someone experienced, hard-headed, and bloody lucky as Koni Malone could have survived something like that."

"Well, whoever he is," replied Escobar, "satellite coverage shows he hasn't moved in almost sixteen hours. Perhaps—"

"Perhaps my bloody ass, Mario!" she snapped. "That's him!"

Escobar blinked and quickly nodded. "I'll start making calls," he replied, rolling up the FlexScreen.

She fell back on her chair and exhaled heavily before adding, "We need a helicopter on that mountain within the hour, Mario. It's already been sixteen *fucking* hours. We don't have time to spare!"

As Escobar scurried away, Stone regarded Natasha with intriguing eyes beneath his freckled forehead.

"*What?*" she asked, her throat tight with feelings she found difficult to suppress.

Stone leaned forward and said, "That Malone's indeed one lucky fellow. Would you also like me to make some calls?"

Unable to prevent her eyes from filling, she replied, "I lost my husband three years ago, Marcus. I can't go through that again."

He placed a hand on her shoulder and said, "Tash, you listen to me now."

Natasha closed her eyes, feeling her stomach filling with molten lead.

"TASH!" he said, giving her a gentle shake on the shoulder.

She blinked, then lifted her gaze. "Bollocks! *What?*"

"I'm going to find Konrad Malone, Tash. I'm going to find him and get him the hell home."

"Then why are you still talking to me, Marcus?"

It was now Stone's turn to blink. Without another word, the large Army colonel stood and headed for the tent's exit.

Her tears blurred his hasty departure.

CHAPTER ELEVEN
COLD, COLD HEART

"Warm weather fosters growth: cold weather destroys it." —Hung Tzu-Cheng.

MOSCOW, RUSSIA. JULY 9, 2029.

The heavy bass echoing off the red-brick walls reverberated in Andrei Vorota's chest.

He sipped a Bacardi mojito at a reserved corner booth next to the spacious dance floor at one of Moscow's first and most popular nightclubs, the Propaganda Café. It was located around the corner from Lubyanskaya Square and just five blocks from the legendary Red Square in the heart of the city.

For the past decade, as most cities in Europe, starting with Paris, declined in quality of life due to the influx of African and Middle-Eastern immigrants, Moscow flourished.

Mostly because we had the balls to close our borders to those fucking refugees.

And the attack in Greenland, which dropped temperatures across most of western Europe, had made Moscow even more desirable than ever because the weather patterns controlled by the Gulf Stream didn't reach that far east.

And even if it had, to Muscovites like Vorota, a few-degrees drop in temperatures just meant an extra shot of vodka. This place was always cold, and therefore it was designed to handle it, meaning that life pretty much went unchanged while places like France, Spain, Portugal, and Italy froze to death.

It was expatriate night at the Propaganda, meaning a lot of single clubbers from the large international community doing business in the Russian capital gathered here to blow off steam and mix it up with the locals. People danced to an energetic and eclectic selection of Pop, Rap, and Salsa tunes by the three DJs working behind the glass booth high above the illuminated floor.

On this lively expat night, English was the language of choice. Those who spoke it well had the best chance of getting lucky. Those who didn't were typically frowned upon as local illiterate trash not worthy of mingling with the wave of affluent, well-dressed, and mostly lonely foreigners. But to get in you still had to get past the bulky doormen controlling access to the club from the long line already formed outside, which by now reached Lubyanskaya Square.

Just as Vorota finished his mojito, one of his two armed bodyguards cruised back from the bar with a fresh drink, which mixing he personally supervised to ensure the health and longevity of one of Russia's wealthiest black-market arms dealers.

Dressed in a gray double-breasted Armani, Berluti loafers, no socks or tie, a diamond-studded Hammer and Sickle pendant hanging from a gold chain around his thick neck, and a Patek Philippe watch worth more than his armored Mercedes sedan, Vorota ignored the twin whores giggling next to him. He reached for the new cocktail and sipped it slowly as his eyes gravitated toward a woman standing alone by the bar.

She wore a cream cocktail dress, which contrasted beautifully with her dark-honey skin, and which he recognized as classic Versace. Red Manolo Blahnik high-heels adorned the denouement of her shapely legs just as a single strand of black pearls lined the base of her swan-like neck. Her short brown hair framed a soft and thin face, like those of models, gaunt but beautiful, including a pair of dark and full lips she compressed while checking her watch before staring toward the entrance, as if waiting for someone.

Vorota, tanned, moisturized, and groomed to metro-sexual levels, watched with growing interest as she pouted ever so slightly, but in a way that attracted him more than the clinically-enhanced sisters he had hired for the evening, and who had long failed to warm his cold heart beyond brief carnal pleasures.

But the ethnically-exotic woman at the bar seemed different, capable of taking him places the whores never could. And he decided it was her eyes, an angelic light-green—also in sharp contrast with her skin tone—which gripped him as she shifted them from the entrance to the cosmopolitan cocktail the bartender slid toward her. She reached for it and took a sip. Leaving a dark-red imprint on the rim, she set glass back down and once more glanced toward the entrance—all done with a subtle grace that exuded class.

She wasn't young, like the twin Slavic beauties cuddling by his side, but appeared more in her late thirties, perhaps even older. But whatever she lacked in youth she more than made up with elegance. Everything seemed perfect with her, even the way in which she produced a small silver case, pulling out a cigarette, which the bartender immediately lit for her while she tapped the rim of her cosmopolitan and whispered something. A moment later, the bartender removed the cocktail and presented her with a mojito. She took a sip and nodded approvingly.

Vorota grinned.

His smile widened as she rejected three different men propositioning her within five minutes, and watched with interest as she checked her watch twice more while frowning and glancing again at the entrance.

Some fool is late.

As he continued to enjoy the mojito while wondering what kind of idiot would stand up someone like her, her emerald gaze glinted in recognition before bringing a hand to her face to cover obvious surprise.

A tall and impeccably attired man stopped by her in mid stride while in the company of a beautiful and much younger blonde who seemed confused.

An argument sparked between the man and the dark mystery woman, surprising the blonde. The man finally whisked away the blonde, leaving the dark beauty visibly upset and scrambling to pull another cigarette out of a case she fished from her purse.

It all happened very quickly, but the same keen business sense that had made him rich—and had kept him alive in this unmerciful town for two decades—now focused on the unique opportunity that had just materialized.

Vorota sprung to his feet, startling his bodyguards and the twin prostitutes, reaching into a pocket to produce a solid-gold lighter just as she freed a cigarette and placed it between her lips.

Her magnificent green eyes, like those of a cat, fell on him and the lighter for an instant, as he thumbed a flame and placed it under the tip of the cigarette.

She took a long drag, exhaling though fine nostrils before mumbling, "*Balshoye Spasiba*," with a heavy American accent.

"You are most welcomed," Vorota replied, smiling, softly inhaling her perfume. "May I offer a more comfortable option in this crowded place?"

She regarded him for a moment, before saying, "Your English... It's very polished for a Russian."

"I split my time between Moscow and New York with my business."

She considered that for another moment before extending her left hand. "I'm Alexandra, but my friends call me Lexi."

"Hello, Lexi," Vorota said, taking her hand and bringing it up to his lips, planting a soft kiss on the top of her palm. "I am Andrei, and it is a pleasure making your acquaintance, yes?"

She gently retrieved her hand and reached for her mojito, wetting her lips before saying, "I'm from New York. What kind of business takes you there?"

"Imports and exports," he replied, before pointing to his booth, where his bodyguards had already cleared the whores. "Shall we?"

She continued regarding him with those magical eyes. "Sure," she finally said. "Why not?"

For the next hour they drank, danced, and talked. He was fascinated by her work as a fashion designer in New York and now here in Moscow working with the Chamber of Commerce and Industry of the Russian Federation to coordinate this year's Fashion Week event. It was all part of the country's effort to gain its fair share of recognition by a fashion world that had shifted from Prada to Pravda in order to propel Russian alabaster-skinned beauties into the world's current top models.

And that certainly explained the dress, the shoes, and the overall glamour. Alexandra was a model-turned-businesswoman, which made her all the more interesting to a man bored with the love-for-hire companions who shared his bed in between business deals.

"Would you accompany me to my penthouse?" Vorota asked after playfully arguing with her about whether one of his bodyguards—whom he had introduced to her as personal assistants—had brought them their second or third mojito.

She leaned away from him, turning serious, contemplating the proposition.

"I promise to be a gentleman," he added, raising his right hand.

"Very well," she finally said, standing. "Show me your place and maybe I'll show you mine."

That was all the encouragement the arms dealer required to leap to his feet and walk with her through the crowd. They stopped by the coat room, where she collected a beautiful mink, which Vorota draped over her shoulders before donning a long Burberry coat. They reached the entrance, and he tipped the staff while one of his bodyguards fetched his car.

The night was cold, clear, and energizing. The distant lights from Moscow's historical downtown glowed toward the star-filled heaven. The envious eyes of a crowd lined up half frozen alongside of the building filled him with satisfaction as his black Mercedes sedan slowly pulled up while he stood there holding Alexandra's hand.

Vorota enjoyed moments like this, at the top of his game, holding all of the cards while a jealous world looked on.

The bodyguard who remained with them opened the door. Alexandra stepped inside first followed by him.

Just as the bodyguard was about to open the front passenger door to get in next to the chauffer-bodyguard, a drunk staggered across the street holding a small flask in a brown paper bag, blocking their exit.

The bodyguard went up to him, screaming, "*Shto s vami! Pashol von!*" *What's the matter with you? Go Away!*

The drunk resisted, shouting back, "*Astaftye minya pakoye!*" *Leave me alone!*

As Vorota exchanged an annoyed glance with Alexandra, a motorcycle approached the building from the opposite direction. The drunk staggered in its path. The helmeted rider swerved the bike, barely missing him, but lost control and struck the Mercedes' left front quarter panel before the rider landed on the hood. The back of his helmet slammed the windshield.

Alexandra screamed.

Vorota cursed and snapped his fingers at the chauffer, who opened the door to inspect the figure sprawled on the shiny hood while the other bodyguard started to shove the drunk towards the curb.

In the same instance, the drunk lifted the paper bag and sprayed something on the bodyguard's face, who then collapsed on the street while screaming. The motorcycle rider surged from the hood and rammed the helmet into the chauffeur's face while driving a knee into his groin.

As Vorota instinctively sprung for the curbside door, he felt Alexandra's hand on his forearm, holding him back.

He tugged to pull free, but her handhold became a vice-like grip that kept him from reaching the door handle.

"Freeze!" she shouted, holding a slim pistol in her left hand. He recognized it as a 32-caliber Beretta Tomcat.

Vorota's eyes locked with this woman who had tricked him. But he complied, watching helplessly as the drunk and the helmeted figure scrambled into the front of the vehicle. The latter floored the sedan, rushing them away from the confused crowd. The former turned to face his passengers while pointing the spray can at Vorota's face.

"Cooperate and you'll be back at your penthouse by midnight."

Vorota's initial shock turned to eerie calm as he regarded his captors. "Do you have any idea who I am? The people I know? The power I have in this country? You are already dead."

"That's the thing, Mr. Vorota," replied Alexandra, the gun trained on him. "We know who you are. We know the people you know. We know the power you think you have in this country. And none of it matters to us. You're nothing but a two-bit arms peddler whose day of reckoning has arrived. Before the night is over you *will* talk to us. You will tell us every last fucking thing we want to know, and then some."

The Russian blinked as the snowy streets of Moscow flashed by. Why were American agents taking the risk of upsetting Russo-American relations by abducting a high-profile and influential businessman?

"What…do you wish to know?" he asked, deciding to play their game for the time being to see where it led, and also to buy himself time as he fully expected his people to find him through the Emergency Locator Transmitter surgically implanted in his right thigh.

Alexandra exchanged a brief glance with the drunken impersonator before replying, "Tell us about your recent business with William Kiersted."

* * *

Rachel watched the arms dealer closely as he considered the question while Case kept the can of pepper spray trained on his face. An officer from the Moscow CIA Station drove them to a prearranged location on the outskirts of the city.

Vorota shifted his weight while compressing his lips, before replying, "Isn't he that Greenland terrorist? Why would you ask me that question?"

"I'll give you one more chance," she warned.

Vorota raised his brows. "You are wasting your time, yes? I am an honest business man who has just been—"

Rachel slapped him with the muzzle of the Beretta across his left cheek, drawing blood from an inch-long gash.

The arms dealer brought a hand to his face. "You will pay for this! You will—"

Rachel pistol-whipped him again, cutting his other cheek. Blood dripped down his white shirt.

Cupping his face with both palms now, Vorota jerked back, getting out of her immediate range as she leaned forward, weapon ready for a third strike.

"WAIT!"

As Rachel gave him a moment to reflect, the driver turned right into Podsosenskij Street, and after checking the rearview mirror for any potential tail, he cut abruptly into the deserted parking lot of a church on the same street. Shutting off the lights, he steered around the towering structure, reaching a smaller lot in the rear bordered by a cemetery veiled in a light haze.

"What are we doing here?" Vorota asked.

Rachel ignored him as the headlights of a Chevy SUV cut through the fog drifting from the snowy graveyard, and drove up behind the Mercedes.

"Let's go, Andrei. Change of vehicles."

Case got out first, opening Vorota's door and guiding the bleeding Russian towards their new ride while Rachel checked the rear.

The Mercedes speed off as she closed the door and settled next to Vorota in the more spacious club-seating arrangement of the SUV. Case sat across from them holding a FlexScreen while another officer from the Moscow Station held the pepper spray in one hand and an object shaped like the handheld metal detector at airport security checkpoints in the other.

"What is that?" the arms dealer demanded in sudden panic.

Rachel grinned. Vorota was implanted, which explained his confidence.

He thinks someone's coming to his rescue.

The CIA officer scanned the arms dealer and quickly zeroed in on his upper right thigh, before flipping a switch on the device and running it again over the surgically-implanted transmitter, disabling it with a localized magnetic field. He then switched to scan mode once more again and confirmed its electronic destruction.

Turning away from the visibly horrified Russian, Case said to the driver, "Takes us home."

"Home?" Vorota asked.

"A place where no one will come looking for you," Rachel explained. "The place where you will tell us what we need to know."

Swallowing while keeping his hands hugging his bleeding cheeks, he offered, "I brokered a deal about six months ago between Colonel Lyov Cherkasski, then the head of the Tessinskij Military Warehouse just outside the city, and a Danish trading company."

Rachel looked at Case, who immediately began to work the FlexScreen. She handed Vorota a handkerchief before saying, "Continue."

The arms dealer wiped his bleeding cheeks, inhaled deeply, and added, "The name was Solaris Exports out of Copenhagen, a company with known ties to Kiersted. It was a clean deal. Six million Euros in exchange for four old Soviet-era machines."

"What kind of machines?" Rachel asked, concern filling her at the thought of Kiersted getting his hands on additional nukes. Ever since Greenland, the world had gone to extremes to eliminate the proliferation of nuclear weapons, but she always feared a handful would still end up in the wrong hands.

Vorota shook his head. "They were not the conventional weapons I typically deal with. They were also not chemical, biological, or nuclear."

Rachel raised her free hand a few inches above her thigh, palm facing the ceiling. "What then?"

"I do not know. I was just the broker for this deal. Cherkasski dealt directly with Solaris after I hooked them up and collected a fee."

Rachel just stared at him.

"I swear to you this is true. But Cherkasski would know. He used to manage the warehouse."

"Used to?" asked Rachel.

"He was dismissed a few months ago."

Case tilted the FlexScreen in the direction of Vorota. "Is this Cherkasski?"

The high-resolution image featured a thin man in his mid-thirties with fine features and a full head of ash-blond hair.

"Yes."

"Very young to be a colonel," offered Case.

Vorota shrugged. "Connections, I presume."

Case flipped the screen back to himself and read, "Our records do show that Cherkasski is no longer with the military. But we have no details why. Was it because he got caught with his hand in the cookie jar?"

Vorota gave him a puzzled look. "I do not understand. Cookie jar?"

As Case frowned, Rachel asked, "Andrei, was he caught stealing or doing criminal deals like the one with Solaris? Was that the reason why he was dismissed?"

"No."

"Then?"

"He was seen in the company of men at...at a gay club."

Rachel and Case exchanged a look. He sighed. She raised her brows, before asking, "Where is he now?"

Vorota became silent.

"No more information until we make a deal. I want full immunity and—"

Rachel flicked her wrist and cut him down the bridge of his nose with the forward sight of the Tomcat.

Vorota jerked back, stung, his eyes filling as a trickle of blood ran down to his lips.

"You're not going to start crying like a baby?" Case teased while grinning.

Rachel remained serious and said, "No deals until we get what we need. First you help us, *unconditionally*, then we may just let you live. Understood?"

Vorota wiped his eyes and nose with the handkerchief, and slowly nodded.

"Now, where is Cherkasski?" asked Case.

"I...I'm not sure," he replied.

Rachel started to move the gun towards his face.

"Wait! I can find out!" he exclaimed, shielding his face. "I can check...I know people."

Rachel slowly pulled the gun back. "Good, Andrei. See how easy that was?"

"Now, where was Kiersted taking this equipment?"

The dealer shook his head again. "I do not know these things. You need to ask Cherkasski after I help you find him."

Case and Rachel exchanged another glance before looking at the bruised and bleeding dealer, deciding to cut him some slack until reaching the safe house.

Rachel shrugged. "We'll see, Andrei. We'll see."

CHAPTER TWELVE
ANOTHER CHANCE

"Then Jonah prayed to the Lord his God from the belly of the fish, saying, I called out to the Lord, out of my distress, and he answered me."
  —Jonah 2:1-2

36,000 FEET OVER THE ATLANTIC OCEAN. JULY 9, 2029.

Dr. Konrad Malone opened his eyes and stared at a red *NON-SMOKING* sign in between a pair of overhead vents.

Taking a deep breath, the glaciologist shifted his gaze about him, recognizing what looked like the oval-shaped interior of a business jet.

What the hell?

How did I get here?

Malone inhaled deeply again, his mouth dry and pasty, his ears discerning engine noise, his body sensing turbulence, which made him think of the collapsing glacier.

He frowned, blinking the thought away as he lay on a fully reclined bucket seat, an IV connected to his left arm. He watched the slow drip from a bottle hanging from the overhead baggage compartment before his eyes lazily drifted to the hazy clouds beyond the round window next to him.

And where are we going?

Malone began to fiddle with the side controls of the seat, locating the recliner button and propping himself up, facing two rows of empty seats.

He checked himself, lifting his legs, moving his feet, flexing his arms. His back sore, a couple of bandages on his arms, a slight headache lingering across his temples, Malone suddenly felt damned lucky not only to be alive but to have survived largely unscathed.

"Welcome back to the land of the living, Doctor Malone," said a commanding female voice in a heavy Kenyan-British accent.

He turned around in his seat and stared at a tall heavy-set African woman wearing white pants and a white T-shirt sporting a red cross above the left breast pocket. A stethoscope hung around her neck. She held a rolled FlexScreen in her left hand.

"I'm Doctor Elinah Varaiya," she said, standing tall over him.

For a moment, he thought he saw admonishment in her dark round eyes as she stared down at him and added, "I am with the Kenyan Red Cross. We rescued you from the top of Mount Kilimanjaro by helicopter yesterday and are bringing you to Alaska now by direct orders from the president of Kenya."

"The president...?"

Varaiya rested her free hand on her hip while using the FlexScreen as a pointing device, aiming it at his face. "You have friends in very high places, Doctor Malone, at least enough for my president to order an emergency rescue operation of such magnitude, pulling many of us away from our work in the villages to search for someone who should not have been at a place closed down by the Kilimanjaro National Park authorities. Hundreds of children die in our villages every day having done nothing wrong, Doctor Malone. You break the bloody rules and get to live. And then, the president ordered me and others to his private jet to escort you back to your home while more children die back at our home."

Malone wasn't sure how to respond to that.

She added, "This is nothing personal, Doctor Malone. It's just that I for one don't understand what makes you so bloody special."

Malone closed his eyes and replied, "I'm not, Doctor Varaiya." He paused, then added, "But the research I was conducting on the glacier certainly is. It could provide answers that may save many lives…millions even."

The Kenyan considered his reply for a moment and said, "Well, your friends in high places seem to agree." She unrolled the FlexScreen, worked it for a few moments with her long fingers, and then added, "You are dehydrated from exposure, still feverish from a bout with malaria, and endured bumps and bruises from your ice encounter…but you'll live."

She produced a clear plastic cup filled with a bluish liquid and a small straw. "Here. Drink this."

Malone took it from her and just stared at it. "What is it?"

"Vitamins and electrolytes."

He took a sip and immediately frowned at the bitterness. "This tastes like shit, Doc. How about a pack of Marlboros?"

She grinned, revealing slightly crooked white teeth, before turning serious again. "Bottoms up."

"A triple espresso then?"

"Maybe...*after* the medicine."

Resigned, Malone chugged it and handed the empty cup back to her, then pointed at the IV bag and asked, "What's in there?"

"A cocktail of antimalarial medicine plus more electrolytes and nutrients; everything you need to get another chance. Make it count, yes?"

Malone nodded. "And the espresso?"

"I'll bring you one. We should reach Fairbanks in another six hours.

"Is there a chance I can get a satellite connection with Doctor Natasha Shakhiva? She's the—"

"We know who she is."

Malone stared at the doctor, and after a moment, she elaborated, "Doctor Shakhiva observed the collapse of Furtwängler on satellite and got your government to contact ours and get this whole thing started. You could argue that you are alive today because of her. You were found very dehydrated and would not have lasted another day or two. You're lucky she pushed so hard, moving Heaven and Earth to get you help. That is one bloody helluva guardian angel you have there, Doctor Malone."

His gaze drifted to the sky beyond the window pane, longing to be by her side. "She is indeed."

"I will speak to the pilot about getting you a connection."

"Thank you."

As Varaiya was about to return to the rear of the plane, Malone asked, "Any word on my two guides? They were with me when I got sick but were not there when I woke up right before the glacier collapsed."

She dropped a pair of thick brows at him and slowly frowned. "We found you alone. No guides and not much camp or equipment left, just a couple of broken tents amidst blocks of ice."

Malone nodded slightly and just shifted his gaze back to the clouds.

CHAPTER THIRTEEN
THE TRUTH

*"And you shall know the truth, and the truth shall
set you free."*
—John 8:32

**NORTH SLOPE BOROUGH. ALASKA.
JULY 9, 2029.**

The Piper Cub on floats taxied away from shore and
pointed its nose into the wind.

Back-dropped by snowy peaks beyond vast fields
of bronzed tundra surrounding Shirukak Lake, Natasha
watched from the edge of the IARC camp as the yellow
and white plane stirred up the smooth surface. The roaring
column of fire from the burn-off vent drowned out the
Cub's engine when Mario Escobar applied full power and
it sprung forward.

Dressed in a gray and black down parka, thermal
pants, and boots, Natasha filled her lungs with the cold air
from a passing Arctic front while crossing her arms.

She had dispatched Escobar to Fairbanks to meet up
with Malone, scheduled to reach UAF in a couple of hours,
courtesy of Colonel Stone, who convinced the White House

to contact the embassy in Kenya and get the American ambassador to personally call the Kenyan president.

The late afternoon sun cast a yellow-gold hue across the region, battling the bluish glow from the plume of pure methane burning atop the vent tower. She watched its flickering reflection on the lake's surface as the Cub climbed into a beautiful Alaska sky.

And for an instant Natasha wished she could have left with Escobar, not just to see Malone but to get the hell away from this time bomb.

But she knew she couldn't.

The same Army who had pulled every string to rescue Malone and bring him home was now soliciting her help in what Colonel Stone loosely described as a new twist in the battle against climate terrorism.

And besides, the unseasonably cold front had the effect of firming up the permafrost enough to reduce the height of the burn-off plume by nearly half in twenty-four hours, lowering the risk of the monster escaping this year.

The Cub splashed down the lake in a whirl of mist and surf, finally escaping its watery grip, and gaining altitude as Escobar banked to the south.

Toward Fairbanks.

She watched it for a few minutes, until it vanished beyond the mountains to the south as the surface of Shirukak Lake regained its mirror-like gleam.

"Hey, Tash."

Natasha turned around. Colonel Marcus Stone stood a few feet away dressed in his camouflage fatigues, matching coat, gloves, cap, shiny black boots, and an equally polished black belt from which hung a holstered sidearm.

He paused a moment, sizing her up. Natasha had let her thick blonde hair down and even applied a touch of eye shadow and lipstick. Something about knowing she would be seeing Malone soon had made her spruce up a bit, and she could see the approval in the colonel's half-embarrassed stare.

"Marcus?"

He cleared his throat and approached her. "Feeling better?"

"Much."

"You look better, too."

"Thanks to you," she said, deciding to reward him with a smile and also a brief hug.

"Glad to be of help," he replied, smiling, before looking into her eyes and adding, "And now we need yours."

"You mentioned a new...development?"

"That's one way to put it."

Stone motioned her towards the large communications tent his team had set up next to the pair of large V-22 Osprey twin-tiltrotor aircraft, plus a third Osprey that had arrived a few hours ago. Unlike the large Army aircraft Stone had used to transport his team and gear to this camp, the latest arrival sported no markings aside from its tail number.

A few minutes later they walked past the soldiers guarding the entrance to the large tent. Inside, she saw a dozen men in black tactical uniforms sitting around a long conference table. They were flanked by four 70-inch FlexScreens depicting remote conference rooms packed with people.

Stone spoke. "This is a U.S. Intelligence Community emergency briefing on the potential threat of climate terrorism on thawing permafrost. Present here is a team of U.S. Navy SEALs tasked with the protection of this camp as well as this vulnerable region. On the screens, we have delegates from the Central Intelligence Agency, the Defense Intelligence Agency, the National Security Agency, and the White House. We have also conferenced-in a dozen officers of the GRU and the Spetsnaz from the Russian Federation, and also present on the phone is the CSIS, the Canadian Security Intelligence Service, as both Canada and the Russian Federation are also vulnerable from thawing permafrost. Leading this cross-functional team by presidential order is Daniel Bennett, Director of Central Intelligence."

Natasha knew that the GRU, the Main Intelligence Directorate of the General Staff of the Armed Forces of the Russian Federation—often compared to the U.S. Defense Intelligence Agency, the military version of the CIA—also commanded the Spetsnaz, the Russian Special Purpose Regiments.

"Who…who is doing the briefing?" she asked.

Stone cocked his head at the climatologist. "You are."

Natasha felt a strong jabbing pain in her chest and she realized she had stopped breathing. Slowly, she inhaled, filling her lungs, forcing herself to relax.

"Doctor Shakhiva," said a voice from the hanging FlexScreen to her immediate right. A man stood at the front of the remote conference room. He was dressed in a dark suit with silver hair and fair complexion. "Dan Bennett. I called this session at the request of the President to get a real-time briefing on the situation up there and understand the potential ways in which climate terrorists could capitalize on this environmental weakness just as they did in Greenland. The people present here in this virtual room represent the largest cross-agency task force ever created under the joint command of the President of the United States, the President of the Russian Federation, and the Canadian Prime Minister."

She turned to Colonel Stone, who whispered, "Just tell them what you've told me for the past couple of days, Tash. I've relayed some of the information already, but they really need to hear it directly from you. Here's your opportunity to tell your story."

Natasha looked about the room, for a moment glad she had actually cleaned up. She cleared her throat, but before she could start, Bennett asked, "Is it true, Doctor? Is it really true that almost two thousand gigatons of methane trapped beneath the permafrost in the northern hemisphere are dangerously close to being released because of climate change? And in your opinion, did such a massive release of methane trigger the Permian-Triassic extinction event 250 million years ago?"

Natasha regarded the man monopolizing the FlexScreen, before her gaze drifted to the other video feeds. The eyes of the world were on her, and for a moment she wished Konrad Malone were here sharing the burden of educating the intelligence community of the dangers lurking ahead.

It's all up to you today, she thought before slowly, methodically——and most importantly, factually——she began to speak.

CHAPTER FOURTEEN
LEATHER AND LACE

"Give to me your leather, take from me my lace."
—Stevie Nicks

MOSCOW, RUSSIA. JULY 9, 2029.

The moon hung high and bright above the Russian capital, its silvery glow staining the Moskva River as it snaked through the city.

Dressed in black leather pants, jacket, gloves, and boots, Rachel glanced at the peaceful sight through the visor of the black helmet while sitting behind the handlebars of a BMW motorcycle.

Trying not to freeze to death while parked a half block away and across the street from Samovolka, a raunchy gay club, the GCCU operative pressed the tip of the gloved index finger of her right hand against her thumb, activating the heads-up display on her visor integrated to her SmartLenses. Rubbing the same index finger lightly against the surface of the thumb brought up a pointer on the screen, which she used to navigate through a couple of menus, pulling up the environmental control of her thermal underwear and cranking up the heat by another two degrees.

In the past two hours, she had seen many same-sex couples going into the club, a three-story dilapidated building, its exterior red-brick walls adorned with green, pink, and lavender neon palm trees glowing with a varying intensity that matched the heavy bass echoing from inside the structure.

Invoking the digital zoom feature on her visor allowed her to digitally probe the faces of everyone coming and going—many dressed in black, just like her. The helmet's CPU performed forty-point facial comparisons with eleven different photos of Cherkasski from CIA files.

Case, also dressed in leather, was inside, walking about, using his combination of SmartLenses and SmartShades, the latter providing much more powerful digital zoom capability than the surgically implanted lenses for close-up work. Wirelessly interfaced to her helmet unit, Rachel could see what he saw, and vice versa.

Contrary to the weathered exterior, the club's interior was flashy, with multi-level platforms where scantily dressed men and women danced under a rainbow of light. All of the floors were clear acrylic, bestowing those beneath with unobstructed views of patrons above, including those wearing leather miniskirts.

Three hours ago, Andrei Vorota had provided confirmation that Cherkasski would be here this late evening. Case and Rachel had left the arms dealer in the company of the local CIA and had reached the club. An Agency chase car with three armed officers parked two blocks away provided back-up for the field operatives.

So far, however, the state-of-the-art facial recognition system had failed to make a match.

Even if Cherkasski had undergone facial reconstruction, the forty-point check should provide enough resolution to identify him. The basic shape of the face, the forehead, the distance between the eyes, and the relative location of the mouth, nose, ears, and eyes typically did not change in the average cosmetic reconstruction.

Rachel continued to watch the street while also glancing at the images from inside the club as well as the digital readouts from the computing unit performing facial recognition. The highest reading of the evening had been a three-pointer, hardly a qualified match.

A young man in a shiny red-leather jacket zippered down to expose his muscular chest, smiled at Case as he walked by.

"I think you made a friend there," she said, speaking into the helmet's built-in microphone.

"Not funny," Case mumbled, the transparent throat mike picking up his voice directly from his vocal cords.

"You should ask him to dance."

"Laugh it up," he replied.

Rachel could hear the laughter from the officers in the chase car.

"Case," she said, turning serious when the software converged on the face of a woman in the club, indicating a possible match. "I'm getting fifteen points from that blonde in the green skirt dancing on the upper left stage."

The camera in Case's SmartShades panned in her direction. "Her?"

"That's the best match we've gotten tonight," replied Rachel. "Get a closer look."

The image zoomed in on a pretty blonde in a ridiculously-short green miniskirt and tight leather black top in the company of three younger girls, also scantily clad. The foursome slow danced to the old Stevie Nicks and Don Henley tune, *Leather and Lace.*

Case tried to focus the video on the target's mini-skirt from underneath, but the blonde kept moving about with her friends, making the task difficult. But as the song reached the spot where Stevie Nicks sang the lyrics, "Give to me your leather," the foursome ripped off their skirts and momentarily swung them overhead, parading about in their lace underwear while singing out loud, "Take from me my lace!"

Rachel narrowed her gaze on the digitally-filtered image of the target's white lace underwear.

"See what I see?" Case asked.

"Blondie may have breasts," Rachel replied as the foursome kept singing while putting their miniskirts back on. "But the parts below don't match."

The image moved to the face, tracking the head movement as she danced until it snapped a high-resolution still the instant the blonde briefly shifted her face down and to the left, directly in Case's direction.

"Twenty-nine points," said Case, reading the same information displayed on Rachel's visor display, which also showed side-by-side an image of the colonel from his CIA file. "Definitely a nose and chin job, but not enough to fool the system."

"And it looks like he ran out of cash to finish the job," replied Rachel, impressed the Russian actually looked so good.

"Maybe Cherkasski likes it both ways," Case said. "Or maybe the girls with him want a woman with a penis."

"Assuming they're real girls," Rachel noted. "Maybe they're guys who went all the way."

"Good point," Case said, panning to them from underneath, finding a bulge suggesting a set of male genitalia on one and either surgical or natural female parts on the other two.

For the next hour, they monitored Cherkasski's activities as he danced, drank, and kissed his companions in a booth.

Case was eventually picked up twice and forced to dance in order to protect his cover—to Rachel's delight; once with two men in drag and a second time with two whip-clutching lesbians dressed in see-through latex skirts and blouses.

She had difficulty containing her laughter, and neither could the guys in the chase car.

"They're leaving now," Case said, relief filling his voice as Cherkasski and his three friends headed for the coat closet before reaching the exit.

Rachel watched them emerge on the street and flag down a taxi.

"No more socializing, Case. Time to go," she said, starting the bike and accelerating towards the entrance as the taxi doors closed and the black and yellow vehicle left the curb.

Case rushed outside, jumping behind Rachel, who took off after it.

"Dancing at a gay club and now riding bitch," she mused, steering them down the street, keeping a respectful half a block through the thin traffic, letting a car get in between them. "And I have it all on high-res video. I own you now."

"Really. Keep it up, and you can kiss that drink goodbye," he said, reaching around her waist with both hands and wedging himself against her as the streets of Moscow rushed past them.

For reasons she could not explain, Rachel welcomed the embrace as she kept her eyes on the road and the taxi's taillights. It continued for another fifteen minutes, reaching a modern apartment complex on Yauzskaya Ulitsa, which, like Samovolka, also overlooked the Moskva River.

The foursome got out and noisily staggered towards the entrance, apparently drunk, as the taxi drove off.

Rachel floored the BMW bike, driving it up on the curb, coming to a screeching halt in between the startled group and the building's entrance.

Case pulled out the same can of pepper spray he had used on Vorota's bodyguard and emptied its content on all three of Cherkasski's companions, who collapsed while screaming. Rachel fired a stun gun at the former Russian colonel, who dropped to the curb in spasms, urinating on himself.

"Time!" Case shouted into his throat mike as Rachel killed the stun gun and Cherkasski stopped thrashing on the frozen sidewalk.

An instant later the headlights of the chase car cut through the night, landing on them as they dragged the semi-conscious Russian to the street.

Two officers got out and shoved him into the rear of the sedan before driving back to the embassy.

Rachel waited until Case jumped back on before taking off after them.

* * *

Thirty minutes later they stood outside a basement holding cell at the American Embassy compound. To Rachel's surprise, a contingent from the GRU had been waiting for them in the ambassador's office. Apparently, the U.S. Intelligence Community had chosen to join forces with their Russian counterparts in this operation given the likelihood of a terrorist-triggered permafrost event in Siberia.

Moreover, the Moscow Station Chief, by orders from the Director of Central Intelligence, instructed Rachel and Case to let the Russians conduct the first round of interrogations.

Rachel, still dressed in black leather, stood next to an equally attired Case Patterson as they watched a flat screen connected to a camera inside the holding cell. Two Russian agents worked on Cherkasski, who was strapped naked to a chair with his hands tied behind his back. The two GRU officers spoke in Russian, which was translated to English by the embassy's AI system and fed to the ear pieces worn by Rachel and Case.

"Where is William Kiersted now, Lyov?" pressed the older of the two officers—a man named Ivenko with a shaved head and a barrel chest in his early fifties—while his much younger but equally robust associate, Alexei, stood behind their bound subject.

"My name is not Lyov anymore!" Cherkasski shouted. "It is Natalia!"

Ivenko punched Cherkasski in his finely-sculpted nose, shoving his head back as blood exploded through his flaring nostrils.

"Answer! Or I will disfigure you!"

"No! Please stop! Please do not—"

The GRU officer punched him again, nearly knocking him and the chair back. Alexei caught him and planted the bleeding transsexual in front of Ivenko, who removed his jacket and tossed it aside. He then slowly rolled up the sleeves of the white shirt he wore underneath, exposing powerful forearms connected to sailor-sized fists.

"I will ask you one more time. Where is William Kiersted?"

"I do not know!" he cried out, tears mixing with the blood on his lips.

The Russians continued their hardcore interrogation for almost thirty gruesome minutes, which included cuts with razor blades, more punching, plus a dozen cigarette burns to the man's breasts.

Cherkasski screamed, jerking and twisting, trying to break free.

As Ivenko and Alexei took a step back to admire their handiwork, Cherkasski dropped his head, crying, bleeding, chest heaving. "Please," he mumbled. "I swear to you...I do not know where he is...I just sold him equipment... that's all..."

Ivenko looked at Alexei and pointed at Cherkasski's groin. The younger GRU officer produced a cigarette lighter and went to work on him.

Cherkasski let out a harrowing scream, his model-like face contorting into a mask of agonized pain as he struggled against the straps, as he tried in vain to break free, shouting, pleading, crying for it to stop.

In her years with the Agency, Rachel had seen her share of brutal interrogations, but there was something particularly dark about this one. Perhaps it was the combination of the subject, who looked like a beautiful model except for the groin, and the simple yet massively painful torture techniques of the GRU. No fancy drugs or equipment. Just a razor blade, a pack of cigarettes, and a cheap lighter.

Russian efficiency.

The GRU officers took turns working Cherkasski for another five minutes, punching, slapping, burning him, and completely humiliating him without even asking any more questions.

Rachel understood their technique. Taking the subject through a sudden and significant amount of pain had a way of letting him know who was in control, lowering any semblance of defense, of self-control, making him want to tell them everything. But every time Cherkasski started to open his mouth, more pain was inflicted, triggering yet more screaming and sobbing.

Ivenko suddenly stopped, grabbed his coat, and motioned Alexei to follow him out of the cell, walking past Rachel and Case while mumbling in heavily-accented English, "He is yours for ten minutes, yes? We get coffee now."

Time for the good cops, she thought, as the GRU men walked down the hallway to the small break room. She went in first, followed by Case, approaching the scourged Russian as the door closed behind them.

"Hello, Natalia," Rachel said, taking a knee in front of the Russian to look him squarely in the eye. The GRU officers had made a mess of what had been a miracle of modern plastic surgery just minutes ago.

The former colonel, whose CIA dossier indicated was fluent in English, coughed, spitting a tooth, which landed on one of Rachel's boots.

She ignored it, staring at Cherkasski's good eye. The other was closed shut from a swelling purple bruise.

"Listen to me, please," she said. "You must tell me everything you know right now. I will then try to convince the GRU to leave you alone. You're currently on American

soil. We can protect you, but only if you cooperate immediately. Do you understand me?"

Lips quivering, nose twisted and bleeding, a dozen
cigarette burns on breasts that actually looked better than
the ones she got after her mastectomy, Cherkasski didn't
take long to consider Rachel's proposition.

Slowly, he nodded.

"Good. What kind of machines did Kiersted purchase
from you?"

"Old...Soviet-era devices...tectonic."

"*Tectonic?*"

Slowly, the Russian nodded, his one good eye losing
focus. "Four of them."

"Get Natalia some water," Rachel said to Case.

He reached for the table on the side of the room and
filled a cup with water from a jar, handing it to Rachel.

She brought it to his lips and got the Russian to take a
sip, which he tried to swallow but instead ended up coughing out onto Rachel's jacket along with bloody saliva.

Rachel ignored it and tried again, and this time
Cherkasski was able to keep it down. She then splashed
some water on his face and wiped it with a towel Case
handed to her.

"Now, Natalia," she continued as the Russian regained
focus, staring at her. "What do you mean by tectonic
devices?"

"I do not have all...information...but they were built
to...induce mechanical oscillations...into the soil...along
fault lines...forcing tremors."

"Who has more information about them?"

"Yuri..." the Russian said, swallowing, breathing
deeply and adding, "Gerchenko."

"Who's Yuri Gerchenko?" Rachel asked while Case worked his FlexScreen.

"Soviet scientist…from the old days. He serviced the…systems before purchase."

Case produced a digital photo on the small screen and showed it to him. "Is this him?"

Cherkasski narrowed his one good eye, spending a moment inspecting it before slowly nodding. "He is older now…but it is him."

Rachel browsed through the dossier headlines beneath the photograph. Gerchenko had been a young engineer in 1989 assigned to Aleksey Nikolayev, the Russian Academy of Science chief engineer overseeing the creation of a tectonic device based on the oscillation machine prototyped by legendary inventor Nikolai Tesla almost a century earlier. The intent of the invention was to induce oscillations in seismic-sensitive regions to reduce the tension between tectonic plates to prevent major earthquakes. The dossier indicated that Gerchenko was in his early sixties, and the sole surviving scientist from that project, which was mothballed when the Soviet Union imploded in 1990.

"Where is Gerchenko?"

"With Kiersted…to help with the machines."

Rachel stared at Case before asking, "Where are these systems now, Natalia?"

"I do not know," he said. "I…swear."

"You know what the GRU is going to do to you next?" asked Rachel.

Cherkasski's lips began to tremble before shouting, "I am telling the truth! I do not know!"

"I don't think you are telling us *everything*, Natalia," Rachel said. "When and where is Kiersted planning to use these machines?"

The Russian slowly shook his head while crying, "I do not know! I want asylum! I want asylum!"

"Listen," Case said, kneeling next to Rachel. "There's no chance of that unless you tell us everything. Only *then* will we be able to convince our people to take you in. Otherwise, we'll be forced to hand you over to the GRU."

"They'll disfigure you, Natalia," said Rachel.

"Plus, they'll finish your...*transformation*," Case said, pointing at Cherkasski's male genitalia and making a scissor motion with the index and middle fingers of his right hand. "Chop chop."

"Please," the Russian said. "Don't let them take me! Please!" he cried, mascara running down his face, mixing with the blood on his cheeks, nose, and chin.

"That's entirely up to you," Case said. "What else can you tell us?"

Cherkasski regarded them with his good eye, inhaled deeply, swallowed, and slowly began to speak.

Five minutes later, Rachel and Case stepped out to confer with their GRU colleagues, sharing the critical information they had gathered.

As the Russians headed for the exit while speaking on their mobile phones, Rachel and Case headed for the ambassador's office. They had to gather every last shred of technical data on these Soviet-era machines. In addition, they needed immediate access to the high-definition video of every satellite within reach of the oil city of Surgat, in the West Siberian Plains.

If Cherkasski's information was accurate, they were almost out of time.

CHAPTER FIFTEEN
BIOMES

"Solutions to the climate crisis are within reach."
—Al Gore, Chairman and Founder, The Climate Reality Project.

UNIVERSITY OF ALASKA, FAIRBANKS. JULY 9, 2029.

"Here, Mario," Malone said, pointing at the large FlexScreen. "This is one of the best samples. I drilled it just last week."

Escobar, standing next to Malone in the analysis room adjacent to the freezer basement of the geology department, zipped up his jacket while leaning closer to the large screen. "Definitely a wide layer of dust, Koni. Over 300 hundred years long."

"Close to *four* hundred," Malone said, sipping his third double espresso in two hours not just to stay warm in the examination room, kept at a constant 25°F to preserve ice core samples under analysis, but also to fight off the jetlag.

For the past four hours, ever since he'd arrived at the university and Escobar had flown down from Shirukak Lake, the scientists had spent a moment exchanging pleasantries before descending to this sacred basement that stored so much of our planet's history.

Escobar worked the FlexScreen and opened a file containing images of the last set of core samples he had drilled in Bolivia from the long-vanished Chacaltaya Glacier, once the highest ski run in South America.

"Look here," the Hispanic glaciologist said, aligning the years to perform an accurate comparison between the sample Malone had extracted from Mount Kilimanjaro to one of the many cores from Chacaltaya, now preserved at -30°F in the large storage freezer next door. UAF kept hundreds of ice cores from the dozens of global expeditions around the world by staff members over the course of thirty years. Malone had added a total of 49 ice cores in the past three months.

"The dust layers overlap," said Malone.

"Not only that, but the element analysis of the particles making up this inch-thick layer, plus the computer analysis of the ice immediately before, indicate a rapid drop in the methane content in the ice, which suggests a release into the atmosphere. That's followed by a decrease of the wetlands thriving in the tropics, replaced by an arid landscape."

Malone stared at the digital readouts on the screen right above ice cores from two separate regions of the world but close to the same latitude, near the equator, noticing the abrupt depletion in oxygen-18 isotopes at roughly the same time, signaling the start of the drought period in Africa as well as a drought period in Bolivia. And that meant as the rains receded, tropical forests turned into wastelands through vast fires that burned the ecosystem to the ground, crystallizing the soil, turning it into sand. In some regions like South America, the land recovered after a few hundred years as the rains returned to the jungles. But in Africa the Sahara remained strong.

"So," Escobar said. "This means that we have just made a similar correlation of dust layers, methane depletion in the ice, and a depletion of oxygen-18 isotopes."

"And that means the famine wasn't limited to Egypt," said Malone, finishing the espresso.

"That's right, *amigo*. It struck both continents."

Malone nodded. "The Egyptians were just better at recording the event in stone."

"Let's upload this into the system," said Escobar, working the FlexScreen, updating the parameters in the master global climate computer model of the UAF.

The AI engine absorbed the new correlation and began to crunch the information.

"It may be a few minutes," said Escobar, leaning against a lab table in the analysis room, which was just large enough to fit a pair of FlexScreens, three lab tables with scanners to analyze ice cores, and a collection of tools should the need arise to desecrate a section of a core to thaw it out and perform further analysis in liquid or gas form.

Malone yawned.

"That was a very stupid thing you did, Koni," said Escobar, arms crossed. "Tash was very worried, and so was I."

"I know," Malone replied. "I spoke to Tash briefly on the flight over here. Look, I'll tell you the same thing I told her. I had no choice. I had to get as many cores as possible before the collapse."

"Then I'm sure you know things aren't so good up there," the Bolivian said. "Methane readings are on the rise. The burn-off vent is now going constantly."

"I heard. At least it does correlate with the theory. The glaciers and the permafrost were created at the end of the last ice age. If they froze at the same time, it figures they would also melt at the same time."

"Man, I wish we were wrong."

"Yeah, but we're not, pal."

"Yeah."

"The question we need to answer," Malone said, "is how bad do we think it's going to get, and if the projections indeed turn out as bad as I think they will be, how do we prepare the world? How do we learn from what happened to the Egyptians—and apparently also in South America—four thousand years ago to minimize casualties?"

Almost on cue, the system beeped, marking the end of the modeling run.

The scientists turned their attention to the screen, and what they saw startled them. Even someone as hardened as Konrad Malone felt a knot in his gut.

The image of the Earth filled the screen as it was that day in July of 2029, with bands of thick jungle in the tropics, ice on the Polar Regions, and heat bands on the desert regions in the correct areas, like the Sahara, Gobi, parts of the Middle East, and also Arizona and Nevada.

But then the computer model began to alter this image in fast-forward time-lapse fashion at the rate of one month for every second based on the data from the ice cores.

"Fuck me," Malone whispered.

"Indeed."

The digitized prediction of the Earth mutating in front of them foretold a radically different world from what humans knew today.

Climate Change wasn't only going to melt the polar caps and trigger floods.

Climate Change wasn't only going to feed monster storms, consume forests with wildfires, and spread droughts around the planet.

If Konrad Malone and Mario Escobar had entered the parameters from the ice cores correctly, and if the computer model was also extrapolating the data accurately, the results showed the creation of entirely new biomes—major ecosystem types like forests, deserts, grasslands, and tundra around the world. The data pointed to the birth of landscapes which humans have never seen before and in the oddest of locations, starting with the rapid collapse of the Amazon rainforest within two decades, taken over by savannas—the next hottest biome after desert dunes—their lush trees replaced by expanses of tall grass. A thick belt around the Earth extending five hundred miles north and south from the equator was modeled to almost reach the boiling point of water—hotter than the hottest point in the Sahara today, meaning everyone in those regions would have to be evacuated within the next ten years, if not sooner.

"These biome displacements are supposed to take hundreds or even thousands of years to play out, Mario," said Malone, not certain if he believed what he was seeing.

"Yep, but our ice cores predict this to occur in our lifetime."

Malone got on the phone.

"Who are you calling?" Escobar asked.

"My grad students. I need another triple espresso."

The scientists spent several more hours holed up in the lab, reanalyzing the cores, triple-checking assumptions, dragging colleagues down to oversee their work, making computer engineers recheck the validity of the simulations, which were predicting landscapes the likes of which modern civilization have never seen before.

This was the kind of drastic shift in weather patterns that had nearly obliterated the Egyptians and created the Sahara Desert where once fertile lands flourished.

"And that's best-case scenario," Malone said.

Escobar was sitting down by now, his bloodshot eyes staring at the FlexScreen. "Yeah," he said. "Worst case is a repeat of the Permian-Triassic event."

At the end of a very long day, Malone and Escobar concluded that with the data in the tropical ice cores, the computer simulations, and the decades of climatology experience under their belts, they were converging on a very simple message to the world.

Mankind would need to adapt…or, like the Egyptians, perish.

CHAPTER SIXTEEN
THE END OF DAYS

"For the form of this world is passing away."
—Corinthians 7:31

NILE RIVER. FIFTY MILES SOUTH OF MEMPHIS, EGYPT (CAPITAL OF THE OLD KINGDOM, 12 MILES SOUTH OF MODERN-DAY CAIRO). 2207 B.C.

The scream made him blink.

Under a blazing late afternoon sun, Pepi II Neferkare shifted his stoic gaze beyond the cedar planks and oars of his barge towards the left bank.

That any scream would rattle him seemed impossible. The pharaoh and veteran of many wars had seen men wail while being skinned alive, or dismembered, or simmered in boiling oil. He had seen his priests pluck out the beating hearts of virgin slaves.

But for reasons he couldn't explain, Neferkare had cared enough about the guards in the adjacent raft to grace them with a brief glance as the fire consumed them while they continued to bail water in clay buckets and toss it in the direction of his barge.

The god-king watched the thatched roof made of papyrus and halfa grass dripping from the incessant barrage of water splashed by overlapping teams of guards in the dozens of escort ships that accompanied him in his short expedition to survey his dying country, cooling off the royal barge at the hefty price of disregarding their own vessels. They had left Memphis six days ago, in the middle of winter, to take advantage of the year's coolest temperatures to venture south. But an unexpected heat wave had swept in from the desert a few hours ago, as they made their way back to the capital city, threatening to consume the volatile vessels.

Sometimes the men aboard the escort ships would be able to divert the water to quench the fire on their own boats before it got out of control. But most often, the dried papyrus would ignite under the merciless sun, spreading too fast across the small boats, narrowing their choices.

Death by fire.

Death by crocodile.

The pharaoh watched as three guards made the latter choice, diving into the reptile-infested water and attempting to swim ashore.

But they didn't make it.

They seldom did.

The same famine that had killed over half of the country's once thriving population had turned the normally aggressive Nile crocodiles into insatiable monsters.

The men screamed as the beasts converged on them, losing themselves in a feeding gorge of howls, death spirals, whipping tails, and foamy blood. The rest chose an even worse death, desperately rowing to shore when the flames engulfed them, finally jumping ablaze into anxious jaws.

Neferkare saw it all; heard it all.

Yet, one by one the escort vessels took their turn, throwing bucketful after bucketful at the barge's roof, at its wooden flanks, on its deck. They persisted until given the order to push back and cool themselves and their vessels while another pair of escorts took their place.

But sometimes the vessels would catch fire before their rotational shift was finished.

And death choices would be made.

Neferkare watched one vessel successfully approaching the shore, half the men aboard quenching the fire while the other half rowed as crocodiles followed.

Teamwork.

They jumped off from the burning ship as its bow went up on the bank, using wooden oars to keep hungry reptiles at bay as they rushed inland.

Unfortunately, the surviving crew would be dead before sundown.

The relentless sun had turned the once fertile banks filled with farms, markets, and villages, into a wasteland of disease, famine, and cannibalism. And if that didn't kill them, the intense heat, enough to ignite papyrus wood, would roast them before they could reach shelter.

Neferkare turned to Harkfuf, his chief military officer who accompanied him on this short expedition.

"My Lord," the elderly general said, his bronzed and muscular chest filmed with sweat as he stood beneath an awning shielding the entrance to the pharaoh's quarters. He pointed at his men measuring the speed of the boat relative to land to calculate their remaining travel time. "At this rate, we will reach Memphis by sundown. I would not recommend such a trip again, even in winter."

Neferkare stared into the aging eyes of his most trusted advisor, military chief, and friend, and said, "As you wish."

The youngest military captain under Pharaoh Merenre, Neferkare's father, Harkfuf had protected the young pharaoh and his mother, Ankhesenpepi II, during his early ruling years until he became of age. In return, Neferkare provided him with a lifetime of power and riches.

Neferkare placed a hand on Harkfuf's shoulder as his loyal subject bowed his head. "I know you will deliver your Lord and your queen home safely," he said, before turning around and going inside his much cooler refuge while two chamber maids drew the entrance curtains.

Dressed in a veil-thin white-linen tunic, her hair pulled back with lapis beads, keeping her long and thin neck clear, Queen Nitocris turned away from the chamber maids fanning her with palm fronds, and walked toward her husband and king.

She used a damp cloth to cool his face.

Neferkare closed his eyes.

Three years had passed since the day she had nearly died on that altar, and yet Neferkare still shuddered at her touch. So much had the former Nubian princess captivated him that the pharaoh had ordered his other wives entombed to wait for him in the afterlife while he broke tradition and made her his sole queen.

Neferkare, who had already birthed him a strong boy, embraced her as all the maids in the royal chamber looked away and froze, like living statues, not uttering a sound as the pharaoh sought solace for the horrors he had witnessed today, and the days before.

Entire cities had been decimated by unimaginable temperatures. A relentless heat wave had turned lush valleys into uninhabitable deserts. An obstinate Nile refused to overflow its banks. Sunbaked and cracked soil replaced the once majestic shores as the angry gods held back the rains to cool his superheated kingdom.

Nitocris held him, washing away the anger and frustration. She took away the fear worming in his gut at the rising number of dissenting Nomarchs questioning his heavenly powers, at the numerous death plots his spies and guards had uncovered, killing traitors almost daily.

Neferkare clutched his wife just as he used to latch on to his mother, tensing at his inability to deal with his growing opposition.

It didn't matter how many he tortured, how many he slaughtered publicly. Traitors would continue to surface, more plots would flare, more rumors would spread about his failing powers, and more priests stopped believing in his divine right, challenging his god-king lineage.

Perhaps he wasn't the son of the esteemed Merenre.

Perhaps Ankhesenpepi II had not been impregnated by the great pharaoh.

Perhaps Neferkare was a bastard, a mortal, incapable of reversing the tide of death sweeping through this once prosperous and powerful nation.

As the maids remained immobile, Neferkare ripped her tunic and took his wife on their large bed made of a thick and soft woven mat on a wood frame supported by legs shaped like the same crocodiles consuming his escorts.

Nitocris accepted him in silence, allowing him to release, to purge his frustration, his rage, his fears.

When he finished, they stepped into an alabaster vase filled with fresh Nile water, where they cooled off while maids washed them. The screams continued outside as another vessel was set ablaze, the flames roaring just outside their windows.

Neferkare stared at his wife, who bowed her head and whispered, "My lord, my love."

The last pharaoh of Egypt's Old Kingdom gazed into the magical eyes of the only woman he had ever loved besides his mother, and whispered back, "When we reach Memphis I will face more danger, more traitors, many more attempts on my life."

The Nubian woman whom he trusted as much as Harkfuf narrowed her eyes, pouting those soft lips, her perfectly-shaped breasts barely breaking the surface of the water.

"I am here for you, my lord, till the end of time."

Neferkare almost chuckled at the irony of her words.

"This too shall pass," she added at his silence.

"Not in my lifetime…not in my lifetime."

She didn't reply. Instead she shifted over to him in the tub and held him from behind, her long arms wrapped around his stomach.

Neferkare closed his eyes and surrendered to her touch, but not before turning his head and mumbling in her ear, "If they wrong me…you must avenge me…and protect our son."

CHAPTER SEVENTEEN
HOLY WARRIORS

"Believers, make war on the infidels who dwell around you. Deal firmly with them."
—Surah 9:121

SURGAT. RUSSIA. JULY 10, 2029.

They advanced silently under a star-filled night in the West Siberian Plains.

Ivenko led the strike followed by Alexei and a contingent of ten Spetsnaz operatives dressed in NanoSuits, clutching automatic weapons. Rachel and Case followed them also wearing the advanced bullet resistant assault gear to shield them from the climate terrorists believed to be holed up in a large waterfront cabin around the bend in a trail at the edge of the vast expanse of forest dominating this remote oil outpost.

Three days ago, high-definition satellite coverage of the region caught a Cessna Caravan landing at an abandoned airstrip west of the place locals called Refinery City. Four figures hoisted strange-looking hardware from the plane into a waiting truck.

Which is still parked in front of the cabin.

Rachel inspected the trail ahead before taking in the towering pines around her, most tilted at varying angles as their roots lost their grip in the thawing permafrost.

Drunken trees.

She wiped the perspiration on her forehead as unseasonably high temperatures plagued an area which had seldom left the high forties even in the height of summer. Yet, today temperatures had climbed into the low eighties, and this early evening they still hovered in the seventies.

Which explains why the ground is so damned mushy.

Rachel frowned as her water-proof boots sunk in the mud, creating light suction sounds every time she took a step, making it difficult to keep up with the well trained Russian forces, who continued advancing single file with a ten-foot spread.

Her thighs burning from the effort, Rachel forced control into her breathing, inhaling through her nostrils and exhaling through her mouth, filling her lungs with the pine-resin fragrance of her surroundings.

Insects hovered about her but didn't settle, their incessant buzzing mixed with the splashing sounds drifting from the direction of the cabin, confirming satellite imagery of a stream running in front of a vacation property. The place was registered to an imports-exports company based in Copenhagen, corroborating the information extracted from Lyov Cherkasski.

Ivenko stopped and signaled the group to spread.

Shifting in the darkness, the Spetsnaz team vanished like shadows, taking pre-assigned positions around the target.

Ivenko dropped to a crouch behind a clump of boulders before extending the middle and index fingers of his free hand at Rachel and Case, signaling to approach him.

They joined him a moment later, and Rachel was glad to take a breather, dipping her right knee into the soft ground.

The large, two-story cabin—what locals called a *dacha*—was nestled between the scenic rapids of a river and a dirt road connecting the property to the main highway that led to the Surgat Oil Refinery complex.

Ivenko, his face and bald head smeared with dark green and black camouflage paint, pointed at the FlexScreen on his wrist, depicting real time satellite infrared imagery of the *dacha*, where four figures moved about.

Rachel slowly nodded, her SmartLenses linked to overhead U.S. Intelligence satellites positioned to observe the cabin from four different angles. Their computer-enhanced, deep-infrared imagery was fed directly in near-holographic form to her ocular implants, providing her with the equivalent of X-ray vision.

In an instant, she could see through the thick walls of the vacation cabin, and so could Case.

Four figures moved about inside, confirming the information displayed on Ivenko's wrist. But unlike the Russian's five-year-old system, the CIA-issued ocular hardware Rachel and Case used didn't require users to constantly take their eyes off the target while trying to read the information on wrist FlexScreens. The American SmartLenses superimposed the imagery over the real world in front of them, also conveying that all four targets were in the large living area in the middle of the first floor.

On the plane ride over here, Rachel had given Ivenko a set of SmartShades for his team. But like anything new, the Russians were hesitant to trust them, especially if it was made in America.

"Where are the SmartShades we gave you?"

Reluctantly, the Russian reached into a Velcro-secured pocket on the armored vest he wore over the NanoSuit and produced them. "Is this necessary?"

"Amuse me," said Rachel, already regretting the arrangement her country had made with these technologically-lagging troops, who were still relying on 2D IR imagery to guide them through an assault. "Try them on for size."

"For size?" Ivenko asked.

"Just put the fucking things on," Case said. "And tell me what you see."

Ivenko pointed at their faces. "But you do not wear them, yes?"

"Ours are surgically implanted over our corneas," she explained.

Ivenko narrowed his gaze suspiciously at them, then mumbled something in Russian, and, visibly reluctantly, slipped them on. The nanotech compounds recognized the shape of his face and adjusted the frame real time to conform to it, creating a perfect fit.

Slowly, the husky Russian turned his head toward the *dacha* and mumbled something else Rachel could not understand but in a tone which indicated surprise.

"This is…impossible…how do you—"

"The technology will be made available to the GRU as a token of our appreciation for the collaborative effort between our governments," Case said.

"Amazing." The Russian inspected the cabin with his newly enhanced vision, and then ordered his troops to do the same.

Rachel smiled a moment later as she heard similar reactions from the rest of the troops.

"Now, Ivenko," Case said, his features softened by the camouflage cream. "We need them alive, especially Kiersted, if he's here. We need to question him to find the other machines."

The Russian nodded solemnly. "We agreed this is our intention, yes?"

Our intention?

Is he fucking kidding me?

But in the spirit of inter-agency cooperation, Rachel decided to be patient with the man. Reaching inside Case's backpack, she produced a black sphere the size of a softball. "First the Orb goes inside and releases the gas," she explained. "*Then* we wait *three minutes* for it to become inert, *then* we go in. Agreed?"

Ivenko stared suspiciously at the black ball in her hand. "This…thing really goes in undetected and neutralize terrorists, yes?"

"Correct. This is *also* proven technology, Ivenko. Like the glasses. You *must* trust it. But if any of the terrorists figures out what's going and manages to run out, then we use stun rounds. Real bullets are a last resort. Agreed?"

Ivenko sighed heavily and finally gave her a slight nod. Then he turned away while speaking into his throat mike, hopefully relaying the objective, before looking back at the American operatives. "My team is ready."

"Okay, hold on," Rachel said. "Tell me *exactly* what you told your team."

Groaning, Ivenko said, "You release your…little ball in one minute, yes? We then wait three minutes before my team goes inside from the south, west, and north ends. You cover the east. Yes?"

Case and Rachel nodded in unison.

"Good. I go now," he whispered, before vanishing in the forest, joining his team.

"I'm too old for this shit," she whispered, placing the Orb back in Case's rucksack.

He looked at her. "They'd better not screw this up."

"Yeah. We need the bastards alive."

They walked in a crouch past the edge of the waist-high shrubbery, her eyes on the weathered cabin, confirming that all four terrorists remained inside and away from the windows.

Their objective, a tall pile of firewood adjacent to a large chopping block and two rusty axes, would place them a hundred or so feet from a side entrance. Her SmartLenses showed that it led to a narrow hallway connecting the entrance to the main room where the terrorists moved about.

She reached it first, breathing rapidly as she slid into place with Case in tow. He huddled by her side, so close she could smell coffee on his breath from the cup he had on the way from the airport.

He took off his rucksack and removed the Orb, the brainchild of a team of nanotechnology scientists from Los Alamos two years ago. The unit, coated with a bullet-resistant layer of Kevlar and armed with a potent sleeping gas, used GPS navigation to reach targets as far away as a mile.

She pressed her right thumb against the Orb's activation window, booting it up. A dozen portholes opened around the sphere, and it immediately started to hover around them under the power of its micro fans.

Case entered a set of commands on his wrist FlexScreen, enabling the stealth mechanism. Micro cameras deployed around the Orb video-recorded their respective fields of view and played them in real-time reverse synchronization on its FlexScreen skin, mirroring its environment, making it almost invisible to the naked eye.

As it blended away, Rachel's ocular implants presented the Orb as a blue sphere floating about them.

"We're in business," she said.

"Showtime," said Case, entering additional commands, which caused the bluish globe to rush towards the cabin. It went up to the roof and vanished inside the fireplace chute.

Twenty seconds.

Case and Rachel waited, their SmartLenses also confirming the Russian troops remained put, per their agreement.

Forty seconds.

The terrorists continued to move inside the cabin undisturbed, when suddenly one reached for his throat and collapsed. As the others began to run toward the front entrance, realizing something was wrong, a new heat signature materialized in the middle of the cabin.

What the hell is that?

The three remaining figures reached the front, running away from the cabin.

A terrorist collapsed by the steps connecting the front porch to the driveway as the gas did its sinister work. The other two, clutching assault rifles, opened fire blindly into the forest while dashing for their truck, managing to escape the gas inside the house.

"How they made it out?" Rachel asked.

Case shrugged. "So much for our little plan."

Seventy seconds.

Somebody from the Spetsnaz team panicked and returned the fire, and contrary to the agreement, did not use rubber bullets.

Rounds tore through the ground to the right of the terrorists, who managed to huddle behind their truck.

The silence was broken by Case as he shouted, "Damn it, Ivenko! Rubber bullets only!"

Three Spetsnaz operatives appeared in the clearing west of the cabin, rushing to the target.

"Ivenko, tell your men to hold back!" barked Rachel, "The gas is active in the cabin for one more minute."

"But the machine is activated!" the Russian commando replied.

"I know," Case said. "But we need to wait!"

Instead of acknowledging, the trio of Russians continued their advance, but all of them dropped to the ground when the terrorists unloaded a barrage of bullets in their direction.

"Goddammit!" shouted Case. "Hold your men back!"

Now fast-spoken Russian flooded the frequency.

More silence followed as the terrorists continued to huddle behind the truck, firing sporadically into the woods, forcing the remaining Russians and also Case and Rachel to remain hidden.

By then, the heat signature from the living room had nearly tripled in size.

"Case."

"I know," he said, checking his watch before shouting, "Ivenko! Cover us!"

A moment later, the Spetsnaz team opened up on the truck, pounding it with a volley of rubber bullets, forcing the terrorists to duck behind it.

Rising from behind the pile of wood, Case zigzagged towards the house. She followed him, the stock of her MP7 pressed against her right shoulder, left hand under the short barrel, right hand on the grip, trigger finger resting on the trigger guard.

Case focused on the picture ahead of them, going around the right side of the property to try to flank their mark. Rachel remained immediately behind him covering the sides in classic close-quarter battle. Meanwhile, Ivenko and his surviving men continued to unload a fusillade of non-lethal rubber hell on the large truck to keep the terrorists distracted.

The smell of spent cordite hovering in the air, Case and Rachel finally got a partial angle on the men huddling behind the truck.

They fired in unison. The rubber bullets struck the two men in the chest, pushing them on their backs. Meant to cause paralyzing pain but not serious injury, the terrorists dropped to the ground moaning.

Case and Rachel were on top of them before they could come around and quickly flex cuffed their wrists and ankles.

"Dammit," Rachel hissed, her ocular software scanning the face of the terrorist who had collapsed from the gas as well as the ones they had just secured. "Kiersted isn't out here."

"Maybe he's the one who collapsed inside?" Case said.

"Area secured!" Rachel said, verifying that the required three minutes for the gas to go inert had passed. "Cabin is now safe, Ivenko. Get your men to—"

It happened quickly. Out of the corner of her left eye, she noticed the terrorist who had collapsed by the front steps, and whose face she had just scanned, was somehow awake now and lifting his rifle toward her.

What the—?

Rachel tried to bring her MP7 around, though she realized she was a fraction of a second too late. The terrorist aimed the muzzle at her face, the only place she lacked armored protection. But as he fired and she tensed in anticipation of the inevitable, Case somehow managed to jump in front of her, taking two rounds in the chest, the impacts pushing him into her as they both crashed next to the two flex-cuffed Russians.

"Case!" she shouted, rolling out from under him.

Ivenko and his men opened up on the terrorist, knocking him out with a short volley of rubber bullets.

Kneeling by his side as he lay on his back, eyes closed, she checked his chest and verified he was still breathing and most importantly, that the body armor had stopped the rounds. But in doing so, the bullets had spread their energy across his upper body delivering the equivalent of multiple blows to his solar plexus, shocking his web of nerves.

As the Russian team stormed the cabin, she cusped his face and shook him hard. "CASE!"

He blinked, coming around, breathing through his mouth.

"Hey," he mumbled. "You…okay?"

"Goddammit," she hissed, keeping her hands on his face as tears filled her eyes. "You need to stop fucking rescuing—"

"Go," he said, blinking rapidly, before placing a hand on his chest and grimacing. "Just…need a minute."

She hesitated, staring at this man she hardly knew who *twice* now had placed himself in the line of fire for her.

"Go...dammit!" he insisted, breathing in and out raggedly.

"To be continued, Mister," she said, before grabbing her MP7 and rushing toward the cabin.

The smell of gunpowder, musk, wood, and garbage tingled her nostrils reminding her of a saw mill as she raced up the steps and onto the front porch, before going inside, her boots clicking hollowly on bare pine floors.

Pictures of people fly fishing adorned walls leading to a large living area with a panoramic view of the river.

That's when she first saw the machine described by Lyov Cherkasski.

Resembling two refrigerators on their side, its charcoal hunk rested inside a hole where the terrorists had sawed off the pine floor, placing it in direct contact with the ground.

With the permafrost.

Lights blinked on the humming unit, but the small solid rocket booster atop one side of the machine had not yet fired.

Ivenko and his troops stood in front of the tectonic device next to the last terrorist, whom they had already flex-cuffed, and who also wasn't William Kiersted.

Damn.

Controlling her breathing, Rachel said, "Cherkasski told us that as the booster fires, its energy drives the oscillator system to inject a resonant frequency deep into the permafrost, inducing a positive loop. We need to stop it."

"How?" asked Ivenko.

Rachel had wondered the same thing since learning about these tectonic units. Kiersted had the only surviving scientist who knew how to work this contraption.

And who the hell knows where they are.

The humming intensified, signaling it would soon go active.

"Well?" Ivenko asked again. "How do we stop this?"

Rachel stared at the Spetsnaz commander, before her gaze landed on this mysterious machine. The increased pitch told her they were out of time. Once the solid rocket booster fired there would be no turning back.

"Shoot the damn thing!" Case's voice boomed inside the living room.

She turned around. He stood by the entryway hugging himself, his face still twisted in obvious pain. "Do it, dammit!"

"What?" Ivenko asked, obviously surprised.

"Yes!" Rachel screamed. "Shoot the damn thing! With real bullets!"

"But the solid fuel?"

"Shoot the *other* side!" she said, realizing Case was right. They were out of choices. "If the machine goes off, it could release the deposits of methane gas under us! Shoot it now!"

Ivenko barked an order in Russian, and his troops quickly swapped magazines in their weapons, before training them on the section of the machine away from the booster and its fuel.

"Stand back!" he ordered Case and Rachel, who rushed behind the Spetsnaz commandos lined up like a firing squad.

The rattling of large caliber machine guns deafened them inside the enclosed structure as a volley of full-metal jacketed rounds tore into the mechanism, tearing it apart.

Rachel stopped breathing, certain that at any moment now a stray round would pierce the fuel cells.

Ivenko raised a fist.

The Russians stopped firing, the smoke coiling from their weapons mixing with the thickening haze hovering above them as the commandos lowered their weapons.

Rachel took a deep breath, the smell of gunpowder filling her nostrils. She stared at the sizzling hunk of metal, relief sweeping through her that somehow the Russians had managed not to blow them all up.

Ivenko raised his brows at Rachel and Case while exhaling through his mouth.

"Let us not do that again, yes?" he said.

"No shit," replied Case, staggering toward them.

"Are you good, yes?" the Russian commando asked, pointing at Case's ribcage.

"I'll live," Case replied.

"The bastard isn't here, and neither are the three other systems," Rachel mumbled.

Case asked Ivenko to get his men to drag the terrorists inside.

Rachel knelt by the one who had shot Case. He was a man in his mid-thirties with ash-blond hair dressed in jeans, hiking boots, and a plain black T-shirt. The red, blue, and yellow emblem of the *Fromandskorpset*, the Danish Navy Seals, was tattooed on his left forearm.

Case used his portable FlexScreen to upload the facial features to the CIA database, where his ocular signature would be matched in chronological order to the terabytes of retinal data collected by the millions of high resolution cameras located at street corners, airports, train stations, hotels, restaurants, and stores across Europe.

"Most terrorist cells operate independently," Rachel told Ivenko as the Spetsnaz team lined up the other terrorists and Case scanned them. "That means that irrespective of the amount of pain you inflict on them, the information they have will be incomplete, or worse, incorrect, pointing us in the wrong direction. But the facial scan system will tell us where they've been for the past couple of months, and that, combined with whatever we can extract, might just be enough for us to piece together the likely location of the other machines."

"And of Kiersted," added Case as he produced four small hypodermics from the rucksack.

"Showtime, Ivenko," said Rachel as his men took each terrorist to a separate room to prepare them for questioning while the rest swept the house for clues.

Slowly, over the course of the next hour, they learned that one of the terrorists, Udo Deppe, had last seen Kiersted at a small airfield outside of Copenhagen, where the mastermind of the Greenland disaster had dispatched them to this corner of the world with orders to activate the tectonic machine. But Deppe claimed he didn't know where William had sent the other units. In fact, none of the terrorists claimed knowledge that other such machines existed, confirming Rachel's suspicions that Kiersted had learned from his mistake in Greenland and had managed to keep each cell operating independently from the others.

"What now?" asked Ivenko.

Rachel did a retinal signature check against the data collected by the cameras at the Danish airfield and got an instant match. Deppe had indeed been there on that date.

As Ivenko watched with interest, Rachel accessed the digitized video of the cameras installed at the airfield on the same day and played it back on Case's FlexScreen, using the computer's retinal and face recognition programs to scrub the video in high-resolution mode in an attempt to get a visual on William Kiersted. Such a detailed search could only be done once the target area had been narrowed down.

Rachel stopped breathing when the computer froze an image of Deppe meeting with a man she recognized as Kiersted, getting a visual on the elusive terrorist for the first time since Greenland.

"Son of a gun," Case said. "That's really him?"

"It is and it isn't," she replied, noticing the slight facial deformation.

"That looks like a facial plate," Case observed, his face a few inches from the screen.

"Jimmy told us he was seriously wounded back then but surgery and implants brought him back."

"It certainly appears so."

"So, they did meet there five weeks and four days ago," she said.

"Now what?" asked Ivenko.

"Now this," Case said, pointing at two Cessna Caravan planes parked on the ramp behind William and Deppe. One stood on a standard tricycle landing gear and matched the description of the Caravan Deppe and team had used to get here. The other had been fitted with large floats for amphibious operations. The master terrorist shook hands with Deppe before heading for the Caravan on floats, where an Asian woman met up with him.

"European Arctic Research Agency," Case said, reading the large emblem on the side of the plane.

"Never heard of it," said Rachel as she commanded the FlexScreen to match the tail number with its registered owner, which turned out to be the agency whose logo was painted in black on the side of the white plane.

"That's because it's probably a front company," said Case as he began to work that lead on another FlexScreen.

Meanwhile, Rachel matched the plane's tail number with the records from Air Traffic Control, which allowed her to access all flight plans for the Cessna Caravan starting on that day until today.

"Case," she said a moment later, as her eyes read through the ATC list. "I think I know where they're going."

"Where?"

"Get Langley on the line," she replied, her finger pointing at a section of text on the FlexScreen. "We need to access our satellites over northern Alaska."

CHAPTER EIGHTEEN
ANGEL OF DEATH

"And in her was found the blood of the prophets, and of the saints, and of all that were slain upon the earth."
—Revelation 18:24

NORTH SLOPE BOROUGH. ALASKA. JULY 10, 2029.

The twilight of an Arctic summer midnight stained the sapphire sky with faint shades of red-gold as Lian arrested the amphibious Cessna's decent at fifty feet above tundra and lakes while maintaining 150 knots.

They had flown in from Greenland via northern Canada and over Victoria Island, refueling along the way. Venturing into the vast oil complex at Prudhoe Bay, Alaska, they took more fuel before heading south, inland.

As soon as they had lost line of sight with the oil complex, Lian had dropped below radar, essentially making them invisible to Air Traffic Controllers. Though overhead satellites could still acquire them either visually or with deep infrared imagery, which could spot the engine heat. But the semidarkness, in addition to the dark color scheme of the Caravan, played in their favor.

As Lian circled the desolate region looking for the right body of water to land on while remaining well below radar, William watched a herd of caribou grazing in the distant flatlands stretching south to meet the rugged Brooks Mountain Range fifty miles to the south.

The steady wind sweeping down the jagged, snow-capped mountains turned into a steady breeze as it combed through the North Slope's rugged vegetation, rippling the surface of countless lakes, before kissing the leading edges of the Caravan.

Many lakes fed braided streams of meltwater flowing to Beaufort Sea as temperatures started to creep back up following a brief cold front—one that did little to harden the permafrost.

Just a few miles to the north, the Trans-Alaska Pipeline System connected the Prudhoe Bay oil fields to Valdez on the Pacific Ocean. Its destruction would provide an added bonus to his plan. In terms of recoverable oil, Prudhoe Bay was the largest in the United States, more than double the size of the East Texas oil fields, the second largest.

And it all gets channeled through the Trans-Alaska Pipeline System right over the thawing permafrost, he thought, watching the unprotected pipeline and the surrounding peaceful scenery while listening to the steady hum of the Cessna's turboprop muffled by the noise-cancellation headphones.

This is too easy.

But William remembered a similar operation two years ago that had also seemed easy on the way in.

You won't get lucky twice.

He flexed the fingers of his iLimb, wondering if he indeed had been lucky, or if he would have been better off perishing in Greenland along with Mathias than living this way.

You survived for a reason.

He stared at the distant mountain range and the sea of tundra dotted with countless lakes. But his eyes probed beyond the majestic sight, beyond the cosmetics, digging deeper, visualizing the monster breathing beneath the thawing land.

You survived to fight another day.

But to win this new fight, he couldn't make the same mistake twice.

This time around William had kept the particulars of the mission completely secret.

This time around no one but those directly associated with the mission—the souls aboard this aircraft—knew that Alaska's North Slope marked the destination of the second tectonic unit. And he had informed them of their destination after departure from Greenland with their precious cargo.

But even that had not been enough to satisfy his paranoid mind.

As William watched his mask-like reflection in the Caravan's windshield and Lian selected their landing site, he thought about the machine he had shipped to Siberia along with an expendable terrorist cell to blast through the permafrost near one of Russia's largest oil refineries. It was a diversion, sure, to keep international law enforcement looking away from Alaska. But he also hoped the team would be able to set that part of the world on fire.

And no one here knows where I deployed the last two machines, he thought, regarding the scenery before unplugging the IV connected to his right forearm feeding him dinner.

Not even Lian.

His eyes gravitated to the Chinese pilot as she used fingertip control to guide the plane over a patch of ash-gold sand bordering a small lagoon.

"That one?" he asked.

Lian nodded while keeping her eyes on the landing ahead, lowering flaps, slowing down, trimming, aligning the Cessna's nose into the steady breeze.

William looked over his left shoulder at Hans-Jorgen and Doctor Yuri Gerchenko sitting directly behind them in the club-style seating of the Caravan's Oasis executive interior. The elder scientist looked puny next to the strapping operator.

"Gentlemen, we're going in. Seatbelts."

Hans-Jorgen gave him a thumbs-up. The scientist barely acknowledged him while working a small FlexScreen. For the past two days, Gerchenko had been computing the settings for the machine in the rear to customize its output.

"Call it," Lian said.

William stared at the radar altimeter, which, unlike the standard barometric altimeter in an aircraft providing altitude relative to sea level, indicated altitude above ground level.

"Forty feet," he spoke into his mike, reading the digital display on his side of the panel.

"Thirty."

The Caravan rushed over the edge of the water at 75 knots, right on target for the amphibious plane.

"Twenty...ten feet."

Lian gently arrested the descent and began the landing flare, lifting the plane's nose, forcing the rear of the aluminum floats down while reducing power to idle.

"Five feet."

William felt a slight vibration as the ends of the floats broke the surface, biting into the water. The sudden drag rapidly slowed the heavy plane, dropping the nose back towards the horizon.

Water surging by their sides as the floats cut through the frigid lagoon like a pair of pontoons, Lian increased power to 900 RPM and lifted flaps before using the rudder pedals to steer them towards a beach-like spot on the west end of the lagoon.

As the Caravan conveyed her footwork to a pair of rudders at the rear ends of the floats, William unbuckled his safety belt and headed aft, signaling Hans-Jorgen and Gerchenko to follow him to the cargo compartment.

The machine monopolizing the rear of the Caravan had two sections, the main oscillator and the rocket booster, each the size of a small freezer. The Cold-War-era device, based on the work of Tesla, was designed to produce mechanical oscillations of a frequency Gerchenko had tuned to the resonant frequency of the thawing permafrost to blast acoustic energy deep into the ground.

As the elder scientist had explained during the equipment acquisition meeting back in Moscow, mechanical resonance was a well-known physical phenomenon.

Today William hoped to use this technology to induce a resonant frequency into the thawing permafrost, collapsing its structure, exponentially increasing its methane flux.

And releasing the trapped methane to the atmosphere.

As the Caravan reached the shoreline, William looked through one of the side windows at the vast sea of tundra expanding as far as he could see.

It was time to scorch the Earth.

CHAPTER NINETEEN
GATHERING STORM

"The sun will be darkened, the moon will not give its light, and the stars will fall from the sky."
—Matthew 24:29

NORTH SLOPE BOROUGH. ALASKA. JULY 10, 2029.

The twin rotors of the V-22 Osprey rattled Natasha as they lifted the heavy aircraft almost vertically above the permafrost north of the IARC camp.

Slowly, the rotors, which faced the skies, began to tilt forward, providing horizontal thrust.

A second Osprey joined them in tight formation carrying the SEAL team. Their call sign for this mission was Hawk Two, while the SEAL team's aircraft was Hawk One.

Colonel Marcus Stone sat next to her in the spacious cabin customized as a VIP carrier for ten, though only three other seats were occupied by the colonel's aides. The rest of his team remained behind in the operations tent to act as mission command. His other Osprey, sporting a utility configuration, remained at the IARC camp on stand-by.

The tilt rotor machines reached two hundred feet while accelerating to 230 knots in thirty seconds, pressing her against the leather seat.

She gave the column of flames burning above the camp a furtive glance before dropping her gaze to the GPS map on the FlexScreen on her lap, which was slaved to the displays in the Osprey's glass cockpit.

Colonel Stone had received word CIA officers in Russia had discovered a climate terrorist plot that included an attack on the Alaska permafrost by some sort of earthquake machine designed to increase the methane flux in the thawing soil.

The CIA, in conjunction with a team of Russian Spetsnaz, had destroyed a similar machine before it could wreak havoc in the West Siberian Plains, including the likely destruction of the oil city complex of Surgat.

Satellite data began streaming into Stone's operations tent thirty minutes ago, pinpointing the shores of a lagoon just fifty miles northeast of their position, where an amphibious Cessna Caravan had landed several hours before.

According to the official FAA flight plan, the Cessna was registered to the European Arctic Research Institute, which the CIA report indicated was sponsored in part by Solaris Industries, a front company from Copenhagen, the hometown of the late Henrik Kiersted and his terrorist son, William.

The Caravan held motion picture permits to shoot caribou movies, but the plane had vanished from radar soon after departing Prudhoe Bay.

Stone had asked Natasha to come along as technical consultant. Their plan called for the SEALs aboard the lead Osprey to neutralize the terrorists and the machine, just as the CIA team and a detachment of Spetsnaz commandos had done in Siberia.

That's the bloody plan anyway.

She filled her lungs and crossed her arms. Natasha had wanted to alert Malone at UAF but Stone had insisted the mission was classified by the Department of Defense as need-to-know. Aside from Stone's team, she was the only one who knew about the terrorist threat, and that meant the rest of the IARC camp would continue with business as usual.

"The whole region is very vulnerable, Marcus," she said into the mic of her green noise-cancellation headset while tilting the FlexScreen in his direction.

Stone frowned. "And our Trans-Alaska Pipeline System goes right through it."

"The same reason this region is rich with oil explains why there is so much methane, just like in Surgat."

"A package deal. Works nicely for the terrorists."

"I'm afraid so."

"A threat multiplier," Stone said, more to himself than to her.

She nodded while tundra, lakes, and rivers rushed past them beneath clear skies as the pilots kept the tiltrotor machines at two hundred feet above the flat terrain. The nap-of-the-earth approach was required to avoid tipping their presence to the terrorists they hoped to still be in the area, though the last satellite imagery no longer showed the Caravan anchored by the lagoon's shoreline. Stone's cross-functional team back at the National Photographic Interpretation Center was still trying to figure out where it had gone.

"Five minutes," the pilot warned.

Natasha watched the sea of tundra expanding south, towards the Brooks Mountain Range. She stared at the jagged peaks, her mind probing farther, across the Alaska Peninsula, reaching Fairbanks, where Konrad Malone was now safe and sound—where she wished she were at this—

"Two minutes. Target in sight," reported the pilot. "Hawk One is going in while we circle at five hundred."

"Any sign of the Caravan?" Stone asked.

"Negative, sir. Just the gear by the lagoon's north shore that matches the description we received from Siberia. Hawk One is dropping the SEALs in T-minus two."

Natasha watched with interest as the Osprey broke formation and descended steeply towards the target and Hawk Two started a shallow turn and climb.

"Prudhoe ATC just advised me of an unidentified contact a hundred miles east of us at one thousand feet," reported their pilot.

Stone frowned. "Is it the Caravan?"

"Can't tell, sir, though its speed matches that of a Caravan. The F-35s we scrambled from Eielson are still fifteen minutes away," the pilot reported, referring to Eielson Air Force Base 26 miles south of Fairbanks.

Natasha felt a chill gripping her gut as she watched Hawk One approach the target zone, the rotor's downwash flattening the shore vegetation and rippling the water's surface.

The Osprey touched down some hundred feet from the suspect equipment and a moment later the SEAL team exited through the rear ramp. But as they rushed away from the V-22, the top of one of the boxes ignited in a plume of fire that reached up to the heavens.

"Dammit!" exclaimed Stone.

"The rocket booster, Marcus!" said Natasha. "The machine is active!"

"Hawk One! Get out of there! Get out of there!"

The ground grew hazy for a moment before fire erupted around the rocket booster, spreading rapidly across the tundra in every direction, swallowing the SEALs and the Osprey on the ground.

Screams filled the frequency as the flames below consumed men and machine.

"The methane!" Natasha shouted. "The machine is collapsing the soil structure! We need to get out of here!" But as she screamed this, another thought entered her mind.

We're too low.

Natasha shielded her eyes as the brightness lighted up their surroundings an instant before an explosion echoed across the land as the flames suddenly expanded, fueled by the sudden free-flow of methane.

"Oh, dear God!" Natasha shouted. "The monster, Marcus! It's out!"

Bright Blue with traces of red-gold, the conflagration licked the Osprey's underside as the pilot fought for altitude.

Gasping, her throat going dry, she grabbed the armrests, terror seizing her as the V-22 trembled. The noise from the twin rotors peaked to a deafening roar, but she sensed no upward motion.

The last thing she saw out of the side windows before the flames and the smoke surrounded them was a towering sheet of fire stretching in every direction, including the IARC camp fifty miles to the southwest.

CHAPTER TWENTY
ARMAGEDDON

"And there will be strange events in the skies—signs in the sun, moon, and stars. And down here on Earth the nations will be in turmoil, perplexed by the roaring seas and strange tides. The courage of many people will falter because of the fearful fate they see coming upon the earth, because the stability of the very heavens will be broken up."
—Luke 21:25

NORTH SLOPE BOROUGH. ALASKA.
JULY 10, 2029.

The resonant harmonics injected into the ground to a depth of fifteen hundred feet altered the composition of the soil as far as one mile in every direction from Ground Zero. It destroyed the semi-frozen balance of the permafrost's crystal lattice, exponentially increasing its methane flux, creating a massive burn-off vent for antediluvian methane deposits.

The gas hissed through this circular tunnel of weakened soil almost as if it were not there, reaching the surface. The resulting fireball, resembling a monstrous torch, spread out radially as the white-hot inferno scorched the walls of this vertical tunnel, tearing into the permafrost, thawing it from the surface down to the methane deposits, enlarging its diameter at the rate of one mile every thirty seconds.

The sheet of fire reached the IARC camp in less than twenty minutes, as scientists, technicians, and even Stone's personnel struggled to evacuate.

The intense heat incinerated every soul in the camp as the wall of flames propagated through the area like a sizzling sandstorm of inky smoke and pulsating lightning, swallowing all that stood in its way. Heavy objects, like the Osprey, vehicles, and other equipment sank in the smoldering quicksand-like soil, as if swallowed by liquid hell itself.

A few souls jumped into the freezing Shirukak Lake, their backs on fire, only to be boiled alive as the inferno heated the surface waters in seconds. Their final agonized screams were shunted by the roaring blaze and blinding smoke.

Within one minute, all life ceased at the IARC camp as the fire continued to eat away the soil, expanding its opening to the deposits, consuming some while igniting new ones in a chain reaction that threatened to devour the entire North Slope.

CHAPTER TWENTY-ONE
SCORCHING THE WORLD

"After there is great trouble among mankind, a greater one is prepared...rain, thirst, famine, and disease. In the heavens, a fire seen."
—Nostradamus

NORTH SLOPE BOROUGH. ALASKA. JULY 10, 2029.

"Mayday, Mayday, Mayday, Hawk Two has double turbine failure! Repeat Hawk Two has double turbine failure. Going down ninety miles southwest of the IARC Camp!"

Natasha clutched Stone's hand as their world blurred past them while immersed in their own smoke spewing from the malfunctioning turbines.

They had managed to rise above the initial blast but the Osprey had endured engine damage as they made a dash at 200 knots south towards the Brooks Mountain Range, where she knew the terrain was firm, solid, where the permafrost ended.

But they were still a couple of miles away.

"We're not going to make it!" Stone shouted as the smoke cleared, as she got another glimpse of the fire burning in the distance but heading their way in what she knew was a deadly positive loop. The monster had been unleashed and only the Brooks Mountain Range would be able to hold it back, sparing the rest of the state.

But to spare themselves they needed to reach it first, needed to—

The pilots kept pushing the Osprey, trying to close the gap, but the craft began to descend rapidly as the main turbines failed while flying at three hundred feet above the tundra.

Just one more bloody mile, she thought, as the mountains loomed in the windscreen.

Her world vibrating around her, quickly losing perspective, Natasha watched in a daze as Colonel Stone opened the V-22's side door.

A rush of cold air and smoke invaded the cabin, the clear surface of a lagoon projecting beyond the rectangular opening as the water rushed up to meet them.

Stone reached across her and unbuckled her seatbelt.

"Wait!" she screamed, as the Osprey continued to lose altitude. "What are you doing?"

"Out! Everybody jump out!" Stone shouted over the intercom, before yanking his headset and also Natasha's, and lifting her frame with one of his big arms.

"Wa—WAIT! Marcus! Bollocks! What are you— "

The colonel stared into her eyes for an instant and screamed, "Run to the mountains! Survive! *Fix* this!"

And he tossed her out.

The blue-gray water, rocky shores, clear skies, and the smoke trailing from the dying aircraft exchanged places as she fell. For a brief moment, the heat from the burning turbines overwhelmed her before she plunged feet first into the lagoon, the water shockingly cold.

She gasped, controlled the urge to vomit from the icy blast, from its chilling, stabbing force. She felt as if she had plummeted into a pool of puncturing nails.

Kicking her legs, she began to swim to the surface, reaching it a moment later, filling her lungs with cold air just as the Osprey crashed a hundred feet away into the jagged rocks lining the lagoon.

A cloud of smoke and debris engulfed the crash site but she heard no explosion.

Get out of the water!

Natasha immediately began to swim as hard as she could, realizing she only had minutes before hypothermia set in. Her eyes focused on the aircraft, praying it would not explode as it lay crushed on the shore, thin coils of smoke rising from its twin rotors.

Her clothes began to slow her down, making it difficult to move, to swim.

Realizing what she had to do to survive, the climatologist removed her water-laden jacket and sweatshirt, and kicked off her boots and thermal pants.

Down to her panties and undershirt, she swam as fast as she could towards the shore just to the right of the crash site.

Her skin goose-bumping, quickly losing sensation in her hands and feet, she pressed on, realizing she would die if she stopped. Fighting off the panic, ignoring the distant fiery storm heading south, she closed the last dozen feet, until her toes touched the rocky bottom.

Straightening up, shivering, she looked for anyone else through the haze enveloping the wreckage as she scrambled out of the water.

Nearly paralyzed by the appalling cold, teeth rattling, Natasha glanced to the north, to the scorching tempest they had managed to escape only to crash short of the protective rocky hills and caves of the Brooks Mountain Range.

Lips quivering, her body trembling, and feeling light-headed, she mustered strength, ignoring the stinging pain, approaching the wreck.

And stopped.

Wedged in a clump of jagged boulders protruding through the surface between her and the Osprey was the body of Marcus Stone. He had tried to jump after her but had fallen on rocks.

She approached him, once more tempering the impulse to vomit from the cold as well as from the sight of his maimed body, broken by the sharp boulders, limbs twisted at unnatural angles.

She put a hand on his cheek. His blue eyes on a face packed with freckles stared at the darkening sky.

Marcus.

Bloody hell.

As she glared into his dead eyes, his final words echoed in her mind.

Run to the mountains! Survive! Fix this!

She continued to the wreckage, reaching the side of the Osprey, and peeked through the same door Stone had thrown her out of two minutes before, saving her life at the price of his own.

Inside the hazy interior, she spotted Stone's aides plus the pilot and copilot—all still strapped to their seats.

Reaching for one of two Arctic survival kits, Natasha unbuckled the front straps of the hard case, opened it, and grabbed a one-piece thermal body suit. She ripped the clear protective cover, unfolded the bright-yellow garment and unzipped the front. The jump-suit-like survival device had a single zipper from crotch to neck.

She unzipped it with numb fingers, before stepping into it with her right leg first, then the left, welcoming the advanced material, waterproof and thermally insulated, against her prickly skin. She slid both feet into built-in foot covers that stretched to conform to her foot size.

Lifting the top over her shoulder, she ran each arm into the long sleeves before reaching down and zipping it up to her neck.

Arms crossed, feeling the material developed by NASA starting to hold on to her heat, she looked towards the still passengers, trying to see if anyone was—

Natasha gasped, bile reaching her throat when noticing their smoking entrails by their feet.

Oh God, she thought, realizing that a section of one of the tilt rotors had sliced through the cabin, almost cutting them in half.

She looked away, rushing towards the cockpit, hoping to find a survivor, but the pilots lay inert in pools of their own blood. The jagged rocks had pierced through the canopy of the Osprey, impaling them.

Bile once more reached her throat.

This time she couldn't hold it. Kneeling in the space between the aviators, she vomited, tears blinding her, every muscle in her body tense, on edge.

Breathing in short sobbing gasps, she stopped, stood, and tried to get a hold of herself.

It was then that she got a glimpse of the scenery beyond the rectangular opening of the Osprey's broken windscreen, and she realized that she could not stay here much longer if she intended to survive.

Run to the mountains! Survive! Fix this!

She had been damned lucky that Stone had thrown her out when he had, but she was still in extreme danger.

Get away from here.
Now.

Hastily, Natasha turned back to the main cabin. She stared at the dead aides next to her, whispered, "I'm so sorry," and unbuckled the restraining belt of the smallest of the three. Nearly decapitated by the blade, his head swung back at a grotesque angle. She removed his thick Army jacket, which albeit bloody, would provide protection from the elements.

Stepping away, she put it over the thermal suit before removing the officer's trousers, which fit her good enough, as well as his Army field boots, which she laced quickly, and finally, the man's gloves.

Her mind on automatic, her survival instincts overtaking all other emotions, Natasha knelt by the Arctic survival case and extracted the survival backpack, putting it on, feeling its weight, not nearly as balanced as her hiking gear but certainly lighter.

She also removed the aide's belt, including a holstered Sig Sauer M17 9mm semiautomatic, standard U.S. Army issue.

Finally, she pulled out both portable ELTs—Emergency Locator Transmitters—from the side wall, and turned them on to verify their operation. In addition, she grabbed a handheld transceiver—two-way radio—from a cubby hole next to the ELTs and powered it on, verifying functionality, before switching it to the Guard emergency frequency.

If she managed to outrun the incoming storm, she would need them in order for a search-and-rescue party to find her in the mountains.

Satisfied they were all operational, she shut off both ELTs and shoved them into Velcro-secured pockets in her Army trousers while hanging on to the transceiver, which she planned to use to broadcast her situation every thirty minutes.

She jumped off the Osprey and headed for the mountains, her eyes focusing on a familiar peak roughly a mile away, where she knew would be many caves for shelter from the elements.

Looking back once, Natasha Shakhiva narrowed her gaze at the distant firestorm heading her way. The boiling wall of smoldering ash rushing south was probably no more than fifty or sixty miles away, devouring everything and anything in its path.

And she began to run.

CHAPTER TWENTY-TWO
ALARM BELLS

"The scientific consensus presented in this comprehensive report about human-induced climate change should sound alarm bells in every national capital and in every local community."
—United Nations Environment Program.

**UNIVERSITY OF ALASKA, FAIRBANKS.
JULY 10, 2029.**

"What the hell is *that*?" asked Malone, sitting next to Escobar in the analysis room adjacent to the freezers dominating the basement of the department of geology.

Escobar stared at the real-time satellite feeding a window on the large FlexScreen, where they had been reviewing core samples non-stop for the past eighteen hours.

The Bolivian dragged the cursor to the window and enlarged it while narrowing his eyes. "It's…please tell me this isn't what it looks like."

Malone stared at a satellite image of the state of Alaska and its neighbor, the Yukon Territory to the east. A deep crimson stain covered one percent of the state, or roughly 6,000 square miles.

"Gotta be a mistake," Malone whispered, his mind doing the math. The methane flux was not high enough to justify such an outburst, at least not in the coming decades. "Check the satellite link and data integrity."

Escobar typed a few commands and shrugged. "It all checks out, *amigo*. Fire's real."

Malone sat there contemplating the surreal image painted on the FlexScreen, his mind going in different directions.

"I'm calling Tash," he said, heading upstairs to the radio room.

Escobar put a hand on his forearm and said, "Hold on. Let's take a closer look."

The Hispanic glaciologist superimposed the location of the IARC camp on the real-time image and zoomed in.

"Oh, God, no," Malone said, staring at the inferno surrounding Shirukak Lake, his vision tunneling at the thought of—

"Maybe they got out," Escobar said. "She was always escorting Colonel Stone, who arrived in those fancy transports. Maybe they all got the hell out of there in time."

A glimmer of hope.

Maybe they got out.

Maybe she got out.

"The video, Mario," he said, taking a deep breath, praying that she'd managed to escape. "Rewind the satellite feed to the hour preceding the fire."

Escobar did. Watching in slow motion as the fire broke out from the shores of a lagoon some fifty miles northwest of the IARC camp. Infrared imaging worked best, clearly depicting Ground Zero as well as the Army Ospreys converging on the site. One of the Ospreys was caught in the initial blaze. The second Osprey managed

R.J. PINEIRO

to head south, before crashing a mile short of the Brooks Mountain Range, but there was no explosion, meaning there was a chance there were survivors in that wreckage.

Escobar zoomed in closer to see if anyone got out, and that's when they spotted a single IR signature of a survivor first jumping off the Osprey before it crashed, then swimming back to it, and finally running south, toward Brooks. But the inferno was less than sixty miles behind her and closing in awfully fast.

"Get the Pentagon on the horn, Mario. These guys were on a mission up there. That's the only explanation why they would be headed for Ground Zero moments before it went up in flames. After we speak to them we're going up there."

"We are? Are we looking at the same images, Buddy?"

"Tasha's up there, man."

"How can you tell? The IR signatures can't—"

"I can't, but neither could she when I was atop Kilimanjaro. You and I are going on a little search and rescue mission. It's non-negotiable."

Escobar shook his head.

"What?"

"You two got some sort of weird connection. It's almost...cosmic."

"The fuck you talking about?"

Escobar headed for the stairs. "Tell you on the way."

CHAPTER TWENTY-THREE
THE ANTICHRIST

"And as you have heard the antichrist is coming."
—John 2:18

NORTH SLOPE BOROUGH. ALASKA.
JULY 10, 2029.

The initial flash reminded him of Greenland, only this time he was in full control.

Sitting in the co-pilot seat of the amphibian Cessna Caravan, William Kiersted watched the fires propagating behind them as they remained at one thousand feet for a few minutes to clear the worst of it.

Lian now descended to two hundred feet while heading back to the ocean at full speed after successfully getting away from the charcoal clouds building up like an apocalyptic storm.

You never really know…until you stare the monster in the eye.

And the monster stares right back.

He took a deep breath, the magnitude of the destruction surprising even him. He never expected the Russian machines to work so well and so fast. But then again, there were *Gigatons* of highly-pressurized methane trapped beneath the permafrost that would have escaped sooner or later. He had simply given nature a head start.

He watched the North Slope vanishing beneath a pulsating blanket of dark clouds alive with flames, redeeming the failure in Surgat even though the Russian oil city had always been the distraction.

"I doubt anyone will follow us. The smoke is too thick and already reaching ten thousand feet."

William almost refused to believe his good fortune. There was indeed something poetic, even elegant, about using a strike to also protect the getaway route by blocking pursuers.

"How long before reaching Canada?" he asked as they remained below radar.

"Thirty more minutes."

William leaned back in the co-pilot seat and watched the navigation system as well as the on-board radar system, which searched the sky for any nearby traffic.

"There's someone on the Guard Frequency," reported Lian, throwing a couple of switches to pipe in the audio to William.

"*Mayday, Mayday, Mayday, this is Doctor Natasha Shakhiva. I'm headed for Brooks to seek shelter. Any aircraft listening please relay the following coordinates to Alaska Search and Rescue.*"

William listened to her GPS coordinates, which placed her just a short distance from the foot of the mountain range.

No one can help you, Doctor Shakhiva.

No one.

William watched the clear skies ahead before focusing on the radar display.

The screen was devoid of any traffic in this remote region of North America, though he knew that was all about to change in the coming days, as the world woke up to this new colossal ecological disaster he had triggered.

They held course and altitude for the next thirty minutes, crossing into Canada and overflying the mining town of Old Crow in northern Yukon.

Lian then climbed to seven thousand feet and contacted the Yukon Territory arm of NAV Canada, the country's centralized Air Traffic Control. She had filed a flight plan for a Cessna Caravan registered under Canada Air Care, a nonprofit organization dedicated to providing free air transportation for medical and humanitarian purposes. According to the flight plan, they were carrying a cancer victim from Old Crow to a treatment center in White Horse, a city in the southern end of the Canadian territory. Their new call sign was Air Care 65R.

"Air Care Six Five Romeo, Yukon Center," came the reply from NAV Canada. "Radar contact ten miles south of Old Crow. Climb and maintain ten thousand, expect fifteen in ten minutes."

Lian read back the ATC instructions, then added, "Yukon Center, Air Care Six Five Romeo. We're noticing strange dark clouds forming on the distant western horizon. Looks like a large wild fire in Alaska. Please advise."

"Six Five Romeo, we've received word of a very large fire on the North Slope propagating rapidly in all directions. Unknown origin. Alaska's Forestry Division in Fairbanks has already been contacted. Not a factor for your flight plan."

"Roger," she replied while grinning at William, who winked back.

He gave one more glance at his handy work monopolizing the eastern horizon before removing his head set and
heading aft, where Hans-Jorgen and Doctor Yuri Gerchenko
sat while watching the fire through side windows.

"Enjoying the show, gentlemen? You have the best seat
in town."

They looked at William momentarily before returning their attention to the incredible sight.

William sat in the rear of the plane and peered at
the extent of the devastation, a feeling of omnipotence
descending over him.

He was punishing an amoral world with Biblical force,
with a global hammer ripped straight out of the pages of
the Book of Revelations.

I have drowned them.

I have frozen them.

Now they burn.

Water. Ice. Fire.

The Earth's basic elements.

He stared at his reflection in the window and frowned
at his deformed face, at the plate he was forced to wear for
the rest of his life. He hated it as much as he despised his
liquid diet, his mechanical limbs, and the knowledge that
he would forever be considered a half-human abomination.

But the fires beyond his reflection gave him solace,
comfort. They filled him with the satisfaction of having
punished those who had taken so much from him.

Water. Ice. Fire.

And I'm just getting started.

CHAPTER TWENTY-FOUR
ASHES TO ASHES

"The first angel sounded, and there followed hail and fire mingled with blood, and they were cast upon the earth: and the third part of trees was burnt up, and all green grass was burnt up."
—Revelation 6:15

NORTH SLOPE BOROUGH. ALASKA.
JULY 10, 2029.

Clouds of smoldering ash spread across darkening skies, swallowing meadows and forests whole, devouring the thousands of rivers and lakes that defined the western tip of North America.

Trees and vegetation ignited in the superheated air, sizzling embers reaching two miles high, exterminating all species in its scorching wake in a conflagration the Earth had not seen for millions of years.

The hungry beast leaped across rivers, stretching its blistering wrath like an insatiable predator. It scourged the woods and all its creatures, heating the streams, boiling alive all living things which had sought refuge from the inferno, as well as all the fish, which floated dead on its simmering surface.

Steam hissed from evaporating rivers and lagoons, their bubbling cries ignored by the roaring flames pulsating from the surrounding tundra. Blue and red-gold fists flickered through the rising haze as millions upon millions of cubic miles of organic fuel fed this unyielding plague consuming the North Slope Borough of Alaska.

Against this apocalyptic backdrop, a lone figure caked in gray dust scrambled across the dying valley at the foot of the mountain range; a lonely creature under the shadow of her planet's darkest hour struggling to escape the seemingly inescapable, the end of days.

At her back, the echoing cries of the dying pushed her to run as fast as her tired legs allowed. She scrambled towards the mountains that marked the southern end of Alaska's North Slope, her only hope in a place losing all hope.

Staring into the barren scarlet tundra at her world's setting sun, Natasha forged ahead. Her back felt the sizzling curtain of death threatening to devour her just as it had greedily consumed any creature failing to flee its blistering grip. From bears, squirrels, wolves, foxes, and caribou, to fulmars, ravens, geese, and swans—all burned alive as they shrieked for a relief that never came. Survivors had long flown or ran past her, reaching the safety of the mountains, beyond the grasp of the inferno.

But a storm was also forming high above the mountain range.

And not *any* storm.

A bloody hail storm.

Her eyes focused on those dense clouds ahead, a gathering squall packed with flesh-ripping hail, powerful enough to stone her to death in mere seconds.

Lightning gleamed over the range beneath a fast-moving curtain of falling ice pounding the rocky peaks, blocking the sinking sun as night fell over Alaska.

Mega hail storms.

They had begun five years ago in this region, their origin still unknown, perhaps the byproduct of shifting weather patterns.

Natasha screamed over the roar of the incinerating cyclone at her back, the incoming hail storm shrouding the mountain range, and the thunder clapping ominously above it all.

She screamed in anger, in frustration, and cursed the dark skies as the world closed in on her.

Lightning flashed as the sun vanished, as a trembling reddish glow spread across the mountains, a reflection of the surging fire on the wall of shredding ice. Scorching clouds of death, accelerated by southern winds, reached beyond the edge of the inferno, stretching mercilessly over the dying landscape like a relentless chastisement, hungry still, threatening to engulf her.

Sheets of lightning arced across the northern sky, bridging the forces of nature accelerating towards each other on a direct collision course. The stroboscopic flashes illuminated the ragged edges of rock formations protruding by the foot of the mountain range; the caves used by her and Malone to escape the elements during previous hiking trips.

Natasha risked a brief backward glance, her eyes assessing the gap separating her from the expanding crimson shroud alive with deadly fire tornadoes, the blazing whirlwinds marking the leading edge of the monster. She then glared at the hail storm before her, pulsating with forks of lightning.

It's gonna be too bloody close.

She grunted, pushing herself a final time, sprinting towards the serrated formations marking the start of the Brooks Mountain Range—back-dropped by the towering wall of falling ice.

The growing heat at her back, her eyes protesting the hazy air, Natasha focused on the looming rocky outcrops, her only way out of this predicament.

Gripped by raw fear, in near-blind panic, her mind pushing everything aside, she took leap after agonizing leap. Her survival instincts refused to give up; a lone figure racing towards her only hope for salvation in the middle of some of the most destructive forces of nature ever seen by man.

Against the fall of night.

At the end of time.

She pushed, kicked, and hurdled, soaring over the tundra while covered in ash, like a white ghost, taxing her endurance to the brink of complete exhaustion.

But through the swirling haze of a world gone mad, through the insane heat threatening to set her on fire, Natasha found solace in the granite terrain she had just reached.

Hard and solid ground.

Methane free.

Almost there.

Her lungs protested the abuse, her tired legs propelling her toward the nearing jagged shapes marking the narrow entrance to a cave leading deep into the mountain.

The tip of the cloud of falling ice reached Natasha as she neared the entrance. Closing her eyes, she persisted, ducking her head, pushing her way through the colliding squall, holding her course, ignoring the pounding hail, until it all vanished abruptly.

The heat, the falling ice, and the toxic fumes were all replaced by the cool humidity of the interior of the cave as she stumbled inside. Its musk brought back memories of yesteryear, of times spent with Malone, enjoying each other's company during their—

The roaring collision outside brought her back. She had momentarily collapsed from the final sprint, had briefly passed out from the heat, the scarring ice, the sheer exhaustion from nearly one hour of nonstop running.

But the misty interior injected her with renewed hope, with new strength as the titanic fronts collided outside in an earth-shaking rumble of fire and ice.

Slowly, Natasha stumbled to her feet, soothing her lungs with the fresh and humid air oozing from deep within the cave.

She blinked repeatedly, clearing her eyesight of ashes and dust, coughing, unclogging her throat and nasal passages before testing the air, confirming the presence of what she needed most besides shelter.

Water.

Inhaling deeply while standing tall, she ignored the world outside exploding in an ear-piercing crescendo that propagated down the tunnel, rumbling the walls, shaking the granite floors.

A few stalactites fell from the rocky ceiling, dislodged by the clashing heavens.

The brittle formations thundered as they shattered on impact, kicking up a cloud of dust that mixed with the sandy haze and heat exhaled by the monsters into the cave's entrance.

Go deeper.

Reaching into her backpack, she produced a flashlight, which she used to guide her in the murky interior as she followed the shallow gradient of a narrow chute with caution. Her rugged boots gripped the damp surface leading to a large chamber, tall enough to fit a two-story house.

Here the air was cleaner, purer, still untainted by the firestorm, its thick rocky walls insulating her.

But Natasha went deeper still, the clashing madness on the surface slowly receding, the crimson glow fading, the deafening sounds giving way to her steady breathing mixed with the gurgling sound of an underground stream as the grade leveled off.

She reached a natural foot bridge that led to a spacious chamber divided by a narrow stream flowing slowly over a gravel fill, disappearing beneath a ledge.

She walked gingerly towards the stream, going around a few stalagmites, thin rock formations protruding from the floor. Kneeling by the water's edge, she closed her eyes for an instant before dunking her entire head in the cold brook, washing away the layer of white dust caking her head, her hair.

She tasted the water, deciding it was safe to drink, before swallowing it.

Resting the flashlight on the granite surface, she removed her backpack, unzipped it, and inspected its contents for the first time.

She found several packs of beef jerky, dehydrated fruits, peanuts, chocolate, and two MREs—Meals Ready to Eat—one with chicken and the other with beef.

She tore the plastic wrapper of a string of beef jerky and took a bite, chewing it slowly while rubbing her aching legs.

As she ate, she rummaged through the backpack, finding a sleeping bag made of the same insulated material as her body suit. It had a built-in inflatable pad and pillow, which she gladly blew up.

As she rested on it, she assessed the rest of her survival gear, including a compass, a handheld GPS, the ELT transmitters, a waterproof plastic poncho, two knives, a stainless-steel dish and canteen, waterproof matches, fishing line and hooks, two flare guns, a signaling mirror, and some first-aid gear.

Enough to last a few days if she rationed the food and also was able to leave the cave and make it to the mountains, where she could fish until help arrived.

After consuming two strings of beef jerky, a pack of peanuts, and a small chocolate bar, she dipped the canteen in the stream, filled it, and then took several sips, before putting it away.

Yawning, thoroughly exhausted, she stowed all of the food in the backpack, crawled into the sleeping bag, and switched off the flashlight.

Clutching the Sig in case a bear ventured into the cave seeking refuge, she quickly fell asleep.

CHAPTER TWENTY-FIVE
CONSEQUENCES

"The era of procrastination, of half-measures, of soothing and baffling expedients, of delays, is coming to a close. In its place, we are entering a period of consequences." —Winston Churchill

PRUDHOE BAY, ALASKA. JULY 10, 2029.

The wall of methane-fueled fire marching south stopped at the foot of the Brooks Mountain Range. To the north, the progressively colder permafrost slowed down the monster, but not before it reached Deadhorse, the oil city on the shores of Prudhoe Bay.

Evacuations started within the hour after the methane gas explosions, but being the height of the drilling season, there simply weren't enough transports to get everyone to safety.

Smoldering clouds reached the oil complex thirty minutes before the flames, unleashing a rain of sizzling embers on the panicked population as they sought shelter that didn't exist. The fire from the sky ignited all wooden structures, from the legendary Caribou Inn in the center of town to all residential and commercial properties. Hundreds perished in the most inhumane of deaths. Even their clothes ignited as they ran towards shore, away from the inferno.

The fires had also pierced the Trans-Alaska Pipeline fifty miles south of the city, propagating north like a fuse towards the storage tanks at the edge of town, detonating them in shocking, Earth rumbling explosions.

The fires continued spreading to the northwest, approaching Barrow, the borough seat of the North Slope Borough of Alaska, North America's northernmost settlement.

And home to 5,000 souls.

Evacuations at the Barrow airport and seaport began almost immediately. The city had long been warned about the possibility of methane explosions by UAF's IARC team and had set up emergency evacuation procedures for the dangerous summer months, when the permafrost was most vulnerable.

But, like in Deadhorse, there wasn't enough time to get everyone out to safety. Women and children boarded the ferries first, chugging out of port and into the calm Arctic Ocean as the wall of fire reached the outskirts of the city, rocketing temperatures, burning hundreds of wooden homes built on pylons due to the thawing permafrost. The blaze and the clouds finally descended over the sea front, engulfing the crowded docks—nearly one thousand men, women, and children—in minutes and in plain sight of those fortunate enough to make it aboard departing ferries. Seagulls and fulmars winged to sea, many failing to escape the accelerating clouds, igniting in midair.

The president declared Alaska a federal disaster area and ordered the immediate evacuation of towns south of the Brooks Mountain Range, including Fairbanks, as a precaution, and had ordered all available forest fire fighting units in the American West to the region.

An unprecedented southerly migration began in the hours following the devastating news from Barrow and Deadhorse as hundreds of thousands of panicked residents took to the highways with every possession they could pack, clogging up the road system.

Above this modern-day exodus, a lone Piper Cub flew at ten thousand feet heading north.

Malone watched the madness below with mixed sadness and anger. The scientific community had issued warnings for years that this could happen, that the thawing permafrost might not be able to contain the methane deposits. And it looked as if it had finally happened, exploding with Biblical power, wiping out in hours a hundred thousand square miles of tundra and everything living within it that failed to make it to the mountain range looming in the distance.

Spread on his lap was a FlexScreen playing back the satellite video feed that had prompted him to disregard the government warnings, convincing Mario Escobar to fly north. The high-definition satellite images of the crashing Osprey by the lagoon just north of the Brooks Mountain Range, followed by the repeated transmissions on the Guard Frequency, confirmed that, somehow, she had survived and was headed for their old hiking grounds.

The world below them in havoc, their radios switched off to stop listening to air traffic controllers instructing them to turn around, Konrad Malone focused on the mountains looming in the distance, growing larger with every passing moment. At this altitude, he could also see the clouds behind the range, charcoal and billowing, but apparently held back by the leeward winds blowing steadily from the south, sparing the rest of the state.

At least for now, he thought. But the unpredictable winds could easily shift in the opposite direction tomorrow, spreading the terror that consumed the North Slope Borough.

The government had already ordered most of its teams of forest fire fighters to the Brooks Mountain Range. These teams of Hot Shots, as they were called, specialized in controlling blazes that consumed millions of acres of forest each year in the American West.

Malone returned his attention to the FlexScreen, to the last known transmission from her emergency beacon by the foot of the mountain range almost four hours ago.

"You realize how crazy this is, Koni?" asked Escobar from the front. "You never get closer to a fire than the Hot Shots. They're the experts, *amigo*."

Malone shrugged. He was asking Escobar to fly to a spot north of where the Hot Shots were headed to hold back the fire. Common sense told him to remain behind the fire-break line the Hot Shots were going to carve along the range to prevent the flames from spreading further south. But then again, common sense had also told him not to camp so close to the dying glacier in Mount Kilimanjaro.

"Just set me down close enough. I'll go the rest of the way on my own. She's a survivor, like you and me. I'll find her and bring her back."

"But the odds are—"

"Fuck the odds, man. She's alive. I can feel it."

"Koni, I also hope she's alive, and I won't just drop you off. I'm in this thing with you one hundred percent," he replied over the intercom as they flew in and out of clouds while climbing to get past the southern peaks. "I'm just concerned there hasn't been any two-way-radio transmission in the past four hours. Her ELT also went dark at the same time."

"That just means she found shelter, Mario. She got to one of our caves and is in deep hiding, riding out the storm, just as I would have done. Like I said, she's a survivor."

"I hope you're right, *amigo*," he replied. "I hope to God you're right."

I know I am, he thought.

Malone had vowed to find Natasha Shakhiva.

Or die trying.

He continued watching the madness below as well as the apocalyptic scene ahead.

The world was on fire.

Just as it had been 4,000 years ago.

CHAPTER TWENTY-SIX
AN EYE FOR AN EYE

"If any harm follows, then you shall give life for life, eye for eye, tooth for tooth, hand for hand, foot for foot, burn for burn, wound for wound, stripe for stripe."
—Exodus 21:25

MEMPHIS, EGYPT (CAPITAL OF THE OLD KINGDOM, 12 MILES SOUTH OF MODERN-DAY CAIRO). 2205 B.C.

Nitocris stood to the side as she watched the enemies of her husband gorge themselves on the most succulent of meals.

It had been months since anyone in Egypt had seen such delicatessen served, and the widow of the late Pepi II Neferkare had saved them for this occasion.

Standing by her side was the loyal Harkfuf, whose role was now to protect the queen as their country imploded, as the relentless heat wave propelled the world's most advanced society into utter chaos, into complete anarchy. Hundreds of thousands had perished, and the priests had finally placed the blame squarely on the shoulders of Neferkare, who died days later at the hand of an assassin, proving to the entire kingdom that he was not a god-king.

And that revelation had also placed Nitocris in severe danger, as a council of Nomarchs and priests took over whatever semblance of an army still existed across the land, a mere shadow of what it had been just two years before.

And this council, which she knew was responsible for her husband's death, now feasted in a special chamber in the bowels of her husband's burial temple, a colossal pyramid constructed over the past decade by the shores of the Nile.

Nitocris smiled politely at them, an eclectic group of priests, Nomarchs, merchants, and military chiefs. They ate, drank, and fornicated with Nubian slaves, before eating and drinking some more.

"How much longer?" asked Nitocris.

"As soon as my messenger arrives we leave the chamber," Harkfuf replied.

"You must protect Pepi III," she said, referring to her son, now almost four years old. "They will come after me for what I'm about to do, but not after the boy. He has my late husband's royal blood."

"I vow to protect him," the military chief said.

Nitocris watched in silence as slaves brought in course after course, as the drinks flowed, as slave girls pleased council members right on their chairs, sometimes while they ate and talked.

Nitocris despised them all for what they stood for, for what they had done to her beloved husband, for the plots she knew were underway to kill her as well.

But I will kill you first, she thought. *You will die here, tonight, in a chamber lower than where my beloved rests.*

Harkfuf's messenger arrived just before dawn, along with a fresh group of slaves and more food, bringing a round of applause from her guests, who were thoroughly impressed at her ability to produce so much fresh food in a time of famine.

Nitocris and Harkfuf bowed while slowly retreating, presumably to give room to the arriving entertainment, but they continued walking back, finally turning around when losing line of sight with the party.

The narrow corridor led to the anteroom, where Nitocris reached for two small stones at waist level protruding just a little more than the rest. To the average observer, they would appear as minor defects in an otherwise perfect work of architecture. But these stones had been placed here as the trigger of a mechanism conceived by her husband's finest builders.

She pressed them in unison, and as designed, the stones glided softly into the wall, releasing the blocks holding back the heavy boulder that formed the roof of the connecting corridor.

In an instant, the boulder dropped into place, blocking the main chamber from the anteroom, sealing the party behind a wall of rock the width of two horses.

Forever.

She wished she could have heard their screams as she entombed them, but perfectly smooth limestone did not allow sound to propagate.

Nodding to Harkfuf, they walked up the incline passageway to the surface.

The predawn skies were indigo with faint streaks of orange on the horizon.

My last sunrise, she thought, perspiration already forming on her forehead and in between her breasts from the blistering temperature, even at this early hour.

As agreed, the chief of the military activated the second hidden architectural feature of the pyramid by pushing three rocks down a long slide towards the side of the structure butting into the crocodile-infested Nile.

A window opened below the surface, sucking water and beasts into the much deeper chamber.

"It is done, my queen," he said as the escorts of the entombed royalty approached the structure to retrieve their principals back to their residences before the sun rose and temperatures became intolerable for humans.

"Then complete your task," she ordered.

Inhaling deeply before slowly nodding, the large warrior proclaimed the crime committed by Nitocris to the dozens of incoming guards.

The queen stepped back as the armed crowd approached her.

And, just as planned, Harkfuf retrieved a dagger beneath his waistband and drove it into her heart.

CHAPTER TWENTY-SEVEN
PERSISTENCE

"Energy and persistence conquer all things."
—Benjamin Franklin.

30,000 FEET OVER THE NORTH ATLANTIC.
JULY 10, 2029.

Rachel settled next to Case on the sofa at the front cabin of the Cessna Citation X as they read the information browsing on the FlexScreen she unrolled in between them. In the rear, three CIA analysts worked the terminals.

"We were too late," she mumbled, staring at what now appeared to be roughly 150,000 square miles of destruction. In plain terms, the north section of Alaska—almost a third of the state—was on fire, and the conflagration was sending clouds of smoldering embers four miles high, where the jet stream carried them around the world.

"This one's gonna hurt...at a global level," he said, before running a finger along the middle of the Brooks Mountain Range and along the western end of the Yukon Territory. "This is where the Hot Shots are going to try to hold the line to keep it from spreading into northern Canada as well as south of Brooks."

"They might not be able to," she whispered. "There aren't enough fire fighters to control something of this magnitude."

Case just stared at her.

During her college years, Rachel had done an internship with one of the nearly one hundred Hot Shot teams in the American West, each around ninety fire fighters strong. She spent three unforgettable and grueling months combating forest fires in Idaho as an intern with the Idaho City Hot Shots. The experience had drilled into her the dire consequences of climate change. Where twenty years earlier the largest forest fires measured tens of thousands of acres, now fires averaged over one hundred thousand acres, with the largest reaching seven hundred thousand acres.

And all that caused by just an increase of one miserable degree in temperature, she thought, also recalling that it took an average of two hundred Hot Shots to control a forest fire of around 100,000 thousand acres. The monster in Alaska was 150,000 square miles, or close 96 *million* acres.

"There aren't enough fire fighters...in the world," she mumbled again. "And besides, the way the Hot Shot teams work is by surrounding the fire and cutting off its fuel supply with burn lines ahead of the inferno to keep it from spreading, letting it burn itself out after exhausting the available fuel in the affected area. I'm not sure how they're going to kill the fuel supply to this one. It's not being fueled from above the ground like a classic forest fire. The fuel is coming from beneath, deep in the ground. Sort of like an oil well fire but multiplied times a million."

"What will happen?" he asked.

Rachel slowly shook her head and said, "Not sure, but there isn't much you and I can do about Alaska. The damage is done. We need to focus on the next strike. There are two more of these damned machines out there. What's our ETA to Toronto?"

"Two more hours," he replied.

The CIA, assisted by the Pentagon, had broadcast a field report about a plane departing Ground Zero in Alaska shortly before the fire broke out, and heading into Canada. The airplane, which Rachel suspected to be Kiersted's Cessna Caravan, mysteriously disappeared as it neared the border with Yukon. But twenty minutes later, Yukon ATC had picked up a Cessna Caravan operating as an Air Care unit heading into Whitehorse. Unfortunately, before any interceptors could be scrambled, the Caravan once more vanished from radar, only to be found abandoned an hour later by members of the Canadian Special Operations Regiment (CSOR) at a remote lake three hundred miles north of Whitehorse.

In the middle of nowhere in Yukon.

"Why are you so sure Kiersted's going for Canada next?" Case asked.

"I'm trying to think like him," she replied. "There are three major permafrost areas in the northern hemisphere. The first is the West Siberian Plains. The second is Alaska and parts of the Yukon Territory. The third is along the eastern section of Canada, including the large area north of Toronto, Ottawa, Montreal, and Quebec City. In fact, archeological records show that people have been living in the region since the last ice age. The entire region is sitting atop a pocket of methane as large as the one torching Alaska. If I were a climate terrorist, that's where I would focus my energy. Imagine a disaster like the North Slope Borough but in a metropolis like Toronto, and then imagine the same clouds of fire raining on the Alaskan tundra burying all of those other Canadian cities under a dozen feet of red-hot embers. I would first go for places like Surgat and Alaska to create a diversion before striking hard in densely-populated areas. Plus the states of New York, Vermont, and Maine are just to the south of the border with Canada.

Case raised his brows and sighed before saying, "What about the fourth machine?"

She lifted her shoulders. "Maybe it's for back-up? Maybe he plans to use them both in Toronto? He sure as hell doesn't need it for Alaska or Yukon, and we destroyed the one in Surgat, and the last report from Ivenko claims they combed the entire area and it's clear."

"Or maybe there's a different target for the fourth one," he suggested, rubbing his chest and grimacing.

"Then it's not related to the permafrost…how are you feeling?"

"I'll survive." He leaned back and sank on the sofa, resting his head, eyes closed, right hand still on his chest, fingertips pressing the spots where he was shot, left arm resting between them. "Not the first time this happened," he added, "but it always feels like getting kicked by a god-damned mule."

She stared at this man who had saved her twice. Those rounds he took had been meant for her face.

And the way he reacted in Paris…

Before she could help herself, she placed her right hand over his left, interlacing their fingers.

He opened his eyes and stared at her. "Rach, what are you—"

"Hush," she said, resting the right side of her head on his left shoulder. "And thank you," she added, staring at the contrasting color of their clasped hands.

"I come with baggage," he said.

She chuckled. "That makes two of us."

They remained like this for a while, immersed in their own thoughts, finding whatever solace could be found as the world burned.

"Rach?" he said after a while.

"Yeah?"

"I hate to ruin the moment...but how else would you use a tectonic machine?"

She lifted her head and gave him a sidelong glance. He still had his eyes closed, head leaned back.

Dropping her head back on his chest, she said, "Well, the original intent was to induce oscillations along fault lines to cause minor tremors and thus reduce the tension between tectonic plates to minimize the chance of a major earthquake. But it's unclear if they actually worked in that application."

"Well, it sure did a number on Alaska, so the design does something to the soil structure."

"No doubt."

Case slowly leaned forward and she also sat back up, but crossed her legs to sit sideways to face him.

"What is it?"

"Is it possible they could be used to actually *trigger* an earthquake?"

"The events in Greenland and Alaska have proven that at this point *anything* is possible, so sure, we can't discount triggering an earthquake. And thinking like a terrorist, I would prioritize places like the San Andreas fault. Biggest bang for the buck."

"Los Angeles and San Francisco?"

"That would be my best educated—"

Case cupped her face and planted a kiss on her lips.

"Have I told you that you're fucking brilliant *and* beautiful?"

Before she could respond, he kissed her again, then looked her in the eye while whispering, "And *this* is to be continued," and rushed to the back of the plane to speak to the analysts.

CHAPTER TWENTY-EIGHT
MASS EXTINCTION

"The end of all things is at hand." —Peter 4:7

BROOKS MOUNTAIN RANGE, ALASKA.
JULY 11, 2029.

The trail beyond the mouth of the cave leading to the first hill was layered with ash and dust.

She regarded the remnants of a colossal battle between fire and ice that had resulted in the temporary retreat of the burning clouds hovering north of the mountain range.

Just past midnight, Natasha trekked up a steep incline as lightning gleamed in the distance, casting a brief flash across the face of the mountain.

She waited to hear the ensuing clap of thunder, but the remote lightning strike was followed by a large quake that shook her high ground.

The smell of fire soon tickled her nostrils.

It's returning.

The shifting winds started to blow charcoal clouds back towards the range, threatening everything and everyone within its vast expanse.

Shaking her head, Natasha peered again at the ominous sight, at the plumes of billowing smoke rising above the scorched land as far as the eye could see. She heard howls and screeches in the distance—bears, wolves, birds of all kinds, some wounded, others scared.

Entire colonies of wildlife were being exterminated as she also noticed the changing color of the whirling fires marking the leading edge of the inferno. They were becoming bluer, shedding the stain of orange and yellow gold from the consumed surface vegetation.

Pure blue.

Pure methane.

Keep hiking.

She continued for six hours straight, finding it increasingly harder to breathe not just because of the altitude but from the reduced oxygen content as the nearing blaze consumed massive amounts of it, which also explained the breeze sweeping towards the flames, drawn by the suction force created by the fire.

She kept one ELT on while conserving the batteries of the second for later, after she cleared the tallest peaks and got a visual of the valleys leading to Fairbanks. She also knew that reaching the other side of the range would increase her chances of being heard on the Guard frequency. So far, her emergency calls had proven fruitless.

She spaced her meals, maintaining a steady pace on trails leading to a passage in between the mountains. Slowly, she left the North Slope valley behind as eruptions burst through the layer of flames now reaching the very foot of the range, pulsating above a sea of flickering fire, licking the darkening sky, obscuring it with ash clouds.

Birds rushed overhead in flocks so dense that at times they blocked the skies. Their deafening screeches echoed against the mountains while winging south. Plumes of fire punched through the blistering valley as the land released more gas, feeding scorching swirls of blue spiraling to the sky.

In a dying world, the climate scientist glared at the devastation she sought to escape, at the extinction event she was witnessing.

Soon the sky would become saturated with ashes and black rain would reach the northern edge of the range, suffocating anything that survived the inferno.

Soon night would also fall.

Vast herds of mammals, mostly caribou, raced south, toward the vegetation-rich valley on the other side of Brooks. Sometime at around midday, she had spotted a grizzly, which made her reach for the holstered semiautomatic. But the beast seemed far more concerned with getting away from the fire than in the prospect of a quick meal.

Following her GPS, Natasha headed for a small lake nestled deep in the mountains, where an old log cabin by its shores provided shelter for hikers from sudden blizzards or hail storms.

It was also the place where Mario Escobar would drop her off for her hikes.

The roaring fires receded in the distance as she immersed herself in the heart of the mountains beneath the twilight of an Alaska summer evening. It provided enough light to see the trails ahead and also her GPS without using the unit's backlight to conserve batteries. It also kept her from having to use her flashlight while continuing her southern escape.

She no longer heard any animals, now.

There were no birds or mammals around, which meant the creatures had either perished or had already reached safety on the other side.

You're all alone.

And that sinking feeling sent a chill down her tired body.

Keep going.

She persisted for five more hours, breathing through her mouth now, fighting off a stinging headache, her mind growing cloudy. She clutched the GPS in her trembling hands and struggled to read it, her eyesight worsening as she fought to keep her footing, to follow the course she had plotted earlier in the day.

Two more miles.

Natasha tried to go on, but her body would no longer obey her.

She fell to her knees on a clearing high up in the mountains, her right hand reaching for the second ELT, activating it as back-up to the first one before she collapsed on her back.

The predawn skies, indigo and stained with burnt orange and yellow-gold, were dotted with stars.

She watched it for a moment before everything faded away. That two miles may as well have been a million.

CHAPTER TWENTY-NINE
RISKY BUSINESS

"Only those who dare to fail greatly can ever achieve greatness."
—Robert F. Kennedy

BROOKS MOUNTAIN RANGE, ALASKA.
JULY 11, 2029.

"Got a signal, *amigo*," reported Escobar over the intercom of the Piper Cub as they circled the southern end of the mountain range at ten thousand feet in moderate turbulence at five in the morning. "Fifteen miles northwest."

"Good girl," said Malone, reading the information on his FlexScreen just as it streamed into Escobar's cockpit display. "She went to the lake; Mario…looks like a couple of miles from the cabin. How come we can't reach her on the radio?"

"Don't know. Maybe her transceiver's out."

Escobar had tried to contact her on the Guard frequency repeatedly in the past hour, after their refueling stop at Coldfoot. The place was a former mining camp reincarnated as a construction town while the pipeline was being built. The town changed again in the early 1980s as a trucker stop and tourist attraction for being "The Farthest North Truck Stop in the World."

They had landed on the nearly deserted airstrip, where a lone attendant topped off their tanks.

"Can you land on the lake before dawn?"

"That's the beauty of Alaska, Koni," the bush pilot replied. "It never gets dark enough. We'll be there in five."

Malone looked towards the north. The glow behind the mountains pulsated now with hues of blue.

Of pure methane.

But he noticed something else. The mountain peaks, clearly visible minutes ago, grew hazy.

"Is that what I think it is above the range?" asked Malone.

"Looks that way."

The winds had indeed shifted, inching the charcoal clouds south, just above the tip of the range.

Malone doubted the prevailing winds would let those clouds venture too far south from the mountains. But the fact they were above the mountains meant not only bad news for Natasha, but also for them if they couldn't get in and out fast enough.

"We can't afford to linger around, Koni. The ash in those clouds will choke the engine and shred the skin of the plane in minutes."

"How much time?" he asked, concern filling him.

"No more than an hour."

"Then you'd better get me on the ground ASAP. We didn't come all this way to quit now."

As he said this, Malone's gaze remained locked on the clouds pulsating with flames looming above the range.

CHAPTER THIRTY
PERMIAN DREAM

"And fire came down out of heaven, and devoured them." —Revelation 20:9

BROOKS MOUNTAIN RANGE, ALASKA.
JULY 11, 2029.

The engine noise hummed in the periphery of her subconscious, as her world spun out of control. She stared at Marcus Stone's face swirling around her, tight with tension while his lips moved, shouting something she couldn't hear.

Natasha tried to listen but the roar from the Osprey drowned his words. And that's when Stone pointed at the other passengers in the rear of the aircraft, and she saw Sergei Shakhiva strapped to a seat across from her.

Sergei?

My love, what are you doing here?

But the Russian climatologist didn't reply, gazing at her with his hypnotizing blue eyes, which shifted to the other passengers in the cabin, Stone's aides. Their bodies maimed, their ghostly faces turning towards her, their lips moving just as Stone's had, their voices drowned by the rotor noise.

She turned back to the Army colonel, his face now as ghostly as that of his aides, highlighting his orange freckles and his closely-cropped orange hair.

He leaned over and yanked open the Osprey's side door.

Run to the mountains! Survive! Fix this!

Natasha fell away from the aircraft moments before it exploded in scarlet flames pulsating across the barren landscape.

But she landed in sand instead of water.

Sand?

That's when she saw the nearing inferno and began to race away from the wall of fire. Sheet lightning gleamed and thunder whipped the valley.

Her legs burned, her lungs protested the heat, and her mouth and throat felt raw from the ashes.

She watched animals rush by; bears, caribou, geese, and foxes—all trying to escape the firestorm.

That's when she saw the strangest of creatures: a mother and two large cubs.

They looked like tigers but bigger—much bigger—with long sabre teeth flanking their muzzles. Their streamlined bodies, light-brown with darker streaks down their torsos, shot past her through the swirling haze. Their strong and elastic muscles pumped against the desert floor in long cat-like strides. They studied her briefly through large oval yellow eyes before darting ahead.

Gorgos!

They're Gorgos!

The mother growled, her powerful roar clashing with the rumbling thunder.

The Permian beasts dashed ahead, leaping over a sand dune as volcanoes erupted in the distance.

Volcanoes?

Confused, Natasha tried to run faster, but her boots sank in the sand and lighting arced across the angered sky as she stared across the arid terrain at an incoming cloud packed with sand.

A sandstorm?

In Alaska?

Lightning sparked in the distance, above a desert hurtled into the dusky horizon by invisible claws stirring up the surface. It blasted tons of sand into the air with the power of a million tornadoes, creating a whirlwind of certain death blocking the sinking sun as night fell over her world.

Natasha followed the Gorgos as they shifted direction toward the ragged edges of rock formations protruding through the desert floor off to their right, the caves used by their kind to escape the day's heat during their winter hunting season.

She followed them while risking a brief backward glance, her eyes assessing the gap separating them from the expanding crimson shroud, before glaring at the incoming sandstorm, alive with forked tongues of lightning. She understood the Gorgos' strategy, their last-ditch attempt to avoid getting caught between the colliding fronts.

But she wasn't fast enough.

The Gorgos reached the mouth of the cave and turned around to watch her, three pairs of golden eyes staring out from the darkness; three lonely creatures from a long-forgotten past roaring at her to hurry, to speed up, to save herself from the apocalypse closing in on her.

The Gorgos vanished as the cloud of sand engulfed her, suffocating, blinding, tearing into her, skinning her alive. The sizzling breath of hell scorched her mind, her senses, her very soul.

Natasha screamed in pain, in agony, in anger at the heavenly chastisement, at the claws tearing her down to the bone.

But through the flames, the shredding sand, the madness, she heard his voice calling out to her in the distance.

He was here.

He had come to rescue her, to save her from this inferno.

Natasha stretched her arms at the spinning darkness and surrendered herself to his embrace.

* * *

Malone pressed Natasha's frame tight against his chest, carrying her as he would an infant.

Racing back towards the lakeshore, his throat sore from the haze descending over the mountains, his shoulders burning from the stress, he forged ahead, finding his surroundings eerily devoid of any animals, any creatures.

He heard nothing except for the distant drone of the fires on the north end of the range mixing with his heavy breathing. Gone were the birds, the caribou, the bears and foxes. And as he struggled to keep up his pace with a gradual depletion of oxygen content—as measured by the wrist-mounted FlexScreen he wore—the scientist understood why, and also understood the reason for Natasha's current state.

Unlike Malone, who had spent the past three months atop Mount Kilimanjaro, becoming quite conditioned to low-oxygen environments, she had lived by the shores of Shirukak Lake, one thousand feet above sea level.

But that doesn't mean you'll last long, he thought, following the same familiar trail he had used twenty minutes ago, after Escobar had pulled up to the shore and Malone had jumped off armed with a handheld GPS map marking the precise location of her ELT transmission.

She stirred in his arms, and he realized just how much he missed holding her.

The trail veered to the right before gradually dropping to the rocky bed leading to the water and the waiting Piper Cub.

A brief upward glance confirmed what his lungs protested: the cloud cover descending over them slowly turned into a dust-rich fog.

His eyes burning and itching, his mouth completely dry, Malone maintained his pace, his rugged boots providing enough traction to keep his momentum pointed straight toward the single-engine amphibious plane looming around the bend in the trail.

"Crank her up!" he shouted at the top of his lungs as he raced across the rocky clearing surrounding the spring-fed lake. "Let's get the hell out of here!"

Escobar ran up to meet him and together they carried Natasha down to the shores as the inky clouds completely blocked the sun and temperatures started to drop below freezing.

Since the Piper Cub was designed as a two-seater airplane, Malone sat in the rear seat first, holding Natasha on his lap. Escobar jumped in the front seat and they were airborne in five minutes.

They remained at two hundred feet above the terrain to stay clear of the toxic and abrasive clouds, which, like volcanic ash, would strip the metal skin of the Piper while flying at 100 knots.

As they reached the southern tip of the range, the skies opened up and they were able to climb while heading straight for Fairbanks, where only military personnel, fire fighters, and scientists were exempted from the evacuation.

"How's she doing?" asked Escobar over the intercom as they reached cruising altitude.

"Steady," he replied, monitoring her pulse as he took a deep breath and filled his lungs with clean air.

Malone looked over his right shoulder at the nearly vanished mountains as dense clouds swallowed the range.

Natasha's breathing became heavier as her body detected the increased oxygen content and started drawing it deeper each time she inhaled, replenishing her system, feeding the cells in her bloodstream.

A moment later her eyelids fluttered, and she opened those hazel eyes he had missed so much. They blinked, gaining focus.

"Hey there," he said, grinning.

"Koni?" she replied.

"Yes? I'm here."

"What took you…so bloody long?"

And she drifted back to sleep.

CHAPTER THIRTY-ONE
11,000-YEAR JOURNEY

"Climate change is the most severe problem that we are facing today, more serious even than the threat of terrorism."
—David King, United Kingdom's chief scientific advisor

THIRTY MILES NORTH OF TORONTO, CANADA. JULY 12, 2029.

William stood in a heavily wooded valley next to Lian as the members of his Canadian cell pulled the machine from a shipping crate. Labeled as weather monitoring equipment from the British Weather Bureau, it had arrived at one of Toronto's piers via a merchant ship the week before.

His cell had loaded up the crate onto a flat bed and taken it to this location. Remote and secluded, the region was layered with the thawing permafrost that gave the towering pines around them the same slant as the forests in Surgat, where his team had failed him.

But not today.

He filled his lungs with cool air, with the invigorating pine resin fragrance of a forest that had been around since the last ice age. In this place, people had lived when mastodons and saber tooth tigers roamed the land, moving into the cold sub-arctic landscape from the south to pursue the big game animals that preceded them.

But it all ends today.

And there would be no one getting in his way.

He had taken the utmost precautions, even ditching Lian's coveted Cessna north of Whitehorse and hiking into town. A charter plane at the regional airport took them to another regional airport just east of Toronto, where Lian rented the helicopter she landed a mile away to meet his cell here an hour ago, right on schedule.

The operatives consisted of four men and one woman, all in their late twenties and hand-picked by William from large pools of revolutionaries and ideologists from South America, Indonesia, Serbia, and the Middle East. Each had a profound reason to hate America and her allies, including Canada and England. William had merely provided them with the opportunity to channel their passion, to achieve their full potential.

To unleash their inner monsters.

This team was hungry, willing to do anything to make a difference, to strike terror in the hearts of Canadians and Americans.

He watched as Doctor Yuri Gerchenko instructed two members of the young team how to complete the assembly process at the bottom of a shallow ravine, below sight from anyone roaming the forest.

The location also provided added protection against an unexpected raid. William had selected it because of its proximity to the gravel road his cell had used to transport the Russian hardware from the major highway out of Toronto. It was the same access road leading to the nearby clearing where Lian had landed their rented helicopter, now hidden beneath a camouflage canvas.

His plan was identical to Alaska. Set up the machine, get everyone on the helicopter, and set the region on fire. By the time a world focused on Alaska realized what had happened, William and his crew would be in Halifax, Nova Scotia, boarding a jet to South America.

Hans-Jorgen and the remaining three operatives had formed an elaborate perimeter defense around the soon-to-be Ground Zero. They stood guard at each point of the compass several meters inside their high-tech defense shield. In addition, William, an old-school commando, had set up his own inner perimeter surrounding the ravine with a dozen Claymore mines linked to a simple handheld detonator.

My last line of defense.

He had also installed mines a few dozen feet up and down the ravine connected to trip wires and to his detonator in case anyone tried to sneak up on him through the creek.

Greenland had drowned the world and had frozen Europe. Alaska was burning, and with it America's largest oil producing state. Despite the failure in Surgat and the physical punishment he had endured in Greenland, he was making a difference.

You never know what you're capable of.

William stared at the iLimb holding his assault rifle while standing firm on his artificial legs.

Toronto would die today.

By fire.

CHAPTER THIRTY-TWO
TIGHTENING THE NOOSE

"This is not a battle between the United States and Terrorism, but between the free and democratic world and terrorism."
—Tony Blair

FIFTY MILES NORTH OF TORONTO, CANADA. JULY 12, 2029.

Her face smeared with camouflage cream, Rachel Daly followed Case Patterson as they approached the terrorist cell from the north. Canadian forces covered the southern perimeter, while a team from U.S. Navy SEAL Team Six out of Naval Air Station Oceana, Virginia Beach, closed in from the east and west.

A pair of General Atomics MQ-9 Reaper Unmanned Aerial Vehicles controlled the sky, and a circling AWACs ten miles away coordinated communications. The UAVs' deep infrared cameras provided an accurate count of the terrorists and overlaid that information on the GPS maps displayed on the wrist-mounted FlexScreens of every member of this cross-functional team. The information was also superimposed on everyone's SmartLenses.

The plan called for the SEALs to go in first guided by UAV imagery, neutralize the enemy—by presidential order after Alaska—and destroy the target with precise surgical fire. The SEALS would take a similar approach as the Spetsnaz commandos did in Surgat, disabling the machine without igniting the rocket fuel—and, of course, the methane.

Her boots sinking in the soft terrain as she followed Case, Rachel came to terms with the reality that they once more were walking over an apocalyptic time bomb. If the methane reached the surface, she would not be able to even register it before the heat vaporized everyone and everything in a ten-mile radius.

Focus.

She stayed the course, continuing the approach, gloved hands clutching a sound-suppressed Heckler & Koch MP7SD assault rifle.

They followed the uneven terrain, past tilted trees rising to a clear sky, and across a dry ravine flanked by clumps of jagged boulders. The leaf-littered ground gave gently to every step. Her heart beat steadily. Her breathing slowed as they reached the outer perimeter of the SEAL killing zone.

Case took a knee behind a row of waist-high bushes bordering the area where only the SEALs could enter for the next three minutes.

"Team Three, Eagle, how do you read?" Rachel called out to the CIA team aboard the AWACs in this joint mission.

"Loud and clear, Team Three."

"Three in position," she reported through her throat mike.

"One in position," answered the Canadian team lead.

"Two moving in," reported Commander John Towers, leader of the SEAL team. Towers had readily understood the nature of the beast they were fighting and had agreed to tone down his team's firepower in order to avoid inadvertently setting off the Russian machine. This meant no grenade launchers or heavy caliber machine guns, limiting his operators to their Heckler & Koch MP7SDs and Sig Sauer sidearms.

Rachel settled down next to Case, shoulder to shoulder, exchanging a brief glance.

He winked while grinning, exposing white teeth beneath a face darkened by hues of dark green face paint.

She returned the smile before checking her FlexScreen, verifying the location of the threat, depicted as crimson dots by the UAVs, as well as the green returns from the SEALs.

"Releasing Orbs," reported Towers.

She watched as fifteen blue specks propagated beyond the SEAL team.

* * *

"Incoming," said Lian, watching her FlexScreen, which showed Hans-Jorgen and his three operatives deployed per the plan inside the orange circle marking their defense system around the shallow trench where Gerchenko was hard at work. Small blue dots—enemy Orbs—were approaching from the east and west.

She looked at William, her dark eyes waiting for his order.

He nodded and said, "Smoke them."

His trusted operative activated the countermeasures unit, which deployed a circular ray of smart blue-green light that expanded from their perimeter system as it became brighter.

The radial proton flare propagated through the forest like blue lightning, altering the molecular structure of any object carrying an electrical charge and lacking the protection password signature embedded in the flare.

The Orbs trembled as the flash damaged their nanotronic circuitry, firing random commands at their propulsion systems, shooting off in multiple directions.

"Movement from the east and west," advised Hans-Jorgen through the radio as his team spotted incoming figures in the forest.

William and Lian took up defensive positions on the east edge of the ravine, and he ordered the two operatives assisting Gerchenko to do the same on the west end, leaving the elder scientist in the middle of the trench giving the final touches to the equipment.

"How did they find us so fast?" asked Lian.

"It doesn't matter," he replied. "Activate the shield."

She tapped the touch-sensitive FlexScreen and said, "We're hot."

"Let's dig in," he said.

William rested his elbows on the top of the five-foot inclined wall of their trench, right hand on the handle of an M60 machine gun, left hand on the forward grip beneath the barrel.

He gathered leaves within reach and used them to shield his exposed shoulder, head, and arms, keeping his weapon just above the edge of the ravine pointed at the drunken trees. Lian did the same, though she held a 9mm Uzi, compact but deadly.

"We have visual," said Hans-Jorgen. *"Two targets east, one west, and two south. Five contacts...they stopped short of the shield...probably SEALs."*

Lian looked at William. "Navy SEALs?"

William inhaled deeply. During his years with the *Fromandskorpset,* he had conducted joint exercises with the American elite fighting unit, and they were virtually unbeatable. They were also invisible. SEALs relied heavily on stealth. The fact that his perimeter team could actually see them told him something was seriously wrong.

"They can see our shield," Lian hissed, watching on her FlexScreen as the incoming team stopped just short of the outer high-tech defense circle.

William didn't reply, his mind considering his rapidly narrowing choices.

"Hans-Jorgen, do you have visual on targets?" William asked.

"Affirmative," he replied.

"Open fire when able. Buy us time."

* * *

"Team Two in position," Towers reported.

Rachel read the downlink from the Reapers. The terrorists had killed the Orbs and were using an active shield of infrared trip wires.

"We've spotted some of their men," the SEAL team commander added. *"My snipers are in position. Four contacts on outside perimeter. Engaging."* Then a few seconds later, he said, *"Targets neutralized."*

Just like that, Rachel thought before Towers said, *"Using flares now to trip the shield and blow a path to Ground Zero."*

* * *

William frowned. Hans-Jorgen should have opened fire by now. Yet the outer perimeter was suddenly silent.

"Come in, Hans-Jorgen," he said.

Silence.

"Why isn't he answering?" asked Lian.

A deep sinking feeling gripped William as he turned to Gerchenko, still fiddling with the hardware. The SEALs must have had snipers in position in addition to the commandos that had chosen to show themselves to draw attention. Hans-Jorgen and his young team had fallen for the ruse.

"They're gone," he finally said, before asking, "How much longer, Yuri?"

"Just a minute," the scientist said, his hands holding odd tools as he worked the Russian machinery. "All we need is—"

The explosions rocked the forest from every direction. The perimeter shield had been pierced, triggering the outer Claymore.

"Let's hope that bought us that extra minute," Lian said.

Peering into the murky forest through the sights of his weapon, William doubted any of his perimeter defenses would make a difference when SEALs were involved.

Still, not all was lost. He still had his inner defense system, the dozen more Claymore mines he had placed just a few feet from the edge of the ravine and also inside the ravine's north and south channels.

His final stand.

"You have less than one minute, Yuri," William announced in a calm voice that even surprised him considering they were about to be overrun.

Almost on cue, the figures appeared in the distance, amidst once towering pines now tilted in every direction.

He aligned the closest figure and opened fire in unison with Lian, though he knew their muzzle flashes would mark their location for the enemy.

The figure dropped but others rushed behind him, and silent rounds stirred the ground around them, though nowhere near the trademark barrage of overwhelming firepower he would have expected the SEALs to unleash.

Still, the incoming fire forced them to duck, to use the terrain as shield.

His back against the inclined wall as rounds zoomed overhead, William watched his younger operatives beyond the equipment on the east wall failing to react in time.

The operatives landed on their backs at the bottom of the creek already corpses, dead eyes staring at the green canopy overhead.

He clenched his jaw in anger, the sight evoking memories of Greenland, of his maimed team.

"Cover that side!" William ordered Lian.

She rushed around Gerchenko, who was still working the system, and reached her new post.

He took a deep breath and resumed his scan of the forest, keeping his head as low as possible while sweeping the terrain with—

Two SEALs materialized from behind trees and opened fire on his position.

A burning pain on his left shoulder told him a round had found its mark.

Cringing, he fired back, taking out the right figure as the left one dove for cover.

Bastards.

Ignoring the wound, he stepped to the right along the wall, taking up a new position, and firing at a SEAL rushing from one trunk to another, a shadow in the darkness, scoring a direct hit.

Two down on this side, he thought, trying to focus despite the loss of everyone but Lian and Gerchenko.

He risked a backward glance at the middle of the trench, and he now saw Gerchenko dead in a pool of his own blood.

And the machine was still not active.

He also saw motion around him in the forest in every direction. The SEALs were closing in. One of the Claymores rigged to a trip wire up the ravine detonated, followed by screams.

"The system!" he screamed at Lian. "Finish it!"

She abandoned her post to finalize the power-up sequence, giving William a thumbs-up thirty seconds later. "Good to go!" she screamed over the noise of gunfire. "Hey, you're bleeding!

"It doesn't matter! We're about to be overrun!"

William reached in his pocket for the detonator and stared into her eyes.

"The moment the Claymores go off, we run north along the bottom of the trench to the gravel road. We need to reach that helo and get the hell out of here."

She nodded.

William toggled the switch and the blast rocked the forest, lighting up the murkiness in a blinding flash of orange flames followed by more agonized screams.

"Now!"

* * *

"Team Two? Come in Team Two!" Rachel spoke into her throat mike right after the Earth-rumbling blast originating from the middle of the SEAL kill zone.

"Not a good sign," Case said, pointing at the two infrared emissions rushing away from the center of the terrorist nest and also at the stationary but growing heat signature in the middle. "Remember Surgat? The machine is on."

"Team One, you copy?"

"Team One here," replied the head of the Canadian detachment.

"Head into the middle of the kill zone," she ordered. "Team Two is not responding. Destroy the machine then search for wounded. Repeat. Destroy the machine *before* searching for wounded. We're going after the bastards."

"Roger that, Team Three."

Case led the way as they raced across the forest, up trails and around bends in the uneven terrain in full pursuit of two terrorists painted red in her SmartLenses by the circling UAVs. Their most direct route took them down into a shallow ravine, which they followed, skipping over rotting logs, branches, and a thick blanket of fallen leaves and pine needles.

"They're about a half mile ahead of us!" she said, staring at Case's dark silhouette as they pressed on. "Team One, are you in position?"

"Almost there, Team Three. My men are almost in position! There's wounded men everywhere. Calling medical evac now."

"First priority is the machine! Please acknowledge, Team One."

"Team One acknowledging."

"Advise when…machine is disabled," Rachel said into her throat mike, taking in large gulps of air as she kept kicking her legs, thigh muscles burning while running as fast as she could.

They had to catch up.

They had to intercept the—

"They've stopped…shit, Case, they have a helo!" Rachel hissed, the SmartLenses providing her with telescopic x-ray vision. "They have a damned helo!"

"How the hell we miss *that*?" Case asked as they kept the pace, closing the gap.

"Camouflaged," she said, looking at the images superimposed on her field of view as fed to her from the UAVs. Two figures were removing a tarp cover and getting inside.

They were still a quarter of a mile away over rough terrain when they heard the high-pitch whine of a turbine revving up.

"We're not going to make it!" Case said.

"Eagle, Eagle, Team Three," said Rachel.

"Team Three, Eagle, go ahead."

And Rachel put in her request with the AWACS controller.

* * *

William watched in satisfaction as the main rotor accelerated, lifting them off the soft terrain. Maybe they would make it after all. Maybe they would—

"Radar contact," she replied, reading the information streaming on her Primary Flight Display system from the onboard radar unit. "Incoming. Three o'clock, two miles, five hundred feet. Closing fast."

As she pulled on the collective and the helicopter lifted a dozen feet off the ground, William slid the door open, unstrapped his safety restraints, and peered in that direction while clutching the M60.

Nothing.

He saw nothing but skies that had begun to become hazier from the fires in Alaska.

"You sure?"

"Three o'clock, one mile, two hundred feet," she said. *Damn.*

William kept the M60 pointed in that direction and started firing blindly, before he spotted the black shadow.

What the hell?

He pressed on, adjusting his fire for a few more seconds, but failing to detonate whatever it was the Americans had fired on them.

"Five seconds to impact! Jump!" she shouted.

Instinctively, as Lian began to unbuckle her safety harness while setting the helicopter in a shallow dive, William tossed the weapon out and jumped.

He fell a dozen feet, landing on his titanium and graphite iLimbs, listening to the hydrogen pistons bleed pressure, cushioning the impact, and immediately forcing his body into a roll.

As he finally landed on his belly, the shadow of the incoming threat rushed above him an instant before it collided against his side of the helicopter, setting it ablaze before Lian could jump.

"NO!" he shouted.

He looked up in horror as the burning wreck plummeted to the ground fifty feet away.

A loud explosion marked the crash site, the flames boiling up to the sky.

Bastards!

Fucking bast—

"Get up!" a female voice shouted behind him. "Hands where I can see them!"

William paused, for a moment considered reaching for the holstered Glock strapped to his utility belt. But after the roll, his shooting hand ended up wedged between his chest and the ground. So, he opted for a fragmentation grenade strapped on his battle vest. He gripped it and inconspicuously pulled the safety ring with his teeth, in essence creating a dead-man's switch. Then he slowly stood, keeping his back to the threat but his hands against his chest.

"Goddammit! Show me your hands!" screamed the same voice. "Show me your hands!"

Slowly, the climate terrorist turned around to face his foe, a woman twenty or so feet away in camouflage gear clutching an MP7 fitted with a slim sound suppressor. A few feet behind her stood another operative, a man, similarly armed.

And William showed her his hands.

"Put it down!" she shouted.

But instead, William looked at the grenade and then back at the operatives.

"Don't do it!" she warned. "Put it down!"

You never really know what you're capable of.

Until…
And he tried to throw it at them.

* * *

Rachel put two rounds through his chest at a distance of a dozen feet, before pivoting on her right foot and diving toward Case, tackling him to the ground just as their world exploded behind them.

The shockwave ripped into the back of her armored battle dress as she landed on top of Case, who quickly rolled out from under her.

She blinked, the impact having kicked the wind out of her. A rush of stabbing pain surged up and down her back as she felt Case picking her up.

Breathing in short, ragged gasps, feeling lightheaded, her ears ringing, she watched the forest around her rush by in a whirl of green.

She tried to cry out but the intense throbbing between her shoulder blades had somehow locked down her muscles tight, choking her throat. All she could do was look up and watch Case as he shouted something she could not hear at someone she could not see.

She closed her eyes as her world began to spin, as she started to lose consciousness. But not before hearing a rhythmic, rattling sound that overpowered the ringing in her ears, followed by a strong downwash.

Many hands converged on her now, picking her up and laying her face down on something soft. She cringed as someone stabbed her in the forearm.

Rachel was about to complain when sudden warmth propagated up to her shoulder and down her back, washing away the pain.

With considerable effort, she managed to open her eyes one more time, just before she felt the sedative lacing her mind, drawing her away from this. And that's when she saw Case's face floating above to her.

"We've got you, Rach!" he whispered, though it looked as if he was screaming. But the ringing in her ears, combined with the roar of what she now recognized as a helicopter, drowned most other sounds.

"You're gonna be fine!" he added. "I've got you!"

Just before the powerful cocktail flowing through her veins lowered a curtain over her current state of misery.

* * *

The motion and the bright light woke her up.

"She's coming around, eh?"

Rachel blinked, then coughed, her throat feeling as if it was on fire.

A middle-age blonde woman in green scrubs held a small flashlight and was moving its very bright beam in front of her eyes.

Rachel turned her face away from it and briefly closed her eyes.

The light went away, and when she opened them again, she recognized the interior of a hospital room. She was on a bed surrounded by blinking machines, plus an IV bag hanging over her. The powerful smell of flowers floated in the air, and as her sight fully returned, she recognized several bouquets lining the table in front of a pair of large windows.

The woman, a stethoscope hanging from her neck, filled her field of view again. She had a round face that reminded Rachel of her own face way back, before Kiersted...

Now she remembered.

The terrorist.

The grenade in his hand.

She wanted to ask where she was, but her throat was too damned dry, so she managed to mouth a barely audible, "Water."

The woman moved quickly, producing a small bottle with a blue straw already in it.

"I'm Doctor Martin."

Rachel took a sip, feeling the water cool her throat. Then she inhaled deeply and took another sip. It tasted like heaven. But as she was about to drink again, the doctor took it away and set it on the nightstand, where she noticed two more flower arrangements.

Before Rachel could protest, Martin said, "Easy there, eh? Don't want you getting sick, eh?"

What's with the damned 'ehs?'

Then she remembered.

I'm in fucking Canada.

"How...long..."

"Two days, Sweetheart. But we've been taking good care of our heroine."

Heroine?

Rachel narrowed her gaze.

"You saved out city, eh?" Martin added. "You and your boyfriend."

Boyfriend?

"It's all over the news," she added.

Rachel tried to take all that in, but before she could ask a question, Martin said, "Poor boy wouldn't leave your side, so we finally convinced him to take a coffee break. And as luck would have it, you wake up when he's down in the cafeteria."

"Where?"

"Toronto General," she replied. "You were flown here in an army helicopter, and I must say, I'm honored to be the chief resident taking care of you."

Rachel nodded slowly, feeling her strength returning, and pointed at the bottle of water.

Martin worked the controls on the side of the bed and lifted the back to sit her up a bit, then she handed the bottle to her.

Rachel took it in her hands, frowning at the IV port connected to the top of her right hand. "What do you... have me on?" she asked, before guiding the straw between her lips and taking a sip.

"Only the finest cocktail to get our heroine back on her feet."

Rachel shook her head. "I was just...doing my job, Doc."

"No, Sweetheart. I'm doing my job, eh? What you and your boyfriend did up there was...well, damned heroic."

Before she could reply, Martin stepped aside and said, "And speaking of him..." Turning toward the door, Martin added, "She just woke up."

As the doctor's figure shifted to the right, Rachel watched the tall figure of Case Patterson emerge in the room. He was holding a cup of coffee.

"I'll leave you to it. Call if you need anything," Martin added. "And I mean, *anything*. I'm at your service."

As the doctor stepped out and closed the door behind her, Case approached Rachel and sat on the edge of the bed, set the coffee on the nightstand and placed a hand on the side of her face, his thumb brushing off a lock of hair over her left eyebrow.

"Hey kiddo," he said. "How're you holding up?"

"Been…worse," she said, licking her lips, which felt as dry as her throat.

In an amazing feat of mind reading, Case reached over the nightstand and produced a small tube of lip balm. He squirted some on the tip of his index finger and rubbed it on her lips.

She wasn't sure if she enjoyed more the ointment or him playing with her lips, but she compressed them to spread the relief and then kissed his finger. Taking another sip of water, she said, "Doctor Martin called you my… *boyfriend?*"

He smiled. "Sorry. Because of our hero status in this place and the fact that I'm divorced, I started getting propositioned by nurses within the hour after we brought you here. That had a way of keeping them at bay."

"I see," she replied.

"So, sorry, Rach," he said. "It just came out."

"Don't be."

"No?"

"Not at all."

He leaned down to kiss her but she slowly shook her face, making him pause in midstride. "You don't want to do that now," she said. "*Trust* me."

Case smiled and kissed her anyway, but halfway through it the door swung open.

He pulled away and they both turned in unison towards the intrusion. It was Martin, and she looked as if she had just seen a ghost.

"What is it, Doc?" Case asked.

"Something's happened in Hawaii," she said, reaching for the remote control and turning on the TV. "Something horrible."

CHAPTER THIRTY-THREE
CRACKS

"The Earth provides for every man's need, but not for every man's greed."
—Mahatma Gandhi

EAST RIFT ZONE. FORTY MILES SOUTHEAST OF HILO, HAWAII. JULY 14, 2029.

Doctor Aeko Nahinu trekked along the bottom of the 50-foot-deep crack collecting samples of Keanakakoi ash to bring back for analysis at the geology department of the University of Hawaii in nearby Hilo.

Nahinu paused to wipe the sweat filming his forehead with the sleeve of his cotton T-shirt, and he took a moment to admire the amazing rift walls towering above him, filled with parallel laminated fine ash deposits.

The East Rift Zone, together with the Southwest Rift Zone—known as the Great Crack—and the Koae Fault System formed the north and west boundaries of the South Flank Block of Kilauea.

Identified as a high-risk landslide that could generate a mega-tsunami, the earthquake-prone South Flank Block had been under the careful study of geologists such as Dr. Nahinu for many years.

Nahinu continued his inspection of the fissure, reaching the first of many steel markers he had drilled into the volcanic rock two decades ago. Using the red marker as a reference, Nahinu snapped photos of opposing walls, before downloading them to his FlexScreen and comparing them for form and fit. Like a giant jigsaw puzzle, the opposing walls continued to fit together well. But a comparison to the same shots from five years ago, revealed an alarming trend.

The crack was widening.

Nahinu frowned. The rifts had been largely unchanged for most of the 20th century and even the first decade of the 21th century, but then something shifted. The rifts began to enlarge. Slowly at first, a mere few inches per year, suggesting possible soil settlement or perhaps underground magma displacements. But in 2023, when Nahinu published his observations that the widening rate exceeded almost three feet per year, the old theory about the South Flank Block breaking away from the island was instantly revived.

Now, six years later, the crack had expanded by eighteen feet, strongly suggesting this section of the Big Island was indeed tearing apart along this seam.

And that meant fifty square miles of land could one day slide into the ocean at great speed, triggering a tsunami of a size and power unheard of in recorded history.

The question was when. In 10 years? In 100 years? In 1,000 years? Longer?

The scientist shook the apocalyptic thought away as he continued to gather the evidence that may provide him with a defendable answer. This was the primary reason behind his monthly tours, collecting more ash, taking more pictures, slowly piecing together the widening rate.

He viewed his methodical approach as the best way to provide factual answers, in a way similar glaciologists used the sliding rates in glaciers to predict their collapse.

The broadening rate so far suggested a linear progression, which further proposed a longer time span before the collapse, probably in a few centuries.

But he needed to be sure.

In the past thirty days, this section of the fissure had widened by eight inches, which could be the start of an exponential trend, drastically reducing the time table.

Or the past thirty days could be just an anomaly in the data, what statisticians called an outlier in a trend chart.

Which is why he had to keep collecting monthly data, and for a moment he wondered if it would be prudent to go weekly for the next couple of months just to be safe.

Nahinu had a number of graduate students returning to school early for the fall term that he could put to good use until the semester began in a few weeks. And he could even keep them taking samples during school by justifying to the board that this phenomenon was worthy of multiple masters and even doctoral theses.

But as far as the world was concerned, he didn't have enough information to recommend any course of action beyond the signs posted every thousand feet along the perimeter of the South Flank Block, warning the public about the danger presented by the shifting landmass.

Unfortunately, like the active lava flow site of Hawaii's Volcanoes National Park, such warning signs only served to attract more tourists, who regularly started visiting the South Flank Block soon after news of the widening crack reached travel agencies.

Fortunately, only scientists such as him were allowed into the deepest and most active crevices after a series of rock slides killed a dozen tourists last year.

And unfortunately for him, this high-risk area was where the best data could be collected.

Nahinu sighed while staring up at the towering walls, deciding not to think about the deadly consequences of falling rocks, before resuming his work.

Over the next hour, he made his way to the deepest and most active section of the fissure, far away from the tourist areas. He photographed walls and checked markers, using a laser to measure distances. He then entered the data into the FlexScreen, which was uploaded real time to a server in the geology department for later analysis.

That's when he heard the strange beeping sounds coming from around a sharp bend in the gorge. And he also heard the sound of a helicopter echoing in the canyon walls.

Intrigued, he hiked over to the jagged edge, by a large metal marker anchored deeply into the west wall. Beyond a cluster of volcanic rocks from a recent avalanche, Nahinu spotted a strange machine resting on volcanic ash at the lowest point in the fissure.

He narrowed his gaze and used the spotter in the laser as a telescope to get a closer look. As large as a pair of refrigerators on their side, the machine sported what looked like a rocket booster with the nozzle pointing up on one side and a number of blinking lights on the other.

What the hell?

As he approached the unit, the *whop-whop* sounds of a helicopter increased overhead, and he watched the dark silhouette of the craft hovering high over the figure back-dropped by clear blue skies.

What is going—

The blast was sudden, deafening even from a distance of a few hundred feet.

The rocket booster atop the machine ignited, its plume blinding, deafening as it shot straight up the walls.

Sweet Mother of—

The rocks began to shake under him, forcing him to reach out for the metal marker, gripping it with both hands as the canyon trembled, as a massive earthquake shook the crack and began to stretch it eastward.

He watched in horror as the rocket booster continued to burn while the east wall slid away from him, shifting towards the distant ocean, the fissure deepening, widening.

A massive roar and an avalanche of rocks rained down the chasm as the floor gave out from under him, swallowing the machine, its gleaming plume vanishing in a black abyss.

His legs swung beneath him as the ripping crust exposed a sea of pressurized molten lava surging a hundred feet below him, its sizzling vapors rising towards him, suffocating, burning him.

Relief came swiftly and mercifully when an avalanche of volcanic rocks careened down the west wall, crushing him, killing him instantly before plunging into the rising lava.

The South Flank Block ripped cleanly from Hawaii's Big Island, as the released pressure shot a wall of lava the length of the fissure a mile into the sky, its roar heard across all of the islands. The land plummeted into the Pacific a great speed, displacing almost one hundred cubic miles of ocean in thirty seconds in an explosive show of earth, foam, and lava.

The resulting swell rose above sea level almost one hundred feet with a forward velocity of nearly five hundred miles per hour propagating east, towards the coast of California.

The mega-tsunami, packing ten times more energy than the Greenland tidal wave, obliterated hundreds of vessels in its first hour, from sailing rigs to megaships, as it rushed towards the mainland, where it would hit southern California first.

Across the entire state, Emergency Broadcasting Systems prompted the largest evacuation in history, but there were just too many people, not enough roads, and too little time.

In the coastal plain of Los Angeles, millions took to the highways trying to reach the San Gabriel Mountains, only to clog all access roads in minutes. Riots broke out, turning the entire metropolis into a death zone. In northern California, residents hoped the high cliffs of the Coastal Range would be enough to protect the state's 400-mile long Central Valley, which encompassed the Sacramento and San Joaquin Valleys. Meanwhile, residents from San Francisco to Silicon Valley fled east towards the Sierra Nevada mountain range.

The tidal wave slowed as the ocean floor shallowed, trading speed for height. It dropped to just under one hundred miles per hour as it reached the continental shelf while rising to a monstrous six hundred feet.

The mountain of water drowned the entire Los Angeles metropolitan area, toppling skyscrapers, ripping buildings and roads apart at their foundations, drowning eight million souls in less than five minutes, before continuing inland for another forty miles until colliding against the mountains bordering the east and north end of the valley.

To the north, the wall of ocean clashed against the Coastal Range in an Earth-trembling explosion that shot foam and dirt two miles high while shifting the tall mountains inland by a dozen feet, stressing the region's tectonic plates to the breaking point, triggering a massive earthquake across the entire state.

As the tsunami collided against the coastal peaks, it gushed inland through the Sacramento and San Joaquin River deltas, at the heart of the San Francisco Bay. It penetrated deep into the Central Valley, forcing millions of cubic feet of high-pressure sea water in the form of a hundred-foot-high tidal wave up the long and narrow bowl-like valley, as high as Redding at the north end and Bakersfield to the south.

In San Francisco, the soaring torrent leveled every structure, from shacks to skyscrapers, uprooting piers, streets, trees, and bridges, including the Oakland and Golden Gate bridges. It tore deep into the soil, triggering landslides in its wake as it flashed down Palo Alto, Mountain View, Sunnyvale, San Jose, and Santa Clara, burying everyone and everything under a hundred feet of seawater, mud, and debris.

The tidal wave spread the kind of destruction the Earth had not witnessed for thousands of years, before the waters finally receded, leaving the state barren, smooth, devoid of any sign of human existence.

CHAPTER THIRTY-FOUR
FAREWELLS

"We must accept finite disappointment, but we must never lose infinite hope..."
—Martin Luther King

SAN GABRIEL MOUNTAINS. CALIFORNIA. APRIL 17, 2030.

Rachel held Case's hand as they walked on the trail leading to Remembrance Gardens, the large memorial park high on the mountains overlooking the San Fernando Valley and the Los Angeles Basin beyond it.

She held his hand as tears welled in his eyes while walking past the recently completed archway leading into the simple, yet powerful clearing visited by so many Americans since it opened eight months after the waters wiped the state clean of its major cities, towns, and highways with the power of a thousand hurricanes.

But unlike traditional storms, this time the ocean took it all, dragging entire societies to the bottom of what now looked like a tranquil sea, the deep grave of nearly forty million people. There were no bodies to bury, no streets to clean, no buildings to reconstruct.

The sea took it all down to soil and limestone, leaving the landscape as Spanish explorer Vasco Nunez de Balboa first saw it in 1513.

Rachel felt Case tightening his grip as they approached the memorial wall, where surviving family and friends of those tens of millions of casualties pinned pictures of loved ones stolen by the sea, by the largest single-most destructive event in all mankind.

Forty million people.

Rachel sighed as Case reached for his back pocket and produced his wallet, where he extracted the small color printout of an image Rachel had first seen on their trip to Russia what seemed like a lifetime ago even though it had only been eight months.

Forty million people.

But to Case Patterson there were two in particular that had had a devastating effect.

Cameron and Ashley.

His hands trembling, Case placed the pictures on the south end of the angled wall, amidst many other photos, messages, drawings, flowers, and cards.

Rachel hugged him as he wept, just as he had wept so frequently for the past several months, since they had seen the impossible on TV in that hospital in Toronto.

Case had experienced a nervous breakdown right then and there, collapsing on the hospital bed.

The CIA had placed him on temporary leave. Rachel had taken a sabbatical under the pretext of recovering from her wounds, but she just needed to be with him in his time of need. Like her, Case now also had no one, and the devastation of losing two kids had been more than the seasoned operative had been able to take.

She had stepped away from the GCCU to become the shoulder that allowed him to mourn, just as so many Americans mourned the coastal disaster in California. And, of course, Alaska, where the fires finally gave way to winter and an Arctic front hardened the permafrost enough to shut off the methane feeding the flames.

But not before consuming more oxygen than the world's ecosystem could replenish, resulting in a reduction significant enough to dilute sea level concentrations to those found at 7,000 feet, which made certain cities up in the mountains, especially in Colorado and Arizona in the United States, habitable only to those who could adapt to living at altitudes over 13,000 feet.

The low-oxygen world also had devastating effects on ocean life, where many species perished.

The mortality rate was on the rise around the world, especially in the population above sixty, whose bodies were less capable of adapting to the Earth's rapidly evolving biomes. Temperatures on the equator belt were already five degrees hotter than normal, triggering droughts, thinning the rain forests, and causing people to start migrations north and south to more habitable climates.

And speaking of climates, the fires in Alaska had only worsened the situation in Europe, where the near-permanent haze from the ashes carried by the jet stream had dropped temperatures another four degrees, propelling the continent into an even deeper freeze.

Although they had indeed prevented Kiersted from repeating Alaska in the densely-populated Toronto areas, the end result reminded Rachel of that old quote from President Kennedy about nuclear warfare...where victory would be like ashes in our mouths.

Her throat felt dry and raspy from the growingly hazy skies as the winds aloft continued to carry the ashes from Alaska around the world, staining the heavens with an eerie orange shade.

But apparently, world leaders had also stared at the same angered skies and felt the same choking smog in the air, finally awakening them to the chilling effect of ecoterrorism.

At the moment, there was a large convention in Rio de Janeiro, Brazil, where the world's nations were meeting to discuss steps towards dealing with that sobering reality.

Case slowly pulled away from her and stared into Rachel's eyes, also filled with tears. It pained her to see him like this, which also told her that for better or worse, she had fallen for Case Patterson.

"I have mourned them, and I have said my farewells," he said, staring at the pictures, then at the vast valley projecting to the distant ocean.

"Time to move on?" she asked.

"Yeah," he replied, starting for the exit. "Time to move on."

CHAPTER THIRTY-FIVE
DENIAL

"The warnings about global warming have been extremely clear for a long time. We are facing a global climate crisis. It is deepening. We are entering a period of consequences."
—Vice President Al Gore

RIO DE JANEIRO. BRAZIL. APRIL 17, 2030.

Natasha Shakhiva-Malone stepped out to the balcony of their hotel overlooking the beach wearing only her husband's white tuxedo shirt.

A full moon hung high on the South American sky this late evening, casting its gray light on a peaceful ocean.

For the past hour, the recently married couple had celebrated the honeymoon they never really had following their narrow escape from Alaska.

So much has happened, she thought, remembering the endless press conferences, media events, and meetings with government officials from ten different countries.

For a while it seemed everyone wanted to hear what Natasha and Malone had to say regarding climate change, the permafrost, the new biomes, and the future of the world.

And this afternoon, it had been a particularly promising event. The couple had shared the stage at the World's Climate Change forum, where high-ranking officials from fifty countries, including the presidents of the United States and Russia, as well as the president of the People's Republic of China, had listened to their theories and the data supporting them. Natasha and Malone had spoken about accelerated rise in sea levels, trapped methane beneath permafrost and Arctic ice, and apocalyptic deserts near the equator. They had presented their findings in the accepted scientific formats of the day. They had issued warnings to the nations where computer modeling showed drastically-changing climates, as captured in hundreds of ice cores from long-melted glaciers. In the end, they had left the stage amidst a shower of applause and praise for their work.

But as to be expected, what started as pure scientific work began to turn political a few hours ago, when a team of scientists from Germany challenged their theories.

Tonight, on the limo ride to the hotel, they heard a story on the BBC about scientists from the École Normale Superieure, in Paris, one of France's most eminent universities and research centers, claiming to have data contradicting UAF's methane threat research. The French proposed that the Permian-Triassic event was nothing more than another asteroid, similar to the one which killed the dinosaurs over a 180 million years later.

Already the online news services were questioning their findings.

"There's my shirt," Malone said, stepping out barefoot to join her wearing just his tuxedo pants and holding two glasses of red wine. He no longer wore a ponytail, though his hair was still long, but above his shoulders, and he was clean shaven.

"Not sure where you took off my bloody dress."

"Foyer," he said, before handing one of the glasses to her and adding, "Courtesy of the hotel manager."

"How nice," she said, taking the glass and staring out to sea while taking a sip.

"The Beijing team speaks in the morning," he said. "Their claim is very reminiscent of the post-Kyoto Protocol talks about curving greenhouse gases on a per-capita basis, which gives them a huge advantage because they have so many fucking people."

Natasha didn't reply, her eyes on the moonlit ocean.

"The ENS team goes after them, and their PR person sent me a note informing me that their theory and supporting data continues to contradict ours," he said. "I guess the French want their five minutes."

"Darling, I don't want any fame," Natasha said, looking at him for a moment before once more staring out to sea. "I'm a scientist, as you are. We look at facts, and we let them speak for themselves."

"But sometimes even facts are not enough."

"Then they have to face more consequences, like Greenland, Alaska, the Hawaiian Tsunami, and much worse, like what's coming our way next summer. The world was told today that of the nearly two hundred Gigatons of methane that escaped the permafrost, less than ten percent was consumed in the Alaska fires before winter closed the valve. The rest is now in our atmosphere, trapping more heat than ever, adding to the destructive positive cycle. Plus, we still don't know how badly those fires damaged the permafrost structure until we analyze the newest core samples Mario is drilling up there. If that isn't enough to scare them, then nothing short of the full Permian-Triassic event will."

Malone rested his forearms on the balcony, standing shoulder to shoulder with his wife. "The world, it appears, has the attention span of a gnat. They forget very quickly."

"But the Earth doesn't forget."

"Nope. It sure doesn't."

The fires in Alaska had added better than four inches of ashes over the polar caps before winter encased them in a few feet of ice, forever preserving the event. And the thickness of that fresh layer of ash, twice as thick as the one in the ice cores he had drilled last year in Kilimanjaro, also told them the events that took place in Egypt would pale by comparison to the nightmare headed their way.

Natasha looked out at the beautiful beach and ocean. "While the world continues mourning, climate change continues its unforgiving trend, Greenland continues to melt, sea levels continue to rise, and Europe continues to freeze. Meanwhile the permafrost is barely hanging in there, holding back a monster that can do to the entire world what that mega-tsunami did to California. Alaska was just a warning, Koni. It just gave us a taste of things to come. And on top of that, there's the continued threat of Kiersted copycats wanting to capitalize on the situation."

"Well," Malone said, "irrespective of any terrorists in the picture, our Chinese, German, and French colleagues intend to show evidence that the Permian-Triassic event was caused by a meteor."

She shrugged. "Summer will most certainly come again, Koni. It's only a couple of months away. It will arrive, just as it does every year. No PowerPoint presentation and well-delivered speeches by the French, the Germans, and the Chinese will stop the Earth from circling the sun. You and I know what's beneath the Earth's permafrost. And when summer does arrive..."

As Malone put an arm around his wife and kissed her gently on the cheek, Natasha peered into the dark horizon and took a sip of wine, her mind inexorably thinking of an event the world still may not be ready to accept.

An event that took place a long, long time ago...

EPILOGUE

"And all living things upon the earth perished—birds, wild animals, and reptiles…all existence on Earth was blotted out."
　　—Genesis 7:21

KAROO BASIN (MODERN DAY SOUTH AFRICA). PANGAEA SUPERCONTINENT. LATE-PERMIAN/EARLY-TRIASSIC PERIOD. 250 MILLION YEARS AGO.

Parting a wall of conifers with a snout full of wicked teeth, the adult female Gorgonopsian, the Permian equivalent of the saber-tooth tiger, surveyed the river bank extending beyond her hunting hideout.

Her quarter-sized nostrils probed further, past seed ferns lining the uneven tundra sloping down to the herbivore feeding grounds by the shoreline.

Her body completely caked in mud, both to hide her scent from potential prey as well as for protection against flying insects that fed at night, the Gorgo, a creature more mammal than reptile, examined the herd.

A pack of Deltavjatias, Triceratops-like creatures just over ten feet long and lacking protective horns, grazed on the herbaceous plants near the water. Their smooth armored plates, dark green with bluish shades, reflected the bright moonlight this breezy and unusually warm evening, when the Gorgo female reached the end of the wide river following a long migration from their winter hunting grounds to the north.

The Gorgo sniffed the familiar dung-aroma of the herbivores, confirming identification.

Among the Deltas roamed several pups, their dark torsos telegraphing the tender skin that would not be protected for another season, though seasons themselves had become less prominent. The warmer weather lasted longer and the white zone retreated farther south each summer.

The mouth of the river and the ocean beyond it no longer remained hardened during the summer, preventing the Gorgo female from completing her migration to the summer feeding grounds of her youth. There was a time when she could march south across the ice sheet that led to a land blessed with cold temperatures, fresh meadows, and many herds of herbivores that also used to migrate there to escape the extreme summer heat.

Instead, the Gorgos had to evolve hunting tactics during this time of the year and cope with the increased heat, the mosquitoes, less water, and fewer herds. Heading back north meant living through little shade as the clouds that used to shield the land in the summer during her youth had all but disappeared. Lacking their shade, the sun scorched the land, triggering droughts even a desert-adapted hunter like the Gorgo would have difficulty surviving.

But adapting to hunt here in the summer had not been easy. As the herbivores' ranks thinned from increasing temperatures and low rainfall even this far south, they grew more aggressive.

The scars on the Gorgo's torso reminded her of this each day. She had endured deep lacerations last year from the sharp claws of an angered Delta female while the Gorgo stole a youngster. Her mate and other Gorgos had perished here then, while trying to adjust, making mistakes, testing new techniques—as well as developing new survival strategies when hunters became hunted.

The vanishing cloud cover and the increased heat this far south had also brought a new threat to the Gorgos: the disease injected by mosquitoes at night. It had claimed many lives in the rolling meadow flanking the river, which had shrunk in size from last year. Protection for the female Gorgo had come by accident one rainy night when her clan ended up covered in mud, whose aroma fended off the mosquitoes.

The Gorgo sniffed the air to the south with melancholy, longing for the hunting grounds barely visible on the distant horizon and beyond the reach of the dreaded flying insects that thrived in the hotter regions.

Her hungry stare returned to the movement of the herd as it slowly made its way down the receding shoreline, where the water was fresh, safe to drink.

She took her time, waiting for a pup to stray from the protection of the adults, giving her enough time to approach silently using the shallow trenches formed over previous seasons in this changing tundra to get close enough to lunge and steal it before the slow-moving Deltas could reach her.

That's when she saw a Delta youngster laying on its side on a bed of river stones where water had once flowed.

The Gorgo's muscles tightened; her salivary glands filled her snout.

But something was wrong. The pup was convulsing.

Her mind provided an explanation: the young Delta was sick.

Exhaling in a barely audible grunt, the Gorgo realized it had probably been infected by the disease from the flying insects because the pup lacked the protecting armor shielding the skin of the adult Deltas.

It is not safe to eat, she thought, watching the herd move downstream, away from her while protecting the healthy youngsters.

Albeit hungry from the month-long migration, she would not touch the diseased pup just as she didn't attempt to attack the herd without a clear opening. She learned a hard lesson a year ago, when such attack had caused the loss of her mate, who was cornered by a mob of aggressive Deltas and clawed to death.

The Gorgo female let go a soft whimper, recalling how her mate had drawn the Deltas to create a distraction while she snatched a youngster. But the attack had backfired. The well-organized Deltas had mounted an effective counter-attack, nearly killing her as well, which would have also resulted in the death of the unborn cubs she had carried in her womb at the time.

But she had healed, in part by rubbing the wound against the dark-green ferns that grew amidst conifers flanking the shores of dry river beds, just as her mother had shown her long ago, allowing her to birth two healthy cubs, a male and a female.

Keep looking, her orange-sized brain commanded, shifting her muzzle to the right of the Deltas. Her sharp eyesight recognized the long and furry silhouette of a Therocephalian feeding on a lizard, a sight the female Gorgo had not seen for some time.

In her youth, the Gorgo's mother had taught her how to approach the three-foot-long slippery hunter from the rear, the creature's blind spot, snatching it by the long and weak neck and clamping hard to rip off the head before the creature had the chance to whip its sharp snout around and bite off an eye.

The Gorgo inhaled deeply, her brain triggering distant memories of the Thero's tender, moist, and salty flesh. The thoughts filled her muzzle with milky saliva, which began to pepper the sand in between her clawed paws.

Withdrawing her head from the veiling conifers, the Gorgo inspected her cubs, nearly half her size and also covered in mud. They sat by her hind legs facing the opposite direction, guarding her flanks and rear as she had taught them, constantly sniffing the air, looking for danger.

The dark and quiet forest behind her had changed significantly following the vanishing clouds in recent seasons. Trees no longer stood erect, as had been the case in her youth, but tipped to one side, as if pushed by some invisible force—perhaps the same force that had robbed the land of its smoothness, shaping the shallow hills and valleys the Gorgo had learned to use to sneak up on prey. The uneven terrain did make it harder to charge in a straight line, but the Gorgo had since developed a technique for half running and half leaping that allowed her to cover much ground very fast without tripping.

The male cub looked back, making eye contact, before purring loudly. *I'm hungry.*

The female Gorgo swatted him with a hind paw for breaking silence. Absolute stealth was paramount for the successful execution of a hunt, and also to prevent telegraphing their presence to larger predators in the area.

The offending cub shook his head and quietly returned his attention to his observation quadrant while exchanging a glance with his sister, who exhaled through her nostrils in silent reprimand for her brother's blunder while leering, exposing two rows of glistening teeth. This was a family effort and all had to perform their jobs flawlessly, or no one would eat tonight.

The Gorgo gave the listing tree line a suspicious scan until she was satisfied that her cub's telegraphing noise had not attracted any unwanted attention before resuming her search.

The Thero continued to work on the dead lizard, apparently undisturbed by the noise. The direction of the wind, sweeping in from the river delta, told the Gorgo her cub's ill-timed purr had been carried away from the prey and into the forest behind them.

It had been a few seasons since she had seen a live Thero, not since the slow-flowing river and the ocean beyond it began to bubble with the gas that turned into fire, causing thick waves of dead fish to wash ashore.

Many species, including Theros, had feasted that day long ago on the fish, only to die soon after.

Most of the Gorgos in her old pack had shown restraint. Her survival instincts, triggered by the faint but different smell, which had also caused flying creatures to fall from the skies, kept her from consuming something already dead.

Larger species, like the dreaded Titanophoneus—nearly five times the Gorgo's size, sporting a snout large enough to tear her in half—had fed on the many dead Theros, and some of them started to die within days.

The Gorgo female, her mate, and other Gorgo's from her old pack had escaped north, away from the poisoned air and the fields of death until the following season, when all that remained were rolling tundra layered with the carcasses of dead Titans.

But that Thero has survived—and has also adapted, her logic told her as her early recollections of the long and furry creature showed it feeding on fish. And just like the Gorgo, the skin of the Thero continuing to feast on the lizard was also caked in mud for protection against the large mosquitoes.

And that realization triggered two additional threads in her brain. First: the Thero would be safe to eat. Second: the Thero had adapted to its environment like the Gorgo.

Those two thoughts led her mind to a conclusion: the Thero would require new tactics to outwit.

Unfortunately, successful hunts had been growing more difficult without her mate, as two predators were far more efficient than one, and her cubs would need another season before they would be ready to assist beyond guarding the rear. In addition, the rest of the Gorgos from her old clan had long perished while trying to adapt to the changing landscape.

I am alone on this one, she decided, once more slowly parting the thin layer of conifers, surveying the landscape, the dark-brown ginkgos beyond her veil swirling in the same breeze that tickled the Gorgo's nostrils, carrying with it the chemical promise of a meal if she could do this right for her and her hungry cubs.

Slowly, she drifted through the vegetation effortlessly, snout first, parting soft branches before her aerodynamic body flowed through while dropping to a deep crouch, her belly brushing the sphenophytes layering the tundra's flood in between ferns, her senses heightened, her eyes on the prey.

Off to her far left, the Deltas continued to graze on the thin shrubbery amidst river rocks, their thick plates mirroring the grey light from the rising moon as well as shielding the youngsters splashing on the shallows while belching soft screeches to the delight of their elders, who groaned in return. One adult female looked back at the dying youngster by the shore, still convulsing, and she shrieked several times, before turning away.

The Gorgo welcomed the noise as it helped mask her own.

The Thero continued to feed, front paws clutching its prize, long muzzle buried in the lizard's entrails.

The breeze rustled the surrounding vegetation, the long branches overhead of a large marattialean tree fern and surrounding conifers, breaking up the moon shadow.

She now advanced swiftly, quietly, with cat-like grace, four clawed paws moving with synchronized precision, barely sinking in the sandy terrain, her adaptive brain transitioning from survey mode to attack mode. Ten million years of evolution combined with multiple seasons of drastic adaptation guided her as she closed on her prey, as she began to—

The Gorgo paused the instant the Thero stopped feeding.

Instinctively dropping to the sandy floor, hiding behind a pair of seed ferns, the Gorgo slowly raised her eyes—conveniently located near the top of her skull—like two periscopes barely protruding above her hiding trench.

The Thero had dropped its meal and lifted its bloody snout to test the air, nostrils flaring.

It doesn't make sense, she thought. The breeze was coming from the water, carrying any smell not covered by the mud away from her prey.

On the periphery of her vision, the Gorgo noticed the Deltas had also stopped feeding, their heads stretched above their stocky bodies, surveying the forest lining the rolling tundra.

The forest?

The Gorgo sniffed the air again, this time deeper, more carefully, identifying a new chemical signature that made her hind legs twitch. She had not smelled it for a long time—not since the day when the bubbling gas killed so many animals.

A shriek echoed on the tundra. It came from her male cub. *I smell something strange!*

As the Gorgo's meal scurried away and the herd of Deltas stampeded along the shore with an earth-rumbling racket that shook the branches of the ferns around her, a single Titan crashed through the tree line, its semi-hunched body towering over the landscape.

Breaking the silence of the feeding grounds with a deafening growl, the Titan stomped onto the sandy meadow kicking up puffs of dust and dirt with its massive paws as it charged toward her cubs.

Charcoal grey with an immense, top-heavy long head at the end of a very thick neck and an equally disproportionate muzzle crowded with oversized white teeth, the Titan moved clumsily. But what it lacked in speed and grace it made up for in sheer size and terror. Powered by muscular hind legs and strong but smaller front legs sporting long and ragged claws—which she had seen it use to disembowel prey, including Gorgos—the Titan roared again.

Her maternal instincts burning in her mind, drowning all other senses, the Gorgo raced up the meadow as her cubs broke through the wall of conifers rushing toward her in long elastic leaps. They were fast, but the Titan took longer strides, and it would eventually catch up to them.

But not before the female Gorgo would plant herself in between. A lifetime of hunts had trained her mind to quickly calculate relative velocities, which told her she could reach the cubs before the Titan did.

Once the Gorgo and her mate had killed a Titan, but it had required a very coordinated effort.

Tonight, she was alone.

Her frightened cubs reached her, their long and slanted yellow eyes displaying raw fear, nostrils flaring. Their whimpering grunts were almost drowned by the roaring growls of the Titan behind them, its colossal head and wide-open snout converging rapidly on the trio.

She quickly ordered them to run in opposite directions as dictated by Darwinian countermeasures to ensure at least one would survive.

Without checking to see if they had obeyed, the Gorgo scrambled towards the incoming threat, her adaptive brain remembering the tactic she and her mate had used.

Her adrenaline-fueled senses rapidly converged on a single-Gorgo version of the attack.

The Titan stopped less than twenty feet from the Gorgo, who also paused, the muddy skin on her snout pulled back, exposing her own teeth. Her front fangs were a third of the size of the massive white daggers facing her.

She growled while planting her paws firmly in the sand, stiletto claws extended.

You will have to get past me to get to them.

The Titan roared back at the open challenge, standing on its hind legs, the massive head and neck, nearly a third of the beast's total mass, rose an impressive height over the

Gorgo, who remained still, in control, knowing precisely what would come next.

The Titan's attack tactics had never evolved, which explained why the Gorgo saw fewer of them each season.

Advancing towards her strong and confident, the hungry monster blocked the moonlight, sniffing the air, savoring the meal to come. Its menacing shadow projected over the Gorgo, who stood her ground, biding her time.

The growls intensifying, claws at the end of muscular front legs slicing the air, the beast's oozing chemicals filled the Gorgo's senses, telegraphing its intentions.

Just a few yards in front of her, the Titan dropped to all fours with earthquake force, covering the remaining distance, jaws blossoming as it drove them with trained resolve precisely over the Gorgo.

Now!

The female rolled on her side just as the massive snout stabbed the sand where she had stood an instant before. The sheer force of the Titan's muzzle cratered the Tundra with soul-trembling vigor felt beneath the Gorgo's paws as she surged from the quick roll.

The Gorgo's thigh muscles exploded into life, shooting her five-hundred-pound mass forward through the billowing cloud of debris, dashing around the Titan like a shadow while the massive animal tore into the Tundra's floor, still not realizing the trick.

The Gorgo leaped onto the Titan's back with elastic vigor before the Titan could lift its lopsided head, drilling her two-inch-long claws into the sides of the monster's neck, clamping on while tearing into the soft flesh just behind the creature's skull.

The Titan roared in anger, in pain, in agony, trying to stand on its hind legs while stabbing the night air with its front legs, jerking its head back, trying to cut itself loose from the Gorgo's deadly embrace.

Her fangs biting through layers of gray skin, blood spurting, the Gorgo dug deeper, the Titan's flesh warm, pulsating.

Nearly erect now, the Titan abruptly dropped back down on all fours while also thrusting its massive head forward, catapulting the Gorgo off just as it bit deep into the monster.

The Titan, the night air, and the sandy tundra exchanged places as she was flung nearly ten yards, but somewhere along the way her brain commanded her legs, and she landed right side up, facing the threat.

The Titan growled, blood jetting from its neck, streaking down its sides in dark streams, as if it had just emerged from the water, staining the sand around it.

The sweet taste of flesh and blood alive in her snout, the Gorgo once more stood still, spitting out a crimson ten-pound lump before leering, exposing bloody teeth at her much larger opponent, challenging it.

The Titan paused, confused, staring at the lump of meat by the Gorgo's front paws, finally realizing where it had come from.

Taking a step back, the Titan roared, standing semi-erect, soaring over the Gorgo, its head listing a little, muzzle wide open. The wounded beast's claws pierced the night as it closed the distance before dropping back down over her.

And once again she rolled on her side, but this time in the opposite direction, surging to her feet just as the Titan claimed another mouthful of sandy tundra.

An instant later she was back on top, landing on the same spot, skewering the sides of the Titan's neck with her claws before clamping her snout on the flesh from the same bleeding cavity, ripping madly, tearing, widening the wound with vicious bites. Burrowing her entire head into the gash, she tried to hang on as the Titan shook its body violently, threatening to fall on its back, crushing the Gorgo.

But she didn't let up. The Gorgo kept gnawing, ripping arteries and cartilage, her sharp fangs reaching the thick muscles controlling the massive head.

The Titan's roars increased in pitch, turning into deafening howls as the Gorgo sank her jaws into the muscles surrounding the vertebrae, triggering a massive seizure on the beast, which remained semi-erect, its head sagging to the right, front legs sticking straight ahead, stretched claws frozen.

The Gorgo clamped her snout of crimson Permian steel over a thick muscle and pulled back hard, ripping it off the bone.

In a deafening howl, the Titan lifted its head straight up, quivering, and in doing so it lost its footing and began to topple backwards.

The Gorgo pulled her head out when realizing the beast was off balance.

Retrieving her claws, she pushed herself off, landing on all fours on the sand while rolling once, twice, scrambling to get out of the way of the collapsing giant, which struck the ground on its side with the force of a massive boulder.

The Titan kicked up more sand and a boiling cloud of dust that shrouded its bulk as the Gorgo stepped back, once more placing herself between the threat and her cubs' escape route, poised for another strike.

She waited as the dust cleared, as the Titan slowly got up, its large round eyes, as dark as the sky, regaining focus, blood now pooling by its paws, flowing faster than the tundra could absorb.

The prehistoric hunters stared at each other.

The Gorgo growled. *I can do this all night long.*

Confused, the Titan shifted its head from side to side with obvious difficulty, studying its opponent, uncertain how such a smaller creature had been able to inflict so much damage so quickly.

Slowly, the Titan snorted, oozing a cloud of chemicals that conveyed a new message to the Gorgo.

I'm finished here.

It then took a step back, and another, before painfully turning around, whimpering, having difficulty keeping the oversized head up, seeking the protection of the forest.

But the Gorgo wasn't finished.

She had come here to hunt, to feed her cubs, and the formidable Titan had suddenly been transformed from threat to meal.

The Gorgo sniffed, savoring the scent of the Titan's flesh, relishing the taste in her mouth, her stomach aching in deep hunger.

The Titan's rear now exposed to her as it tried to retreat to the forest, the Gorgo charged, easily climbing on top, positioning herself, claws glistening, digging into tender flesh, securing herself.

The injured monster was too weakened to fight back, barely shaking, emitting a high-pitched cry as the Gorgo bit into another thick muscle, and shredding it with incessant bites, losing herself in a primordial frenzy of tearing, ripping, and digging.

Howling in agony while dragging its dying mass towards the forest step after agonizing step, the Titan made a final attempt to resist, jolting, shaking its back, but it could not break the Gorgo's vice-like grip.

The Gorgo's snout struck bone beneath strands of torn ligaments, exposing the vertebrae.

Clamping her jaws around it, she cracked it.

The beast collapsed on its belly while breathing in short sobbing gasps, foam and blood oozing from its nostrils. Its whimpers echoed across the quieted meadow, before all movement ceased.

Standing tall on top of the most feared creature of her time, the Gorgo raised her bloody muzzle to the star-filled sky, to the grey moon hanging full above her. For an instant, she became the top predator of this warming land and growled twice in victory.

And it was at that moment of complete control, as the moonlight cast a grayish glow on her atop the Titan, that her nostrils detected a new chemical signature.

At the same time a gurgling sound erupted from the river, sweeping across the rolling tundra, followed by more eruptions, on water and then through the sand, irritating her nasal cavities, her eyes.

Her cubs cried out for her as the eruptions intensified, as a massive explosion in the distance shook the valley.

The wall of fire propagated across the meadows at lightning speed, incinerating everything in its wake.

The Gorgo tried to warn her cubs of the imminent danger as flames swallowed their world.

AUTHOR'S RESEARCH SUMMARY OF CLIMATE CHANGE ISSUES*

PERMAFROST.
The permafrost is thawing during the summer months in Siberia, northern Canada, and Alaska, causing buildings to collapse and also creating "drunken trees" due to the softening of the soil in affected forested regions. The biggest threat, however, comes from the potential release of as much as two thousand gigatons (billions of metric tons) of methane, an extremely effective greenhouse gas trapped beneath the permafrost since it was formed 11,000 years ago at the end of the last ice age. This release could take place over a very short period of time (a few years up to a decade), exponentially accelerating the rate of climate change. This has been hypothesized as a cause of past extinction-level events. In addition, methane clathrate, also called methane hydrate, is a form of water ice that contains a large amount of methane within its crystal structure. Extremely large deposits of methane clathrate exist under sediments in the ocean floor. Increasing ocean temperatures can release large amounts of this runaway greenhouse gas and could increase the global temperature by an additional ten

*Compiled from multiple sources, including NASA, IPCC (Intergovernmental Panel on Climate Change), The United Nations Climate Change News, EcoWatch, Nature Climate Change, and Wikipedia.

313

degrees. This is on top of the warming done by the released methane under the permafrost. The theory also predicts this massive methane release will greatly affect the available oxygen content of the atmosphere. This theory has been proposed to explain the most severe mass extinction event on Earth known as the Permian-Triassic extinction event. This, I think, is a very intriguing inflection point.

RISING OCEAN LEVEL.

With increasing average global temperature, the water in the oceans expands in volume, and additional water enters them which had previously been locked up on land in glaciers. To put things in perspective, if all the ice on the polar ice caps were to melt away, the oceans of the world would rise an estimated 70 meters (229 feet). However, with little major credit melt expected in Antarctica, sea level rise of not more than 0.5 meters (1.6 feet) is expected through the 21st century. Thermal expansion of the world's oceans will contribute, independent of glacial melt, enough to double those figures. This means that at the current rate of global warming from carbon dioxide released into the atmosphere, sea levels could rise as much as 1.5 meters by the end of this century. The "methane event" could multiply this number by a factor of 5 or more while also pulling in the sea rise timetable.

STORMS.

Hurricane power dissipation is highly correlated to temperature, reflecting global warming. Computer modeling has found that hurricanes under warmer, high carbon-dioxide conditions, are more intense than under present-day conditions. Hurricanes such as Katrina and Rita, and more recently, Michael and Florence, gathered most of their destructive power during their days traveling over the warm waters of the Gulf of Mexico or the Caribbean. The "methane event" could result in much warmer waters, creating storms never yet experienced by modern civilization.

FOREST FIRES.
Rising global temperatures might cause forest fires to occur on a larger scale and more regularly. This effect releases more stored carbon into the atmosphere than the carbon cycle can naturally re-absorb, as well as reducing the overall forest area on the planet, creating yet another positive feedback loop.

OCEAN ACIDIFICATION.
It is estimated that oceans have absorbed roughly half of all carbon dioxide generated by human activity since 1800 (around 120,000,000,000 tons, or 120 petagrams of carbon). But in water, carbon dioxide becomes a weak carbonic acid, lowering the pH of the ocean. This acidification results in the methodical destruction of coral reefs, reduction in fish reproduction as well as the plankton on which they rely for food. Scientists are trying to assess the effect the "methane event" would have on the acidity levels of the world's oceans.

MELTING POLAR ICE.
There are large reductions in the Greenland and West Antarctic Ice Sheets. Excepting the ice caps and ice sheets of the Arctic and Antarctic, the total surface of glaciers worldwide has decreased by 50% since the end of the 19th century. The loss of glaciers not only directly causes landslides, flash floods, and glacial lake overflows, but also increases annual variation in water flows in rivers. The melting of glaciers at

an accelerated rate in Venezuela and the Peruvian Andes is a particular concern because of the direct reliance on these glaciers for water supplies and hydroelectric power. The sea absorbs the sun, while ice largely reflects the sun's rays back to space. The retreating sea ice will allow the sun to warm the now exposed sea, contributing to further warming in yet another positive feedback loop. The "methane event" would be a significant accelerator.

DROUGHTS.

Large-scale experiments have shown that rising atmospheric temperatures, longer droughts, and side effects of both, such as higher levels of ground-level ozone gas, are likely to bring about a substantial reduction in crop yields in the coming decades. The "methane event" would also accelerate this.

HEAT WAVES.

Global warming leads to increasing frequency and strength of heat waves. The European heat wave of 2003 killed around 30,000 people. In the United States around 2000 people die each year due to extreme summer heat.

DISEASE.

Climate Change is expected to extend the favorable zones for vectors conveying infectious disease such as malaria and west Nile virus. In poorer countries, this may lead to higher incidence of such disease. By 2050, snow melting in the Himalayas and increased precipitation across northern India is likely to produce flooding in India, Nepal, Bangladesh, and Pakistan. Climate Change is expected to increase the geographic range of infectious diseases such as malaria, dengue fever, schistosomiasis. Except for east central China and the highlands of west China, much of the Asia Pacific region is exposed to malaria and dengue.

INSURANCE COMPANIES.
An industry very directly affected by the risks of Climate Change is the insurance industry. A June 2004 report by the Association of British Insurers declared, "Climate change is not a remote issue for future generations to deal with. It is, in various forms, here already, impacting on insurers' businesses now."

MIGRATIONS.
The U.S. and Europe may experience mounting pressure to accept large numbers of immigrant and refugee populations as drought increases and food production declines in Latin America and Africa. Numerous African countries suffer from famine and civil strife. Darfur, Ethiopia, Eritrea, Somalia, Angola, Nigeria, Cameroon, and Western Sahara hit hard by reduced water supplies, reductions in agriculture, triggering the instability on which warlords capitalized. Reduced rainfalls and increasing desertification of the sub-Saharan region will result in migrations to Europe. Increases in temperature can expand the latitude and altitude for malaria. Flooding is also conducive to cholera. The major impact on Europe from global climate change is likely to be migrations, now from the Maghreb (Northern Africa) and Turkey. Precipitation is expected to decrease in the central and eastern Mediterranean zones and southern Russia, with acute water shortages projected in the Mediterranean area, especially in summer. Places like the Balkans, Moldova, and the Caucasus will be unable to cope with the droughts, resulting in massive migrations north. The Italians today already deal with a large Albanian

immigration, and others may press north from the Balkans. The U.S. will face the potential demand for humanitarian aid and a likely increase in immigration from Latin America—all the while the U.S. is dealing with its own climate change issues. In the past, U.S. military forces have responded to natural disasters. The military was deployed to Central America after Hurricane Mitch in 1998 and to Haiti following the rain and mudslides of 2004.

WATER AND THE MIDDLE EAST.

In the Middle East, climate change has the potential to exacerbate tensions over water as precipitation patterns change, declining by as much as 60 percent in some areas. In addition, the region already suffers from fragile governments and infrastructures, and as a result is susceptible to natural disasters. Overlaying this is a long history of animosity among countries and religious groups. With most of the world's oil being in the Middle East and the industrialized nations competing for this resource, the potential for escalating tensions, economic disruption, and armed conflict is great.

CRITICAL FACTORS.

The critical factors for economic and security stability in the 21st century are energy, water, and the environment. These three factors need to be balanced for people to achieve a reasonable quality of life. When they are not in balance, people live in poverty, suffer high mortality rates, or move toward armed conflict.

ABOUT THE AUTHOR

R.J. PINEIRO is a thirty-year veteran of the computer industry as well as the author of many internationally acclaimed novels, including *Without Mercy, Without Fear, Ashes of Victory,* and *Avenue of Regrets*. His new novel is *Chilling Effect*. Pineiro makes his home in Texas with his wife, Lory.

To learn more about R.J., please visit:
www.rjpineiro.com
https://www.facebook.com/rjpineirobooks/